THE FIRST FIVE STAR WESTERN CORRAL

Western Stories

THE FIRST FIVE STAR WESTERN CORRAL

Western Stories

Edited by
JON TUSKA
and
VICKI PIEKARSKI

Five Star
Unity, Maine

Five Star Western

Published in conjunction with Golden West Literary Agency.

Cover photograph by Robert Darby

March 2000

First Edition

Five Star Standard Print Western Series.

The text of this edition is unabridged.

Set in 11 pt. Plantin by Minnie B. Raven.

Printed in the United States on permanent paper.

Library of Congress Cataloging-in-Publication Data

The first Five Star western corral : western stories / edited by
Jon Tuska and Vicki Piekarski.—1st ed.
    p.   cm.
  "A Five Star western"—T.p. verso.
  Contents: The mystery dogs / Fred Grove—For the good of
the service / Tim Champlin—So wild, so free / T.T. Flynn—
Night ride / Peter Dawson—Wild challenge / Robert Easton—
Day of the dedicated / Cliff Farrell—"Give-a-damn" Jones /
Bill Pronzini—The last ride of Gunplay Maxwell / Stephen
Overholser—Ruby's cape / Jane Candia Coleman—His personal
prisoner / Les Savage, Jr.—Horse tradin' / Rita Cleary—
A question of faith / Ray Hogan—Eagles over Crooked Creek /
Max Brand—Favorite son / Cynthia Haseloff.
  ISBN 0-7862-1848-7 (hc : alk. paper)
  1. Frontier and pioneer life—West (U.S.)—Fiction.
2. Western stories. I. Tuska, Jon. II. Piekarski, Vicki.
PS648.W4 F57   2000
 813′.087408—dc21   99-055130

Table of Contents

Foreword

by
Jon Tuska

It is perhaps the greatest benefit afforded the true historian that he or she is able to transcend the accident of having been born at one time rather than another by being able to know enough about a past time to enter actively into the feelings and thoughts of the people who lived then. Unfortunately for all of us the 1990s can be characterized as a time when all sense of historical reality in most American popular culture seems to have been bravely abandoned.

James Bowman, movie critic for *The American Spectator*, wrote an article for *The Wall Street Journal* (3/19/99) in which he examined all five of the films from 1998 nominated for an Academy Award in the category for Best Picture. Looking over the ridiculous scenes to be found in SAVING PRIVATE RYAN (DreamWorks, 1998), Mr. Bowman could not help commenting on the many moments in the film that struck him "as the intellectual flailings of a man of the 1990s trying to understand the men of former times and driven back on contemporary assumptions in order to do so." He had to wonder at how director Steven Spielberg was compelled to hypothesize on behalf of the American soldiers in the Second World War "a sort of utilitarian calculation when Mr. Hanks's Captain Miller confides in his sergeant that he is only able to function by telling himself that for every life lost under his command another ten lives will be saved—as if the reason for going to war were to save lives! True, the captain shows other signs of coming unhinged, but in 1944 even crazy people would not have reasoned like that. Why should they, when they could take for granted what we no longer can—namely the sense of what it means to be a man, and that the shame of being thought a coward, or having let down your pals, was more to be dreaded than death itself. For those of us accustomed to the post-feminist and therapeutic assumptions of the 1990s, such ideas are at best faintly disreputable and at worst comically old-fashioned."

It is, of course, always a most difficult task to divorce yourself from the social and philosophical assumptions that predominate the time in which you are living, but to do so is one of the objectives of the author of Western stories or Frontier fiction, and perhaps in the end this is the most significant of objectives. When I was three years old, my father gave me an album of six ten-inch 78rpm sides issued by Capitol Records of Tex Ritter singing songs and ballads of the West. Three of these sides in particular—"Billy the Kid," "The Pony Express," and "Night Herding Song"—I listened to so often that the groves turned a dull white from the needle of the tone-arm having tracked them so many times. The original ballads in this album were partly narrated and partly sung by Tex Ritter with orchestral arrangements provided by Merle Travis and his Orchestra. The short biography of Tex Ritter included as liner notes on the inside back flap of the album jacket told about the singer's career in motion pictures, and in later years I managed to see all of the Western films he had made.

It was many years after this, when I was doing the background research for my book, THE FILMING OF THE

8

WEST (1976), that I first met and spoke at length with Tex Ritter. It is occasionally granted to you in life to encounter another person with whom you find you have a spontaneous rapport, as if you had known each other all of your lives. One such person for me was Tex Ritter. Following that interview, we remained in touch over the years, primarily via the telephone, because even in the late 1960s Tex was on the road, performing fifteen days out of every thirty. I recall that he once was thinking of getting together a retrospective of his Western movies, wondering if he might tour with it to various colleges and universities, since in those days there was a keen and avid interest in films of the past among university students. Tex had early on married one of his leading ladies, Dorothy Fay, and they had had two sons. But it was about another of his leading ladies that I asked him, more than once—Eleanor Stewart—who had appeared opposite him in HEADIN' FOR THE RIO GRANDE (Grand National, 1936) and ARIZONA DAYS (Grand National, 1937). She was, I had told Tex, one of the most strikingly beautiful women who had ever been in a "B" Western. He remembered that Eleanor was under contract to Metro-Goldwyn-Mayer, but he had no idea what had become of her.

It was nearly three decades later that I "found" Eleanor Stewart, and it was ultimately as a result of our conversation that she sent me a fine book manuscript, THE FAIR VISION, that was published in late 1999 as a Frontier story in the Five Star Westerns. As it happened, I was copyediting this book when James Bowman's article appeared in *The Wall Street Journal*. Among the many historical absurdities in the films he mentioned was that of Queen Elizabeth I, speaking somehow as a "flower child" four hundred years in advance of her time in ELIZABETH (Gramercy Pictures,

1998), when she addresses a group of Roman Catholic bishops: "I ask you why we must tear ourselves apart for this small question of religion. Catholic? Protestant? We all believe in God." Of course, Elizabeth's predecessor had been known, quite accurately, as "Bloody" Mary, and her successor, the erstwhile James VI of Scotland who became James I of England, agreed with both Mary and Elizabeth that the matter of religion was no "small" question. Indeed, it had been literally the most burning question throughout Europe since the 16th Century and was no less so in the time of Queen Elizabeth I. It was primarily to escape religious persecution in Europe that the Separatists boarded the *Mayflower* and sailed to the New World. As a youth I had had a chance to tour this ship, and, even then, I found myself surprised at how small it was, and how vast, by comparison, the Atlantic Ocean.

Yet, size meant nothing for the Separatists—or Pilgrims, as they came to be known—as for so many after them for whom the frontier in the American wilderness was just that—a *New* World—the chance to start anew and to be something new, to do something new, to create something new that would never have been possible at all had they stayed in the Old World. It was so easy amid "the post-feminist and therapeutic assumptions of the 1990s" to forget this entirely, if it ever came to mind at all. But it is to be found always in the very best of Frontier fiction and Western stories. The American frontier, in the early years and ever after, as it continued pushing ever farther into the West, was so attractive because of the hope for freedom that it embodied, personal freedom, social freedom, economic freedom, above all spiritual freedom. The driving force of people in previous centuries in what became the United States was precisely this desire for, this quest after, this unwavering belief in freedom.

Where very often conflicts arose between factions in the New World, they had to do with how far this desire for freedom could, or should, be taken. Ultimately this was at the heart of the struggle between the so-called Free States and the Slave States. In a land which professed to believe that freedom was an inalienable right due to every human being was it right or just or truthful were it denied to any race or class of people? In THE KIOWA VERDICT (Five Star Westerns, 1997), Cynthia Haseloff explored this very question again, but from a totally different perspective, when she wrote dramatically of the first time members of an Indian nation were tried in federal court not for acts of warfare but on a civil charge of deliberate murder. Among the Kiowas in this story, as among many Indian nations, one of the freedoms that was regarded as the right of every man, woman, and child was the freedom to kill an enemy with impunity. The majority of Texans in that time, and probably the majority of Americans of all colors and races who were not Indians, did not believe in such an expanded definition of personal freedom. There had to be, they believed, some limits to personal freedom, or it would not be possible for all of us—coming as we did from every continent and every ethnic group and every race on the globe—to live together peacefully in this New World. None of these questions, and no aspect of personal and political and religious freedom, admits to an easy answer, ever, and the struggle toward some resolution has been a national preoccupation, and probably will continue to be so well into the new millennium.

It is possible, now that we have departed from the 1990s, to realize just how ludicrous it was to have thought of that time at all as the age of information. What had been widely lost even before it began were the critical tools so important to the historian to double-check everything, to verify every statement, and most of all to realize that without documents there can be no history. Budd Boetticher, who directed several of the finest Western films in which Randolph Scott ever appeared, told me how one day Randy had called him on the telephone. Karen Steele, who had had the rôle of the heroine in several of these films, was present with Boetticher at the time and answered the telephone. Randy sounded very upset, so she summoned Budd at once to the phone. The cause of Scott's consternation, as he informed Boetticher, was what he had observed on a studio street at Universal Pictures where he had been on a visit. Randy had seen Rock Hudson walking down that same studio street, holding hands with Tab Hunter! Scott told Budd it was one of the most disgusting things he had ever witnessed.

Years later, Charles Higham and Roy Mosely coauthored CARY GRANT: THE LONELY HEART (1989) in which they recorded the following anecdote. "Randolph Scott, happily married, apparently had preserved a sentimental feeling for Cary. In the 1970s, Cary and Scott would turn up at the Beverly Hillcrest Hotel late at night, after the other diners had gone, and in the near darkness of their table at the back of the restaurant, the maître d' would see the two old men surreptitiously holding hands." In their notes to this book, the authors admitted that "the maître d' who saw Randolph Scott with Cary Grant at the Beverly Hillcrest Hotel does not wish to be identified." Boetticher, when he heard it, called up Cary Grant's ex-wife, Dyan Cannon, and wondered where this story had really come from. Cannon admitted that it had come from her, but only at third-hand, and so the name, or even the actual existence, of the maître d' was impossible to determine, and there was even some question if this scene had really occurred at the Beverly Hillcrest Hotel or at the Beverly Hills Brown Derby. I knew and talked to Randolph Scott, and, of course, this kind of question never came up; but I have also known many people who worked with him, both in front of the camera and behind it, and there does not seem to be a shred of documentation for this rumor that there might have been a sexual relationship between Scott and Grant. C. H. Scott, Randy's adopted son, in his WHATEVER HAPPENED TO RANDOLPH SCOTT? (1994), probably was closer to Scott than anybody else who has written or commented on him, and he concluded there was no truth in it.

Now, an historian might cite as a footnote the assertion by Higham and Mosely for those avid for gossip, but not without also noting that the preponderance of the evidence and testimony in the case is to the contrary. Even were this allegation the truth, it would make no difference in the high regard I have always had for Randolph Scott's many, many Western films—beginning with his splendid embodiments of Zane Grey's Westerners at Paramount in the early 1930s to his final films directed by Budd Boetticher and Sam Peckinpah. Moreover, I wouldn't even bring up the matter except it served as the framing story for an article written by John Mort on the Five Star Westerns, among other Western publishing programs, in *Booklist* (3/1/99) titled "Buying Westerns; or, Whatever Happened to Randolph Scott?" He concluded this satirical overview with the observation: "You probably already knew that Scott and Cary Grant were a scandalously gay couple through the 1930s, happier, no doubt, than either of them were in their marriages. There's a tale of the West."

This is not responsible history, and it can scarcely pretend to be valid literary criticism. Yet, as editors, in selecting the stories for this collection, as for the Five Star Westerns in general, Vicki Piekarski and I have insisted that our authors be accurate historically, truthful to the time, whenever it might be, to the place, wherever it might be, and to the people, whoever they might be. Mari Sandoz, that remarkable Western author who was a first-generation descendant of a true Western pioneer, once commented how it is almost impossible for a white man *ever* to create an American Indian as a point-of-view character because it is very difficult for a white man ever to think about, much less regard, the world from the perspective of an American Indian. Notwithstanding the fact that Mari Sandoz accomplished what was so difficult in her life of Crazy Horse, and I believe Will Henry and Cynthia Haseloff have managed to do it in their Western fiction, it also became fashionable in the last decade of the 20th Century for white men to write books projecting "the post-feminist and therapeutic assumptions of the 1990s" into their native American characters, as Win Blevins tried to do with Crazy Horse in STONE SONG (1995). This practice, ultimately, proved as dissatisfying and ridiculous as the scene in BLOODY SEASON (1988) where Loren D. Estleman would have his readers believe that Doc Holliday, in preparing to spend a night out of doors, would make himself a mattress of mesquite branches, or the way in THE HIGH ROCKS (1978) Estleman has his timber wolves attack armed human beings, hiding in a cave, rather than to prey on the horses they have left standing defenselessly just behind the cave. People who live in the American West, or know something about it, can only laugh at these kinds of stories.

It is perhaps only natural that human beings in every period find themselves inflated with the arrogant conceit that those presently living know so much more and so much better than anyone who was cursed with living in an earlier time. To this in the 1990s in the United States was added an aberration borrowed from totalitarian cultures of the recent past that called for the revision of history according to the dictates of what in the era of Soviet Socialist Realism was called political correctness. Of course, it may well have been at base only a disguise for a most virulent manifestation of conformity and herd psychology, but foremost among the tenets of this political correctness was the reliance on historical revisionism. The past, and the people who lived in that past, were to be re-invented according to idealized icons that conformed to the images and thought of these new politically correct standards. It was no longer important, or even relevant, to know what people had thought or what they had been like in the past. They were, and had always been, only self-fulfilling prophesies embodying the virtues being celebrated by the revisionists.

It was by such means as these that many were comfortable in abandoning entirely the greatest freedom of all enjoyed by true historians: the ability to transcend contingency—the terrible limitation imposed on any real hope for understanding—of having been born at one particular time as opposed to another. Such a posture destroys any possibility of ever being able to penetrate into the thoughts and feelings of a former time, much less to understand what once were the pressing issues for a former generation. Understanding anything was replaced by the solipsistic response that the most, indeed, the only really important, thing was not what had once been, or knowing of what a thing consisted, but only what a politically correct person should *feel* about it. This was the only response any longer deemed relevant.

Yet, if the Western story suffered due to this confluence of tendencies, the ultimate culprit—if I may use such a term—was even easier to identify. It was bad writing. Too many authors of Western stories lacked the tools and imagination to create real characters and recreate situations about which a reader came to care deeply, to engender an empathy that called into play the moral sensibility so inherent in the best Western stories of even the relatively recent past. Such writers did not realize that the Western story at base has always been a story of renewal and that this is what has made it so very different from any other form of literary enterprise. Yet, it remains refreshing, even revitalizing, in these days of a medically over-educated culture obsessed with health and terrified of old age and dying to behold once again generations of Americans to which such obsessions and terrors meant nothing. It is spiritually encouraging in these days of political correctness, timidity, and herd-notions such as one-settlement culture that wants everyone to believe in a lock-step approach to life to contemplate those generations where individual, cultural, and ethnic differences were abundant, where not one culture but many co-existed, even if warfare between them was unceasing. We have benefited from that time. There is no one idea and no one cause that can possibly ever win endorsement from everybody. We still live now with that reality of the frontier as part of our social existence.

Above all, the greatest lesson the pioneers learned from the Indians is with us still: that it is each man's and each woman's *inalienable* right to find his own path in life, to follow his own vision, to achieve his own destiny—even should one fail in the process. There is no principle so singularly revolutionary as this one in human intellectual history before the American frontier experience, and it grew from the very soil of this land and the peoples who came to live on it. It is this principle that has always been the very cornerstone of the Western story. Perhaps for this reason critics have been wont to dismiss it as subversive and inconsequential because this principle reduces their voices to only a few among many. Surely it is why the Western story has been consistently banned by totalitarian governments and is sneered at by the purveyors of political correctness. Such a principle undermines the very foundations of totalitarianism and collectivism because it cannot be accommodated by the political correctness of those who would seek to exert power over others and replace all options with a single, all-encompassing, monolithic pattern for living.

There is no other kind of American literary endeavor that has so repeatedly posed the eternal questions—how do I wish to live?, in what do I believe?, what do I want from life?, what have I to give to life?—as has the Western story. There is no other kind of literary enterprise since Greek drama that has so invariably posed ethical and moral questions about life as a fundamental of its narrative structure, that has taken a stand and said: this is wrong; this is right. Individual authors, as individual filmmakers, may present us with notions with which we do not agree, but in so doing they have made us think again about things that the herd has always been only too anxious to view as settled and outside the realm of questioning.

The West of the Western story is a region where generations of people from every continent on earth and for ages immeasurable have sought a second chance for a better life. The people forged by the clash of cultures in the American West produced a kind of human being very different from any the world had ever known before. How else could it be for a nation emerging from so many nations? And so stories set in the American West have never lost that sense of hope. It wasn't the graves at Shiloh, the white crosses at Verdun, the vacant beaches at Normandy, or the lines on the faces of their great men and women that made the Americans a great people. It was something more intangible than that. It was their great willingness of the heart.

If there has been an overall literary objective in the Five Star Westerns, it has been to bring again to the fore the true elements of the Western story and the Frontier story at their finest. As editors we have gathered fourteen stories in this first Western corral of fiction by authors of Five Star Westerns. Only five of these fourteen stories have been published previously, and in each case only in a magazine. Nine of these stories are being published for the first time anywhere. Something about each of these authors and their most recently published work will be included in the headnotes to the respective stories. In general, however, it is perhaps worth stating that what alone brings you back to a piece of music, a song, a painting, a poem, or a story is the mood that it creates in you when you have experienced it. The mood you experience in reading a Western story or a Frontier story is that a better life *is* possible if we have the grit to endure the ordeal of attaining it; that it requires courage to hope, the very greatest courage any human being can ever have. And it is hope that distinguishes the Western story and the Frontier story from every other kind of fiction. Only when courage and hope are gone will these stories cease to be relevant to all of us.

The Mystery Dogs

Fred Grove was born in Hominy, Oklahoma. While working on newspapers in Oklahoma and Texas in the early 1950s, Grove began publishing short stories in some of the leading Western pulp magazines. His first four Western novels were published by Ballantine Books and include some of his finest work, especially COMANCHE CAPTIVES (1961) which earned him the first of five Spur Awards from the Western Writers of America. COMANCHE CAPTIVES also won the Oklahoma Writing Award from the University of Oklahoma and the Levi Strauss Golden Saddleman Award. THE BUFFALO RUNNERS (1968) won the Western Heritage Award from the National Cowboy Hall of Fame. Grove's Western fiction is characterized by a broad spectrum of different settings and time periods. THE GREAT HORSE RACE (1977) and MATCH RACE (1982), both of which won Spur Awards, are concerned with modern quarter horse racing. PHANTOM WARRIOR (1981) and A FAR TRUMPET (1985) are set during the time of the Apache wars. Two of Grove's most memorable novels, WARRIOR ROAD (1974) and DRUMS WITHOUT WARRIORS (1976), focus on the brutal Osage murders during the Roaring 'Twenties, a national scandal that involved the Federal Bureau of Investigation. NO BUGLES, NO GLORY (1959) and BITTER TRUMPET (1989) are notable for their graphic settings during the Civil War. Grove himself once observed that "thanks to my father, who was a trail driver and rancher, and to my mother, who was of Osage and Sioux Indian blood, I feel fortunate that I can write about the American Indian and white man from a middle viewpoint, each in his own fair perspective." Fred Grove's most recent novels include some of his best writing: MAN ON A RED HORSE (Five Star Westerns, 1998), INTO THE FAR MOUNTAINS (Five Star Westerns, 1999), and A DISTANCE OF GROUND (Five Star Westerns, 2000).

* * * * *

He lay slumped against the rocky wall, sweat runneling his slim brown body, naked to the waist, his heart laboring heavily, his legs and arms strengthless. He ran a hand through his straight black hair, now cropped short, and gazed about him. In the fitful light of the torches, he could see the forms of his young Navajo friends, like him, becoming weaker day by day, some already unable to stand. Soon they would all die in this dark hole where they dug out the shiny metal for the Hairy Ones. Then others would take their places, and others after them.

He dozed. Hardly had he begun to rest, it seemed, when he heard the harsh voice of a Hairy One ordering them up. The voice drew nearer. He heard the snap of a whip and the unwilling stir of bare feet. He saw his friends struggling to rise; some could not. He watched in growing despair.

Of a sudden his smoldering defiance burst through. He did not rise, even when he saw his captor moving upon him. This white-skinned man had hair on the backs of his hands, under his long nose, and on his chin and cheeks like the fur of an animal, so thick that his narrowed eyes seemed to glint behind vines, and his mouth was like the den of a beaver overhung with roots. These Hairy Ones also imprisoned their bodies in heavy clothing. There was an odor about them that nauseated a Navajo. Although no stronger than drying hides and other camp odors, the smell was strange and discernible this moment, despite the bad air in the tunnel.

He tensed but kept his face inscrutable as the Hairy One said: "Get up, Roberto."

"My name is Hosteen." His words came awkwardly in the alien tongue he was learning, the tongue he detested.

"On your feet. Remember, you are a slave and a heathen."

Hosteen, not rising, continued to stare at the muscular figure towering over him, the whip dangling like a long black snake.

"I am a Navajo. My name is Hosteen."

"Heathen! Your name is Roberto."

"Hosteen."

It struck him as he knew it would, quickly and powerfully, as it had before when a slave lagged, the whip slashing his naked legs, now his arms and shoulders. He took each blow without expression, refusing to show pain before an enemy, while inside him he cried out. He heard the voice again: "If I punish you much more, you cannot work. Say your name is Roberto and get up."

"Hosteen," he breathed. "My name is Hosteen."

Again the rain of pain. Just when he was about to cry out, it ceased. He sank back. The arm-weary Hairy One was turning away to herd the others to their work.

Hosteen swayed up and fell into line, a grim awareness coming over him. Another beating like that and he would not rise to see another day. He must try to think. One must be brave, but not foolish brave.

Trailing back into the dimly lit tunnel, he chose a pick

and began digging and filling the stout sacks. His hands bled. Dust filled his nose and throat and filmed his eyes. He coughed. All around him there was coughing. And before him, like a sweet dream, rose the wind-swept red rock country where he was born, far to the north, bright and high and clean. Would he ever see it again? He feared not.

A nearby clattering broke his musing. He turned. A boy lay face down across the handle of his pick. Hosteen knelt and lifted the boy over on his back and touched his slack face, seeing the glazed eyes. He stood, eyes smarting tears, as the boy was hauled away by his heels.

Afterward, with the others, Hosteen strained at the lumpy sacks and fell to dragging and carrying them to the entrance of the tunnel, then down the mountain to the high-wheeled *carretas*. Here, for a few moments before he was shouted and lashed back up to the tunnel, he always rested his fascinated eyes on the "Mystery Dogs" inside the log corral. That name, which the Navajos had given these four-legged creatures because they were burden bearers and carried people on their backs, did not fit them somehow, for they were too beautiful and did not look like dogs.

He had seen them first when many Hairy Ones raided Hosteen's tribe and took only young captives, slaying the elders. On the long walk down the Río Grande to this stony mountain he had constantly observed the Mystery Dogs, which the Hairy Ones called *caballos* and which the Navajos were not allowed to go near. Astride their *caballos*, the Hairy Ones had come like gods and left in evil.

"Stay away," Hosteen had been warned. "Don't touch the *caballos*. *Caballos* eat heathens."

Terrified, he had obeyed. And yet, he asked himself many times, why did not the beautiful *caballos* also eat the Hairy Ones, since they were like the Navajos except for the paleness of their skins and the furry hair on their bodies? It was strange. It challenged his reasoning.

Hosteen also noticed that his captors handled these mystery creatures with great care on the trail, feeding them corn and staking them at night to eat the sparse grass, and leading them to water several times each day, and brushing their smooth skins, which glistened in the sun, and combing their glossy manes. And when the Hairy Ones wished to ride, they placed a thing of leather pieces sewn together on the creatures' heads and a straight thing in their mouths and controlled them by pulling on long leather reins attached to the straight thing. And on the creatures' backs the Hairy Ones placed a blanket and on top of that a horned thing of leather that made a seat. How lazy his captors were to ride! How puzzling it all was!

His mind whirled. Could it be that these beautiful beings were the Hairy Ones' secret medicine or power, more powerful than the medicine sticks his captors possessed, that made noise and smoke and hurled tiny objects that killed Navajos? Indeed, everything the invaders did was strange and destructive.

Straining, his body streaming sweat, hacking for wind, Hosteen helped lift the last sack into a *carreta* and stepped back, his eyes fixing on the corral, searching for the *caballo* he had seen yesterday for the first time. His throat caught. There it was now, curiously watching among its fellow creatures, its wide nostrils flaring. He caught their pungent smell. He liked it.

He stared in awe, momentarily lost to his surroundings. This *caballo*'s skin was as red as the Navajo sun, and a broad streak as white as snow ran the length of the proud face. How beautiful! How swift! For he had seen the *caballos* run. His spirits lifted higher. If only he might possess such a wonderful creature, if only he dared touch one and not be eaten alive. Still, why would a being with eyes so intelligent and brave, so warm and gentle, devour a helpless Navajo boy and not the evil Hairy Ones? He yearned to know the truth.

As he stared, a Hairy One ordered the Navajos back to the tunnel. Hosteen lingered a moment longer. Instantly a whip lashed his shoulders. He turned and followed his tribesmen, conscious of an unlooked-for strength. Somehow the whip didn't hurt so much now. Had the red *caballo*—which he decided he would not think of again as an undignified dog of burden—working in its mysterious way made him braver? Perhaps he could ride the *caballo* to freedom. The moment the bold thought sprang to his mind he shrank from it, stiff with fear.

When he staggered into the sunlight again to start loading, there was a noisy commotion in the camp of the Hairy Ones, a rushing about. Looking off to the south, he saw a line of bobbing *carretas* and many four-footed creatures bearing packs, the braying ones with long ears that did not approach the beauty of the proud Mystery Dogs. Watching, Hosteen remembered. One moon ago he had seen such an arrival. Tonight, he knew, the Hairy Ones would drink much crazy water and shout and sing and fight among themselves until it was time for Grandfather the Sun to leave his robes and look upon the world.

Twice during the long afternoon Hosteen saw boys drop in their tracks and be dragged away. That evening, as he ate the watery corn gruel which the Hairy Ones fed them like dogs, a somber realization crowded his mind. He could not endure much longer. He must try to escape. He must be brave. Better to die under the open sky, eaten by a beautiful red *caballo*, than here in the darkness of a foul cave.

Presently, two guards entered to tie the slaves for the

night, weaving and talking boisterously as they went from boy to boy, binding their wrists behind them and then their feet with leather thongs.

"Why tie them?" the first Hairy One asked, "when they are too weak to run away?" His laughter spilled. He gave an enormous belch and reeled against the wall.

"Because," said the other, drawing himself up stiffly, "our illustrious *commandante* so orders. It is our sacred duty to save these heathens from their savage ways."

"Their wrists are as thin as reeds."

"Tie them anyway."

"Save them, it shall be." Attempting to deliver a mocking salute, the first Hairy One lost balance and fell backward. His companion roared with laughter.

When the captor came to him, Hosteen smelled the sourness of crazy water like a further taint on the fetid air.

"Because of your heathen stubbornness today," the guard said, "I will double-tie you tonight."

Hosteen was dismayed. He hadn't expected this.

After the guards left, taking the torches, the tunnel was still but for the coughing and an occasional low moan. Now and then, faintly, Hosteen caught shouts and snatches of song from the camp. *Tonight*, he thought. *If I do not escape tonight when the Hairy Ones are full of crazy water, I will not be alive when the supply carts come again in another moon.*

Twisting about, he felt along the wall behind him for a cutting rock. There was none. Struggling to his feet, he felt higher and to each side. There was none. Now he worked at his rawhide bonds, hoping to slip his wrists free. He could not. Instead, the rough leather seemed to bind him tighter, and in his squirming he knocked over his water gourd.

Next, he scooted forward and with hands and feet searched clumsily for a sharp rock on the tunnel floor, but it was deep in rubble and dust. He found nothing. Weakness overcame him. He lay there for a while. Worming back, he groped for his water gourd. It wasn't there. He had lost his bearings in the darkness. When morning came and he wasn't in his place, the guard would whip him again. He sagged against the wall to rest.

Something dug into his back. Something sharp.

He turned with new strength, feeling for the jagged edge of the rock, and began sawing his wrists back and forth.

A long time later his raw arms dropped free. He sank to the floor, spent. But in moments he was untying his ankles and jerking up and freeing the nearest slave.

"Listen to my words," Hosteen said, when they were all around him. "There is only the guard between us and freedom. I will take him. Then we will ride away on the *caballos*."

"No . . . no!" He could feel their fear, their shrinking back. "The Mystery Dogs will eat us. You know what the Hairy Ones say."

"I have not seen this thing happen. Why do they not eat the Hairy Ones if they like human flesh?"

"We are afraid, Hosteen. We will walk."

"And the Hairy Ones will catch you on the *caballos*. Well, come. You will need your water gourds if you are going to walk."

As he slipped toward the mouth of the tunnel and saw the first dull glow of light, the voices of the camp sounded stronger. With the yelling and singing was a rapid, string-like music not unpleasant to his primitive ears.

He stopped. There was no one at the entrance. But he could not believe the Hairy Ones would leave the slaves unguarded. He moved to the opening, then froze at a whistling sound.

The guard lay flat on his back, snoring steadily, deeply. Crazy water smell was strong. Hosteen stiffened as the guard mumbled and stirred. Another moment and the snoring resumed, rising and falling. Hosteen relaxed.

Stepping back, he led his young tribesmen out and down the trail, past the noisy, torch-lit camp at the foot of the mountain, and onward to the clutter of *carretas* loaded the previous day. Just beyond rose the corral. From here a valley beckoned toward the north. He paused to draw in the sweet-smelling air.

"The Mystery Dogs will eat you," someone said. "Come with us, Hosteen."

He did not quite understand himself. It was strange and compelling. He said: "I must find out about this thing. Go on."

He watched them hurry away, becoming smaller and smaller in the moonlight until their small figures dissolved. A sense of loneliness stabbed him. Would he live to see them again?

His heart leaped faster as he turned and approached the corral. The warm pungency of the *caballos* sent excitement racing through him. He had covered but a few steps when he heard snorts and a ruffle of hoofs. Although he had made no sound, the four-footed beings had discovered him. Did they fear him, a mere boy? Or were they hungry? He was both puzzled and frightened.

He had seen the low house near the corral where the Hairy Ones kept the leather things that went over the *caballos'* backs. Entering, he took one of the leather things and examined it closely. The attached straight thing, which he remembered went between the *caballos'* teeth, was as hard as rock.

Now, going outside, he called on all his courage and

slipped between the bars of the gate and stood motionless. Would the *caballos* rush upon him with teeth bared?

To his relief they trotted to the far end of the corral and swung about, trampling and snorting. How beautiful under the golden light! For a moment his fear left him. One head stood out. The white-blazed face of the red *caballo*. Hosteen stared, entranced. Did he dare touch this most mysterious and powerful of all creatures? For to touch an enemy was the bravest feat of all.

He did not remember stepping forward, but he was, drifting, as silent as smoke. He was some ten steps away when they milled and trotted off. He froze. And an insight came to him: Was it his smell that made them turn away? Did they fear him? But why, when they were the powerful eaters of human flesh?

He became stone still for so long that the *caballos* seemed to lose interest in him; some strayed from the bunch. He began a slow drift again toward the blaze-faced *caballo*, pausing at longer intervals. The creature was blowing softly through its wide nostrils, watching him, more curious than afraid.

By now Hosteen was quite close. He extended his hand, although he never remembered lifting it, toward the quivering nose. He took another careful step, fascinated by the beauty he saw so near, the large eyes more luminous and soft in the moonlight. One more step and he would touch this fearsome Mystery Dog. He was trembling. He had no breath.

With a suspicious snort, the red *caballo* bolted away. And suddenly all of them were running around the corral.

Hosteen glanced in alarm toward the camp. Had the Hairy Ones heard? He listened. As the *caballos* quit circling, he picked up the unbroken strains of stringy music and the hum of voices.

Once more he stalked. Once more he stood close. Only this time, as he reached out a trembling hand, he murmured softly: "O *caballo,* you are beautiful and strong. As red as Grandfather the Sun. As swift as the great wind. You are not a dog. Now I tell you this thing . . . I would rather you ate me here than die in the Hairy Ones' dark hole. If you must do this bad thing which the Hairy Ones say, do it now. I am afraid, but I am ready to die brave like a Navajo."

Little by little he stretched forth his hand. Would the dreaded moment come when he touched the nose? He felt dwarfed as he sensed the creature's enormous strength. Its pungency, strange yet warm, flowed over him, making him even weaker.

He felt the tip of his forefinger graze the nose; to his surprise it was sensitive and also warm. Now he touched the nose with his hand, while his mind spun. Why didn't the creature open its mouth and devour him? Still, he did not draw away, letting the creature breathe his Navajo smell. A shudder ran through him as he felt the lips move. But nothing happened. He felt no pain.

Emboldened, he stroked the white blaze while murmuring all the while. Breathless, he very gradually brought up the leather thing and held the straight, rock-like thing against the *caballo*'s mouth. It opened, and, when he glimpsed the great, even rows of teeth, his fear jumped again. But when he slid the straight thing against the teeth, they parted and did not bite, and, quickly, he drew the leather thing over the short ears as he had watched the Hairy Ones do.

He was bathed in cold sweat as he stood back, holding the reins. Would the *caballo* follow him out of the corral? Would it eat him when he attempted to ride? Or would it devour him now, when he turned his back? He did so, feeling the tingling up his spine, and pulled on the reins and marveled when the other followed him obediently. *I am not fooled,* Hosteen reminded himself. *The Mystery Dog acts friendly, but so did the evil Hairy Ones when they came to my people.*

When Hosteen let down the wooden bars to go out, it occurred to him that the Hairy Ones could not pursue his friends if the other *caballos* ran away, so he left the bars down.

At last he halted. He no longer heard the camp or hoof sounds. He stood in a lake of moonlight. *Now,* he thought. *It will happen now.*

With dread, he drew the reins over the *caballo*'s arched neck and moved to its side. Grasping the long mane, he pulled himself to its back and waited, resigned—for the blinding crash to the earth, the thud of hoofs, the ripping of his thin flesh. He closed his eyes. He must be brave to the end.

A moment. More moments.

He opened his eyes, bewildered. It was strange, but he felt nothing. To his astonishment the *caballo* stood quietly. It seemed to wait.

Shifting about, Hosteen happened to touch his heels to the *caballo*'s flanks. And instantly he was aware of gliding movement beneath him, of being carried away as if on the wings of an eagle. A rhythmic drumming reached his ears. Faster and faster he was moving. He had the headlong sensation of the moon-drenched night rushing past. Cool wind teased his face. A sudden knowing came and deepened, absolute and true. He had found his power, and beauty as well. Above all, he was free again.

For the Good of the Service

Tim Champlin was born John Michael Champlin in Fargo, North Dakota. He began his career writing Western adventure fiction with SUMMER OF THE SIOUX (1982) and has said that the American West represents for him "a huge, ever-changing block of space and time in which an individual had more freedom than the average person has today. For those brave, and sometimes desperate, souls who ventured West looking for a better life, it must have been an exciting time to be alive." Champlin has achieved a notable stature in being able to capture that time in complex, often exciting, and historically accurate fictional narratives. The saga of Jay McGraw, a callow youth who is plunged into outlawry at the beginning of COLT LIGHTNING (1989) later to become a Wells Fargo agent, continues in THE SURVIVOR (Five Star Westerns, 1996) and in DEADLY SEASON (Five Star Westerns, 1997). In all of Champlin's Western stories there are always unconventional plot ingredients, striking historical details, vivid characterizations of the multitude of ethnic and cultural diversity found on the frontier, and narratives rich and original and surprising. His exuberant tapestries include SWIFT THUNDER (Five Star Westerns, 1998), a story of the Pony Express that has been compared favorably with the fiction of Mark Twain, and LINCOLN'S RANSOM (Five Star Westerns, 1999), based on the actual historical event of the theft of President Lincoln's body from its mausoleum. THE LAST CAMPAIGN (Five Star Westerns, 1996) is a vivid account of the final campaign against Geronimo. The story that follows concerns another Apache war chief, Victorio.

★ ★ ★ ★ ★

It was a futile chase, and Lieutenant Miles Justeen had known it would be from its beginning, six days ago. His only hope had been that this knowledge wouldn't leak into his voice when he was giving orders to his troops. The emptiness in the pit of his stomach had felt as vast as the vacant New Mexican landscape. Experience and instinct had told him that Victorio's Apache raiders were miles away to the south by now, moving as swiftly and silently as a buzzard's shadow over the desert.

The mounted column of ten troopers and two officers now topped a slight rise, revealing more endless miles of nothingness, bounded only by several flat-topped mesas in the far distance that might have been forming a broken wall at the edge of the world. In the clear air, the purple mesas looked to be thirty miles away, yet Justeen knew they were closer to eighty.

From a vulture's viewpoint, the column could have been a dying centipede, crawling across this ancient, powdery seabed of gypsum and salt crystals. Captain Stanislaus Ingersoll raised his right hand, and the column came to a rattling, shambling halt behind him, leather squeaking. The thick tail of yellow dust they dragged along caught up and wrapped softly around them, sticking to everything but eyeballs and the undersides of tongues.

"Justeen!" Captain Ingersoll barked without turning his head.

In spite of his fatigue, Miles Justeen's stomach roiled at the sound of the nasal voice. He kneed his mount forward from the back of the column and reined in beside Ingersoll. "Sir?"

"Fraternizing with the enlisted men again?" the captain said in an insinuating undertone, his eyes still to the front.

Justeen suddenly had a bitter taste in his mouth and spat to one side. "No, sir. Just conferring with Sergeant Burke."

"From now on, I want you riding at the head of this column where you belong."

"Yes, sir."

"While you wear that uniform, you will act like an officer whether you want to or not. Understand?" The venomous voice was just loud enough for Justeen to hear.

"Yes, sir." He had to swallow the gorge that was rising in his throat at the arrogance of this man who was ten years his junior in age and seven years behind him in experience. Justeen had learned early in his own career to take full advantage of the experience of men of lesser rank, such as career non-coms like Sergeant Patrick Burke. He wanted desperately to swing his balled fist and knock this man from the saddle, crumpling that slim back that was as straight as a rifle barrel, but, with accustomed discipline, he thrust the fleeting urge aside. While such an action might provide some temporary satisfaction, it would quickly end his career, and he had invested too much time and effort to let his contempt for this pompous West Pointer end it now. Justeen had tried hard not to hate this man who had gained a captaincy in the cavalry only four years out of college, thanks to a father-in-law in the War Department. Not only did Justeen believe hate to be morally wrong, but he also knew it was a self-destructive emotion that could eat out a man's insides, leaving him hollow inside.

"What do you make of that?" Ingersoll pointed.

Justeen's gaze swept over the aching glare of the near distance and then farther out to their left where piñon-studded foothills finally sloped down to meet the level, arid plain they were traversing.

"What's that, sir?" he was finally forced to ask when he saw nothing.

"There! That smoke," Ingersoll said impatiently, handing over the field glasses.

Justeen adjusted the focus and aimed the glasses in the direction of Ingersoll's pointing finger. He picked up a dark smudge on the horizon with threads of black smoke trailing upward, like strands of hair brushed against the brassy sky. Justeen handed the glasses back.

"Well? Smoke from a homestead chimney?"

"No." Justeen shook his head, squinting at the position of the sun. "Three reasons . . . no cooking fire in mid-afternoon . . . and it's certainly not for warmth. Thirdly, wood fires usually give off white smoke. That's a large fire burning something oily."

"Huh?" Ingersoll took another look, then shoved the glasses back into their leather case and hung them on the saddle horn. He considered it an inherent sign of weakness ever to acknowledge a subordinate's ideas or wisdom. Even his leading of this patrol, which usually required only one junior officer, was Ingersoll's way of showing Justeen how it should be done—and, Justeen believed, to grab a little glory for himself should they come up with Victorio's band. Justeen was painfully aware that Ingersoll's belittling atti-tude was obvious to the men, and he prayed it would not undermine their respect for his own authority.

"Move out!" the captain ordered, motioning with his hand.

"Stagger the column," Justeen said to Sergeant Burke who had ridden up, unnoticed.

Justeen was startled at the look that flashed like a hurled lance from Burke's gray eyes to the back of the captain's head, but the sergeant quickly recaptured the demon and replied with a respectful—"Yes, sir."—as he turned to relay the command. Every second trooper moved out of line to ride twenty yards to the side, a maneuver that not only kept down the plume of dust but also allowed the horses room to breathe.

The men rode silently, numbly, down the gentle incline toward the valley floor. Conversation and jokes had long since been pounded out of them by the brass hammer that swung overhead in the heavens. No longer did they borrow or lend chews of twist. In mouths with no saliva, the tobacco only balled up in dry lumps of leaf.

In the mistaken notion that it would enhance their speed and mobility, Ingersoll had directed that no pack mules were to accompany the column. The resulting subsistence rations hardly mattered to the depressed appetites of the men who were making do on hardtack, beans, and bacon, and to ensure their bellies remained flat, the bacon had slowly melted down to mostly lean and rind, the fat saturating the cotton sacks and leather saddlebags. Hot, metallic-tasting water in nearly dry canteens; carbine barrels that blistered bare hands; blue shirts bleached and faded, whitened with salt; stained campaign hats that kept the foreheads damp and the sun from boring into the top of the skull; red-rimmed eyes and unshaven faces; perspiration chafing the crotch and armpits where saddles and shirts were damp, then dry, then damp again, adding to the sour smell of old sweat, and mingling with the smell of horses— these were the things that had replaced the glory and the guidons when the post was left behind. Yet, these men were lean, hardened veterans, uncomplaining and accustomed to hardship, accepting their lot, men who referred to their trials only in terms of wry and biting humor. If Justeen could have winnowed a select few from the hundreds of men in the ranks, he could hardly have done better than those who rode behind him now. From Privates Atkins, Norbert, McLeary, Murphy, Slater, Bungart, Johnson, to Corporals Stern and Duffy, to First Sergeant Burke, they had all proven themselves, time and again. Each had his own reasons for enlisting and reënlisting, but all had a sense of duty and would give their best efforts while they wore the colors.

Justeen twisted in his saddle and ran his slitted eyes over their faces. He knew them as individuals and as a fighting unit, and he was proud of them. But of their former lives he knew little. He again faced front and eased his position in the saddle to one slightly less uncomfortable and thought of his own life before the war. That life was as dead as last year's grass. Only in his mind's eye could he still see the broad, tree-shaded street and the two-story, white, clapboard house of his boyhood. He could almost feel the cool breeze and hear the shouts of his friends, almost taste the numbing cold of iron-tainted well water drunk straight from the pump, sniff the sharp smell of dill weed coming from his mother's kitchen, see his father in white shirt and suspenders sprawled in the porch swing on a summer's evening. How long ago all that seemed! Yet it was his mental salvation, when he needed to escape. He could call it up at will, savoring the small details of a life that he had once taken for granted.

The troop halted for ten minutes every hour, and the horses were unbitted to allow them to crop whatever grass they could find. During the next four hours, this proved virtually none. The standard procedure was to trot for twenty minutes every second hour, and to dismount and lead the horses for a full hour before a watering stop. But, on his own initiative, under the harsh gaze of Ingersoll, Justeen modified this to a ten-minute stop every hour and a leading of the animals for thirty minutes every two hours, with no trotting at all.

"The mounts won't stand it, sir," he explained after Ingersoll heard him give the command to Burke. "They have no water at all, and we won't reach the tanks in those foothills until dark." Ingersoll grunted something that Justeen took for agreement.

Although time in this country was measured in terms of the number of daylight hours, Justeen, from long habit, consulted his silver-nickel pocket watch. It was six-thirty, and they were approaching the still-smoldering embers of the fire it had taken them four hours to reach.

While they were still a good hundred yards off, Justeen noticed something moving. As he turned to see if Sergeant Burke could make out what it was, he was startled when Burke yelled: "Git away from there, ye black spawn o' Satan."

The sergeant fired his revolver once, then twice, the booming explosions racketing away to be swallowed up by the massive silence. Several black vultures took off, flapping heavily away.

"That'll do, Sergeant," Justeen said. "Put it away. They're just nature's clean-up squad."

When the patrol reined up a few minutes later, Justeen saw at a glance that the charred heaps of rubble had once been two large wagons. Whatever animals had pulled them were gone, but the bodies of their human masters were still there, horribly mutilated. He dismounted stiffly, and had to hold onto the slotted McClellan saddle for a few moments before enough feeling returned to his legs and buttocks to step away.

It was hard to tell if the three bodies had been Mexicans or whites. The naked corpses were already swollen and blackening after several hours in the fierce sun. Their thighs and arms were split open, and they had been disemboweled, the strings of thick viscera swarming with green flies. As a final indignity, their genitals had even been amputated. One of the three was lashed to a rear wagon wheel, head down over a small fire, where his brains had slowly roasted. Justeen fervently hoped the man had not been conscious long.

"Ah, those red devils have taken their revenge, and that's for certain," Burke muttered, surveying the carnage.

"Select a burial party and get started," Justeen said to Burke, before walking toward Ingersoll who was some distance away, avoiding the bodies and looking at the wagons. "Apparently a small freighting party," Justeen said to his superior officer.

"That's very obvious, Mister Justeen. When we catch up to those savages, there will be no prisoners taken." The tall, lean captain was poking at the smoking wagon with a piece of burned board. Justeen caught a faint whiff of coal oil. Apparently that had been part of the cargo. It probably accounted for how thoroughly the wagons had burned—and for the amount of black smoke they had seen from such a distance. The wagons were now only piles of charcoal and pieces of iron.

"Anything left?" Justeen wondered.

"Nothing. What they couldn't carry off, they burned."

Justeen looked at the officer. His blue tunic was buttoned to the neck, his hat was on straight, and besides the thin mustache decorating his lip he had somehow managed to remain clean-shaven, no doubt using precious drops of his canteen water.

"What could they have wanted with a couple of freight wagons?" Ingersoll asked. "Probably just their savage, destructive vengeance against the whites." He kept his eyes averted from the burned body that two soldiers were cutting away from the wagon wheel only a few feet away.

Justeen nodded. "Vengeance was part of it, all right. But it was the mules."

"What?"

"They wanted the mules, or horses . . . whatever was hitched to these wagons. Fresh mounts and food. The men were just in the way, and provided some entertainment."

"Savages!" Ingersoll murmured grimly. "We'll run them to ground."

Justeen was not as optimistic, but said nothing as he walked away toward the six men who were already using entrenching tools, attached to their carbine barrels, to scrape out shallow graves in the sandy soil. The stench of burned flesh and fecal matter was strong in the late-afternoon heat. "Sergeant Burke, do you believe in reincarnation?" he heard himself asking.

"Heaven forbid, sir!" The wiry Irishman recoiled at the idea. "With my luck, I'd come back as me horse!"

Before he could stop himself, Justeen snorted with laughter.

Ingersoll shot him a hard look, but Justeen hardly cared. *Ingersoll doesn't matter now,* he thought. *His opinion of me and my methods has been formed. Now all he needs is some justification for disciplinary action.*

"I do believe in a heaven and a hell," Burke was saying. " 'Scuse me, sir. . . ." He suddenly interrupted himself and walked toward the soldiers. "Slater! Murphy! I said *three* separate graves . . . not one big one. And move back off the trail a ways."

Justeen decided to do some scouting on foot around the attack site. The signs he read in the scuffed earth showed the attackers had swept down out of the pine-covered hillside to hit the freighters where the faint wagon track skirted the base of the hill, before tracing its twin scratches across the crusty wastes to the next low mountain range many miles to the northwest. But what disturbed him was that all the shod and unshod hoof prints leaving the scene did not go south or southwest, following the easiest route on the arid plain. The tracks, instead, curved away and then started back into the foothills through a rocky defile. Why? Maybe to take advantage of the cover and whatever water tanks were available. But it would be rougher going, and slower, if they were headed for the border.

He returned to stand beside the first sergeant. "Do you think Victorio is headed straight for Mexico?" Justeen asked.

"Beggin' your pardon, sir, but I don't carry the rank to be offerin' opinions on such as that." He glanced toward Captain Ingersoll who was watching them from a distance.

"But I'm asking, Sergeant."

Burke removed his hat and mopped his wind-burned face with a shirt sleeve. "Well, sir, if I were guessin', I'd say they would be heading that way. But, like a riled-up rattlesnake, they might strike a time or two more before they get across the line where we can't follow." He replaced his hat and watched his men, yellow neckerchiefs tied over noses and mouths, dragging the bloody corpses into the hollows dug in the ground. "There's a lot of hate in those heathen hearts," Burke went on, averting his eyes from the horror that had so recently housed human spirits.

"Hurry with those burials!" Ingersoll barked, looking up

from the small notebook where he was now scribbling something. "We're losing daylight. It'll be dark in an hour."

"Yes, sir," Justeen replied.

"The man is all heart," Burke muttered under his breath. "Get a move on," he said in a full voice.

"Sarge, this ain't a job we'd be a-draggin' out just for fun," a muffled voice retorted through a yellow bandanna.

The fiery orb turned to an orange disk and slipped down the sky toward the other side of the world. The air temperature began to moderate slightly. A touch of breeze stirred as the cooler, heavier air high in the mountains began to slide downslope into the arid valley. On this faint movement of air, Justeen caught a whiff of woodsmoke, and he was standing well upwind of the smoking wagons. A prickle of cold fear went up his back under the damp shirt. The raiding party was still close by, or else they had left a cooking fire burning somewhere above them.

He quietly conveyed his suspicions to Burke. "Get those bodies covered and let's get mounted," he concluded.

"Yes, sir."

Without appearing to hurry, he walked toward Captain Ingersoll. "Sir, we need to move out of here quickly."

"Have you forgotten how to salute, Mister Justeen?"

Justeen came to attention and snapped a salute. This formality was usually dispensed with on such patrols, but apparently it was still a necessity for a man whose authority was upheld only by his shoulder straps. Justeen repeated his concern to Ingersoll.

"Nonsense," the captain said, glancing at the silent hillside. "Once this carrion is buried. . . ."

"Those were *men,* sir," Justeen interrupted, barely able to control his temper.

"As I was saying, *Lieutenant,* we'll then proceed into the foothills to find that water tank you said was nearby. Then we will make a night march down the valley. There will be a partial moon to light our way. If those Indians went into the hills, it was only for water. We'll head down the valley and likely cut them off when they come down the other side."

"Sir, I think we should wait until dark to go for the water. Less chance of an ambush."

"If you're afraid to lead this column, Mister Justeen, I'll be glad to relieve you of command," Ingersoll snapped, a predatory gleam in his black eyes.

"No, sir. I'm just urging caution. We don't want to walk into a trap. Victorio knows we're hot on his trail. He's likely posted a rear guard to slow us down."

"If you remember your military history, General George McClellan could have ended the war much sooner, had he not erred on the side of caution. Besides, an officer does not act on hunches, especially those he gets from non-coms. I heard you discussing this with Sergeant Burke."

Justeen ground his teeth in frustration, but snapped a parting salute, and turned on his heel. He was saved from any further thought on the matter when a crashing of sudden gunfire ripped the air. Several mounted Apaches came riding out of the rocky defile, yelling and firing as they came.

Justeen yanked his long-barreled Colt and ran toward the horses, his heart pounding. The war party had caught them afoot and probably hoped to stampede the animals and wipe out the surprised and scattered soldiers at the same time. But Bungart, Stern, and Duffy had taken the precaution of hobbling all the horses.

"Get your carbines and get down!" Justeen yelled.

The startled horses were plunging but were too tired and restricted by their front feet to get away. The three horse guards grabbed their .45-55 Springfields from their saddles and flopped onto their bellies, facing the oncoming Apaches who were still seventy yards away.

The burial party was scrambling to get to the burned wagons, the only cover around. Ingersoll had his revolver out and was already firing.

"Wait until I give the command!" Justeen shouted. "Then give 'em a volley!"

The Apaches closed to thirty yards.

"Now!"

Carbine and pistol fire flashed and roared in unison, and three Indians pitched from their horses. One pony went down, kicking, throwing its rider.

Then the firing became general as the remaining five mounted warriors rode past them, still yelling and shooting. Three of them were armed with repeating Winchesters, Justeen noted in a flash.

After the first volley, the soldiers fell back on their six-guns, with no time to reload the single-shot carbines, all but Burke who could load and fire a trap-door Springfield faster than anyone Justeen had ever seen.

Hitting a moving target from a stationary position was easier than hitting a stationary position from horseback, so the defenders had the advantage. When the first attack swept past without securing the horses, the Apaches wheeled and rode back through, firing rapidly. With a daring quickness, they retrieved two of their three wounded comrades before riding into the shelter of the rocky defile, leaving the field to the soldiers. A pony lay thrashing on the ground. One Apache lay dead or badly wounded, too close to the defenders to be retrieved.

"Get reloaded!" Justeen yelled. "Is everyone OK?"

"McLeary got it in the head," a husky voice answered.

Atkins had a flesh wound in the upper arm and was cursing softly, trying to grip it with his other hand.

A bullet had grazed one of the horses across the withers, Bungart reported.

Captain Stanislaus Ingersoll was also down, his knee shattered by a lead slug. Justeen knelt by the wounded officer who was lying near one of the wagons, feebly clutching his leg. Part of his pants leg was soaked in blood, as was the top of his boot. He was gritting his teeth, and sweat was popping out on his pale forehead. Justeen tied his own bandanna tightly around the thigh, just above the wound, to help stanch the flow of blood. When Justeen tried to ease him into a more comfortable position, the captain gasped and fainted. Justeen took his pocketknife and slit the trouser leg. Even with a layman's eye, he could see this was a severe injury. If the leg could be saved, and the officer lived, he would, at the very least, have a stiff knee for life.

At such a moment, ingrained discipline assumes control of a man's actions. Justeen was once more in command and did what he had to do—prepare for the next Apache onslaught and attend to a seriously wounded officer. There was no time to entertain a sudden vision of himself parrying thrusts from a Board of Inquiry—a board that would surely be convened because of Ingersoll's political influence.

He looked toward the men. There had been no panic. The battle-hardened troopers, weapons ready, lay quietly, awaiting the next attack.

But no second attack proved forthcoming. The only sound in the stillness was the snorting and thrashing of the dying pony. A carbine crashed, and the pony lay still, mercifully dispatched by one of the soldiers. An acrid pall of fine dust and spent gunpowder drifted slowly away on an imperceptible breeze.

★ ★ ★ ★ ★

The sun finally died in a welter of red and gold twenty minutes later, and the patrol stirred and made ready to depart. There would be no pursuit of the Apaches. Victorio's band, with three wounded or killed, had paid a price for the lives of the three freighters, and the Apaches could ill afford the loss. It was only another minor skirmish in this hard war of attrition, Miles Justeen thought, but it would somehow all add up to a conclusion down the years.

He unstrapped the bedroll from the cantle of his saddle. They would have to fashion some sort of blanket litter in order to sling the wounded officer between two horses. It was the only way he could be transported. But it was many rough, jarring miles to the nearest post, and Justeen wasn't at all sure the captain would make it.

Several yards away, Duffy and Johnson were preparing McLeary's body for burial. Another man was helping Atkins bind a neckerchief around his wounded arm. Justeen dropped the blanket on the ground and reached for a bottle of carbolic he always carried in his saddlebags. As he uncorked the disinfectant and squatted to pour a little of it on Ingersoll's still oozing knee wound, Sergeant Burke walked over and looked down at the unconscious captain.

"What a shame that a fine young officer is cut down so early in his career," he observed.

Justeen looked at him sharply, but couldn't detect any hint of sarcasm in the voice or behind the gray eyes.

"But, on the other hand," Burke continued, "he'll probably be reassigned to a desk job at one of the posts back East, if he isn't given a hero's medal and disabled out of the Army. But, whatever happens, it will be for the good of the service," he concluded firmly, turning away. "Our next problem is to get a couple of volunteers to scout for water in those hills."

Burke's uncharacteristic remarks triggered a thought process in Justeen's mind. As he squatted on his heels, he recalled details of the march—a look here and a comment there, insignificant at the time, which now took on an ominous clarity, especially when he remembered that Patrick Burke had been situated directly behind Captain Ingersoll during the attack.

"Sergeant Burke," he said to the retreating back, "if the post surgeon removes a four-hundred-grain Springfield bullet from this man's knee, I'm having you court-martialed."

Burke kept walking. "Lieutenant, I'm *sure* I saw some stolen Army Springfields in the hands of those filthy, heathen redskins." He stopped and turned around. "And I wouldn't be at all surprised if several of the men noticed 'em, too."

And there, Miles Justeen decided, the matter would forever rest.

So Wild, So Free

T. T. Flynn was born Thomas Theodore Flynn, Jr., in India-napolis, Indiana. He was the author of over a hundred Western short novels for leading pulp magazines. He moved to New Mexico with his wife Helen and spent much of his time living in a trailer while on the road exploring the vast terrain of the American West. His descriptions of the land are always detailed, but he used them not only for local color but also to reflect the heightening of emotional distress among the characters within a story. Following the Second World War, Flynn turned his attention to the book-length Western novel and in this form also produced work that has proven lasting. Five of these novels first appeared as original paperbacks, most notably THE MAN FROM LARAMIE (1954), featured as a serial in *The Saturday Evening Post* and subsequently made into a memorable motion picture directed by Anthony Mann and starring James Stewart, and TWO FACES WEST (1954), dealing with the problems of identity and reality that served as the basis for a television series. He was highly innovative and inventive and in later novels, such as RIDING HIGH (1961), concentrated on deeper psychological issues as the source for conflict, rather than more elemental motives like greed. He was so meticulous about his research that he once spent days to determine the exact year that blue- (as opposed to red-) checked tablecloths were introduced because all anachronism was anathema to him. Flynn is at his best in stories which combine mystery—not surprisingly, he also wrote detective fiction—suspense, and action in an artful balance. The world in which his characters live is often a comedy of errors in which the first step in any direction frequently can, and does, lead to ever deepening complications. His most recent books have been NIGHT OF THE COMANCHE MOON (Five Star Westerns, 1995), RAWHIDE: A WESTERN QUINTET (Five Star Westerns, 1996), LONG JOURNEY TO DEEP CAÑON: A WESTERN QUARTET (Five Star Westerns, 1997), DEATH MARKS TIME IN TRAMPAS: A WESTERN QUINTET (Five Star Westerns, 1998), and THE DEVIL'S LODE: A WESTERN QUARTET (Five Star Westerns, 1999). Reprints of all of his Western novels from the 1950s have been published in hardcover editions by Chivers Press in the Gunsmoke series. His Western stories are available in full-length audio editions from Books on Tape and D H Audio, while NIGHT OF THE COMANCHE MOON was recently published in paperback for the first time by Leisure Books. The story that follows was the last fiction T. T. Flynn wrote, and this marks its first publication anywhere.

★ ★ ★ ★ ★

The buggy had been halted by force. The man on horseback by the front wheel was holding the long reins. Kelly saw that much as he looked down the last, long slope to the road.

Any road, Kelly had been thinking as the still-wild black stallion ran tirelessly down through the lower hills and rough breaks, meant ranches, farms, settlements, where good men were bogged in burdens and worries. For Kelly, none of that, ever; he stayed in the mountains and high hills, more free and satisfied than the wild horses he hunted.

It was the buggy top, cut frugally from an old wagon tarp, remembered well, that made Kelly drop his carbine across the pommel as he rode down the brush-dotted slope toward something which was probably none of his business. That he might regret it never occurred to Kelly. His days, and sometimes nights, held zest and few regrets.

His hat had a tilt; a sunburst of gay yellow silk kerchief draped his neck. His grin was easy and carefree as he halted the stallion so that the carbine muzzle just happened to point at the scowling rider who still held the reins.

"Kelly!" Ruthie Duval's surprised gulp from the sun-cracked buggy seat sounded relieved. "It's years. . . ."

Kelly chuckled. "Almost three years, Ruthie. I move around." Ruthie, he recalled, must be past twenty now, still small-boned, still slender, with a new, surprising maturity on her honest, attractive face. Kelly's glance went to the buggy whip in the road dust—to the thin, red line on the man's jaw and cheek. A Morrison, by the slabby build and pointy face, one of the younger Morrisons, about Ruthie's age. They were a tribe, look-alikes, the Morrisons, clannish and dark-tempered.

Ruthie swallowed with visible effort. "I'll take the reins now, Breck." She was flushed, from temper or fear. A little of both, Kelly decided.

Fight a Morrison and you had to fight them all, sooner or later. They made common cause against outsiders. This one, Breck Morrison, was near-handsome, despite his sharp face. Long brown hair had a vain curl; checkered shirt had a bold look. Cartridge loops were fat on his belt, gun heavy in his holster. And he held stubbornly to the reins, scowling.

Kelly's finger slid to the carbine trigger.

Breck Morrison noted it. His look was venomous as he tossed the reins to Ruthie. "Me 'n' Ruthie were talkin'."

"Talk on." Kelly's smile widened. "I'll wait . . . got all day."

"Some other time!"

The retreating horse drove dust spurts as spurs gouged hard. Kelly frowned over that as he dismounted and picked up the whip. He liked horses. His grin was restored as he returned the whip and settled back in the saddle. "Your buggy stopped much like this, Ruthie?"

"I don't see Breck often," Ruthie evaded. She changed the subject as she gathered the reins. "Kelly, when are you going to stop living like a wild horse, and settle down?"

"I come in." Kelly's eyes were laughing.

"I've heard," Ruthie said. "Drinking, gambling, fighting. . . ."

"Only a little." Memories widened Kelly's grin.

Ruthie's face pinked. "And . . . and saloon girls. . . ."

"Everything you hear."

"Is true, isn't it?" said Ruthie relentlessly. Then she drove on.

Kelly rode easily by the creaking wheels. Years ago the buggy had been rickety; it was more so now.

Ruthie said: "I'm almost twenty-two . . . you were five years older. . . ."

Kelly thought back to Ruthie's long braids and crisp bright ribbon bows, to himself lofty with overwhelming age, five years older. His smile was reminiscent.

"I know girls," Ruthie said firmly, "many girls. . . ."

Kelly jested: "So do I."

"Not that kind! Earnest, Christian, home-loving girls, who could do a lot with you, Kelly."

Kelly almost shuddered. "How," he inquired hastily, "are little Johnny and Uncle Tobe?"

Ruthie's face shadowed. "Little Johnny is eighteen now.

He . . . he thought everything you did, Mike Kelly, was perfect and wonderful. He still does . . . wants to be like you . . . he's trying hard." Ruthie sounded bitter.

Kelly cleared his throat and tried to adjust to this new Johnny. After all, being Mike Kelly wasn't so bad.

"Rheumatism," Ruthie finished, "has almost crippled Uncle Tobe. Stop by sometime, Mike, and sit with him."

Gaunt Uncle Tobe, the rock, the pillar—rearing two small kids on the scant ranch land that had been left to them. Kelly had the picture now. This look of full maturity had been forced on Ruthie by work, responsibility, worry.

"Are the Morrisons," Kelly asked mildly, "giving you trouble?"

"No . . . that is. . . ." Worry shadowed Ruthie's face again. "It's Johnny, really. He ordered Breck off our property . . . warned Breck not to speak to me again . . . and did it across Uncle Tobe's shotgun and a buckshot load."

Kelly's grin returned. "Good for Johnny!"

"Wild like you . . . trying to be like you, Kelly!" Ruthie drew a worried breath. "Did you ever hear of a Morrison who would forget a shotgun threat?"

Kelly hadn't, but passed over the fact. "What did this Breck say when he stopped your buggy back there?"

"Breck wanted to take me to the *fiesta* at the Campas Ranch today. He said he'd take me out from now on, or no one else would. He . . . he hinted that Johnny might get hurt if I didn't keep Johnny out of it."

"This Breck," Kelly said with amusement, "must have it bad. What do you do to a man, Ruthie?" The thought brought his chuckle. "I rode in for the *fiesta* . . . go with me."

Ruthie's quick glance was suspicious. "So you can laugh at Breck . . . and make it worse?" Her shrug denied Kelly that. "I couldn't go, anyway. Pete Radwick sent for me. Another baby today. I promised to help."

"Another?" Kelly was wryly amused. "What do they do with so many?"

"You wouldn't know, Kelly. They love them, of course." Ruthie's clouding concern returned. "Johnny will be at the *fiesta*. So will Breck. Will you watch Johnny?"

"No one ever starts trouble at the *fiesta*," Kelly reminded airily. "But I'll ride herd on Johnny. Don't worry."

Rancho Campas had been an immense Spanish Grant, where proud dons had been lavish with hospitality, indifferent of money or business, hot-bloodedly reckless in gambling. Ricardo Campas bore his ancestors no ill-will for the vastly shrunken ranch he had inherited. Enough remained for the good life, and some of the traditions, including yearly *fiesta*.

Kelly knew what he would find on the broad, grassy flat beside the green willow thickets along the Creek of the Angels. *Fiesta*—great beef chunks slowly pit-roasting in the old way; deep iron pots simmering fat chili beans; beds of tender shuck corn steaming over hot coals; buckets of fiery red chili, of deceptively cool-looking green chili; hillocks of platter-size tortillas on snowy cloths; steam drifting from huge, smoke-darkened coffee pots—and *fiesta* radiating from the beaming, portly figure of Ricardo Campas, elegant for the day in silvered-studded *charro* clothes, welcoming all.

Kelly arrived with an exuberant flourish, as usual, the burnished black stallion bursting into the lower end of the flat in a skimming run, Kelly's hat tilted, wind-rippling yellow silk folds at his neck, warming laughter on his face.

He called greeting at the long hitch racks and shook

many hands on his way to the cook pits and the shifting group around Ricardo Campas.

"¡Miguel . . . *amigo!*" Ricardo's English was better than Kelly's—but this was *fiesta*. Arm around Kelly's shoulder, Ricardo spoke through his graying mustache into Kelly's ear. "Add a hundred to any offer for that big black devil of a horse."

Kelly's chuckle was soft between them. "Took me months to run him right and corral him. No Spanish jawbreaker goes into his mouth."

"Two hundred . . . *ai!* . . . three hundred," urged the heating blood of earlier dons, who had wished and got, at any cost.

"That horse remembers, Ricardo. He'd trample you and take off . . . like he's waiting to do with me."

"*Por Dios* . . . a killer?"

"He could be . . . listen," said Kelly under his breath. "I've been watching a blood-bay stallion, with more mares than this one had. First offer, if I corral him?"

"Sold . . . *now!*" A hasty palm sealed it. "But for the love of every saint, *amigo,* not all my skin to pay."

A good life Kelly had, Kelly thought complacently, as he heaped a tin plate and dropped cross-legged on the grass. That big, blood-bay mustang stallion would take outwitting. But he was as good as corralled, already sold. And what a trip that would be after Ricardo paid. The town would remember Kelly for weeks.

"Gee, Mike . . . Mister Kelly . . . 'member me . . . Johnny Duval?"

Inches taller, shoulders broader. Glancing up, Kelly remembered how it was at eighteen, cocky and confident, juices fermenting. Johnny, Ruthie had said, was like Kelly.

Johnny's gaze admired Kelly's yellow neck silk, Kelly's lank, weathered toughness. "Wish I had a horse'd match that black you rode in," Johnny said enviously. "Need help next time you hunt a bunch?"

"Can't tell." The shiny-eyed admiration was making Kelly uncomfortable. Johnny had a gun belt, a gun—suppose he heard that Ruthie's buggy had been stopped? Breck Morrison was here at the *fiesta,* and other Morrisons. "I'll let you know," Kelly said noncommittally. He sat thoughtfully, absently crumbling a bit of tortilla, after Johnny moved jauntily on.

A half hour later Kelly's face was blank when he confronted Breck Morrison. "If Ruthie Duval is stopped again . . . or Johnny's egged into gunfight . . . I'll track you," Kelly said softly. "Pay heed."

The slabby, near-handsome face turned red. "You makin' threats?"

"Promises," said Kelly coldly. "To you . . . and anyone helps you." He walked away.

Jump one Morrison, you jumped them all. Kelly's grin broke ruefully. He'd ridden in for fun today, and now he was a cat's whisker from a feud, and it would be a mean one. All the Morrisons were vindictive. The thought lurked back in his consciousness as he watched the horse race, another Rancho Campas tradition. To a wagon at the falls of Angel Creek, west to distant cottonwoods, back to the flat— some four miles, all in view of the spectators gathered near the finish rope.

Kelly's black could have won, but four furious miles punished any horse. In the gathered crowd, Kelly watched over thirty riders string dust across the distance, and leaders quirt and spur back to the flat, four almost neck and neck ahead. But Johnny Duval's straining claybank broke the rag-hung finish rope.

Kelly shook his head as Johnny tumbled off to a grinning strut of victory, leading his blowing, lathered horse to Ricardo Campas for the winner's prize—a new revolver with pearl grips. A heady boost for a cocky, wild, young rooster. Not good for Johnny; not good.

There was dancing, as always, on a wide plank floor, put down each year. Kelly was a tireless dancer, but today his mood held him off the floor. Ruthie Duval was on his mind—and Johnny, who wanted to be like Kelly. Ruthie had made it sound accusing—Kelly, roaming the far hills, enjoying life. Girls like Ruthie, Kelly decided, simply couldn't understand. But someone did want to understand. Kelly's roving glance stopped, locked with near and boldly inviting eyes.

He had noticed her honey-colored hair from a distance, her dress cut low, the way she walked—drawing men's eyes even while she looked discreetly down. Kelly drew a breath—and the quick flame fizzled, a sparking moment of promise went soggy. The inviting smile never reached his mouth. Feeling sheepish, Kelly watched the honey hair toss disdainfully as she turned away.

Sundown blazed. Oil flares on tall poles around the dance floor fought back the creeping blue twilight. The first few of waiting fire piles around the flat lifted flames. A scattering of wagons, buggies were leaving. But the guitars, fiddles, laughter, and dancing grew louder, faster. And when, early in the evening, Kelly saw young Breck Morrison loitering near the dance floor, staring off into the night, grinning faintly, Kelly looked that way with interest.

That was how he happened to see Johnny Duval moving

from the firelight into the shadows under the willows—and the honey-colored hair at Johnny's side. Trouble, Kelly sensed, but what? He started toward the spot where Johnny had vanished.

Sparks swirled up from the nearest fire as a wood chunk toppled, and the screech that lifted back into the willows sounded like a furious, protesting cat. Music stopped, and the silent tension through which Kelly ran now had an uncertain, explosive quality. Not even his worst forebodings had guessed what happened next. The honey hair fled back into the first firelight in disheveled outrage, the low neck of her clinging dress visibly ripped.

Kelly groaned as he ran. Johnny would never live this down—if Johnny lived. Ahead of Kelly, Breck Morrison was bolting into the willows, gun in hand. No way to stop him.

Back in the willows a gunshot slammed heavily, another gun fired, and the echoes were reverberating as Kelly reached the first low willow branches and black shadows. Twigs, leaves slapped at his face. He lifted a guarding arm—and stumbled over prone legs.

"Johnny?" Swinging back, Kelly thought of Ruthie, whom he'd have to tell, whom he'd promised to look after Johnny.

"Kill 'im!" called thickly from the ground. "He shot me an' run!"

Not Johnny's voice—but Johnny's trouble. Breck Morrison had been cut down with a bullet. First the girl, then a Morrison. Kelly could have groaned again over Johnny's thinning chances.

"I hope he gut-shot you," Kelly said savagely as suspicions crystallized. Other men were rushing to the spot. "Here's one!" Kelly shouted. Covered by that, he headed out of the willows, trying to think like Johnny would be thinking.

Fiesta had ended in confusion. Outraged women had closed protectively around the honey hair. Kelly ran, unnoticed, toward the long hitch racks. The shadowy, bolting run of a horse faded from the racks ahead of him. When he reined his own horse the same way, ominous, fire-silhouetted figures were running to the racks.

South, the ranch road, and town. North, beyond the black line of willows, Angel Creek scoured against a high cutbank on the other side. Where the willows thinned ahead, wagon ruts dropped into the creek, lifted through a narrow slit in the high bank to open range. Instinct guided Kelly. Johnny was rattled, desperate. North lay fastest escape. The black horse splashed across the shallow creek and topped the high bank. A slash of the rein ends exploded into a tremendous run.

Kelly had no solution for this unholy mess. They might not have hanged Johnny for decently stealing a horse, forgiving youthful error. Shooting a proddy gunman might have been approved. But this: virtue—Kelly snorted—defiled. A righteously indignant Morrison shot down. Kelly groaned, once more. Johnny, strutting his new, thin shell of manhood, had dug a dismaying pit.

Eyes adjusting to the pale starlight, black horse running like a scudding ghost, Kelly thought how this would crush Ruthie. Her burdens, heavy enough, did not deserve this. And Ruthie's eyes would condemn Kelly.

A straight line led quickest away from danger. The line this way was north to the Lone Rock Tank, on to the higher breaks beyond, and twenty-odd miles of dry, lifting hill country to the next water. Dubious safety lay that way for Johnny, and angry men coming behind him, Kelly knew, must be thinking the same thing. He hoped instinct was right—and it was. Off to the left a gun muzzle blossomed red.

"Johnny!" Kelly veered over, shouting again. He saw the shadowy horse and rider slow, and halt. Johnny was peering suspiciously, gun in hand, when Kelly reached him.

"I thought. . . ." Johnny was hoarse.

Kelly swung off. "Swap horses! You'll never get anywhere on that raced-out claybank!"

"I never touched her," Johnny said fiercely, despairingly, as he dismounted. "Sudden-like, she let out a scream an' run from me."

"If you can stay on my horse," Kelly said swiftly, "get to Ruthie and tell her what happened. Then head for the hills. On the west shoulder of Little Baldy, you'll cut a deer trail. Follow shod tracks to a small pole cabin. Wait there for me."

"That's more'n s-seventy miles. . . ."

"If you make it," Kelly said coldly. "Who is that girl? I never saw her before."

"Rose Ella Bunker. Her old man started a jackleg blacksmith shop in town."

"You'll learn, maybe," Kelly said curtly. "Now get going, if you can sit that horse. I can't stand the sight of you."

He held breath while Johnny stepped up. The edgy black sidled nervously, snorted, then obeyed the reins. Johnny vanished into the night, shaken, stripped of swagger and, Kelly knew, in real danger.

At Lone Rock Tank, a shallow seep pool, Kelly watered the claybank and left trampled sign, easy to read. Beyond the tank, a cattle trail angled up into the first rough breaks, where tracking was almost impossible on a moonless night. Some two leisurely hours later, Kelly tied the claybank to a dead cedar stump beside a scoured wash, and stretched comfortably on the scanty grass tufts.

Stars dusted the sky. Coyote clamor lifted eerily in the

distance, died away, broke out again as Kelly gazed at the sky and thought of Johnny, Ruthie, the Morrisons—and Kelly himself. A mess, he decided—and he was sleeping soundly on it, hat over his eyes, when rattling hoofs up the wash brought him standing in full daylight.

A shirt-tail posse that must have waited for dawn at Lone Rock was tracking Johnny's horse at a gallop. The bony, white-mustached old man in the lead, Kelly saw, was Old Rance, first and worst of the Morrison clan.

"He ain't Duval!" Huck Morrison, father of Breck, slabby son of Old Rance, shouted it.

Riding at Old Rance's stirrup was Ed Powers, the deputy from town, and Kelly relaxed a little. Impartial and friendly, Ed Powers was stubborn only in holding closely to the law.

Kelly's humor drew crinkles at his eyes and bent his mouth as the blowing horses pulled up around him.

Old Rance glared at the claybank. "That 'n's the hoss young Duval rode in the race!"

"My horse now," Kelly said.

"Don't fog around it, feller. Where's the kid?"

Kelly yawned. By now they all knew he'd swapped horses with Johnny, and baited them off into the empty breaks.

"Why ask me?" Kelly said reasonably. "I've been asleep. If you're the law, find him yourself, you back-shooting old fence-cutter."

Huck Morrison erupted angrily: "Drag it outen him at a rope end."

They'd drag him, too, Kelly was aware. Any Morrison would. But Ed Powers spoke sharply from his horse. "Kelly didn't shoot anyone and wasn't near the girl."

"That," Old Rance blared, "ain't the point! He helped Duval git scarce on a fast hoss! Makes him guilty to us! He'll git the same."

"Not here," said Ed Powers with stubborn calm. "I'll take Kelly in . . . no help needed, or advice."

"We c'n wait!" Old Rance was malevolent.

The deputy rode beside Kelly, and spoke under his breath. "You're safer this way." Powers was regretful. "You shouldn't have helped Johnny Duval. That girl business . . . he don't have a friend."

Kelly grinned. "One friend," he reminded, and after a moment Ed Powers grinned, also.

This was to have been Kelly's day in town—one to remember. It still was his day, Kelly reflected wryly as a fast trot brought them in through the hot, gray dust of Main Street. Kelly saw the old buggy with an ancient tarp top waiting in front of the deputy's small office, next door to the saddle shop.

"I'd like to talk to Johnny's sister alone," he told Ed Powers.

"That ain't surprising," Ed drawled. "Well, go ahead."

Ruthie had been sitting listlessly inside the front window of Ed's office. She was on her feet when Kelly stepped in and closed the door.

"Johnny said they'd probably catch you," Ruthie said. She hadn't slept, Kelly guessed. She had a tired sound, a tired look, crushed, as if the burdens, finally, were too much.

He had an urge to comfort her, but there was scant comfort in Johnny's trouble. Kelly's chuckle covered that. "Johnny stayed on my horse and got away . . . that's the important thing."

"Anyway for a time, I suppose," Ruthie said. "But what's ahead for him? Breck's limping around town with Johnny's bullet in his leg and . . . and that girl and her story?"

Ruthie's unhappy eyes said that the blame was Kelly's. It

was Kelly who had set the example. And that was the moment that Kelly, being Kelly, was inspired.

"Breck Morrison's in town here . . . able to walk?"

"Yes."

"Mmm-mmm . . . Ruthie." They were alone, but Kelly lowered his voice cautiously, humor lighting his face as he spoke rapidly.

Red surged into Ruthie's cheeks; tired worry in her eyes flared into indignation. "You would think of something like that!" she said bitingly. "You and . . . and your saloon girls!"

"If it would help Johnny . . . ?" Kelly held his breath.

"I'd never get over being ashamed." Ruthie's cheeks were flaming. "Why, I've never. . . ."

Kelly believed that, too, but if Ruthie could bring herself to do it. . . . He patted her small shoulder reassuringly as Ruthie left the office.

Minutes later Ed Powers said: "Sure, I mean to talk to the Bunker girl. Didn't have a chance last night." Ed frowned across the pine table that was his desk. "Breck Morrison watching them and grinning don't mean a thing."

"Ed, when I see a wolf start a stalk, I look where he's looking. She'd already passed me a let's-walk-out look."

"You collect them kind of looks, Kelly. I'll get her story, and Breck Morrison's . . . and they'll tack Johnny Duval's hide high, and salt it. Yours, too, for mixing in."

"Just do like I asked," Kelly urged. He was still inspired, confident.

But when the honey-haired girl walked into the small office, drawing glances even from across the street, Kelly had first doubts. She looked like a church-choir girl now, a bruised flower, still frightened.

"Here, ma'am," Kelly said, offering the chair by the front

window, where Ruthie had been sitting.

The honey-haired girl looked at him appraisingly, Kelly decided. She looked at the window that would display her to all the street, and sat down like a satisfied cat. And the dusty, bare little office suddenly seemed full of Rose Ella Bunker, honey hair, clinging dress, and a deal of Rose Ella which came readily to imagination.

Ed Powers looked at her, and drew a breath. *You, too,* Kelly thought, less inspired by the moment. He had not expected Old Rance Morrison to stalk in, trailed by Huck Morrison, Breck's father. Or other men to gather in the doorway, inspecting Rose Ella with interest and Kelly with dislike.

Ed Powers closed the door against the curious faces. "You two can stay, I guess," he told the Morrisons. "Breck's coming to give his side of it."

"We got Breck's side . . . a lead slug in his leg!" Old Rance said coldly. "Gal, tell your'n."

Rose Ella faltered. "I'm still so shamed-like. Didn't seem no harm, likely, walking out like that. . . ."

The last of Kelly's inspired confidence slowly faded as Rose Ella Bunker tearfully nailed Johnny's hide barn-roof high and completely salted. Standing beside her chair, looking across her honey hair, Kelly could see through the dusty window to the street, and not even Breck Morrison, emerging from the Yoke Bar across the street gave much hope.

Breck was using a knob-headed cane, limping painfully, Kelly hoped. He was barbered, slicked up in a new loud shirt and wool pants, and looked, Kelly decided, well pleased with himself.

It won't do, Ruthie! Kelly wanted to open the window and shout warning. *Shouldn't have talked you . . . !*

Kelly stopped thinking. Ruthie's small figure was already

running lightly, swiftly from the walk into the street.

"Breck!"

Not a cat screech, like last night, but it carried—it carried, even through door and window into Ed Powers's office, into Rose Ella Bunker's ears. She looked out the window. She stopped talking. She stiffened.

Breck Morrison halted in the street, alarmed, it seemed to Kelly, then stunned as Ruthie wrapped tearfully around him—or so it appeared to Kelly. The town, Kelly guessed, had never seen anything like it on Main Street. Nor had Breck Morrison, anywhere. Rose Ella's frozen look watched through the window.

Kelly himself was fascinated as Breck Morrison's near-handsome head bent down—or Ruthie pulled it down. That kiss—Kelly winced, then was queerly resentful as he waited for it to end. Ruthie didn't have to be so convincing, as if she were blindly enjoying it.

Breck Morrison's enjoyment could not be doubted. His arms closed around Ruthie in full possession—and Rose Ella Bunker hissed like an aroused cat. "After all I done for Breck . . . tricking Johnny Duval that way. . . ."

"Gal," Old Rance shouted, "what's that you're sayin'?"

Rose Ella, shriller by the breath as she watched through the window, said spitefully: "Breck put me up to it last night . . . to even a grudge, he said!"

"Your dress was tore, gal!"

"Breck said I was to do it that way. Seemed like I couldn't deny him."

"Breck!" Old Rance said it like an oath as he yanked the door open and plowed through the men outside, who were looking at the street. Huck Morrison followed. Kelly was at their heels in dark, hard temper, for the first time since he could remember.

Old Rance, white mustache quivering, saved him the trouble. Breck Morrison had unwrapped himself and was grinning hugely, foolishly down at Ruthie when Old Rance's heavy revolver barrel belted him squarely on the side of the head.

Old Rance did not stop to see Ruthie gasp or Breck's staggering fall. "Drag your low-down pup home, Huck, an' keep 'im there!" Old Rance rasped over his shoulder as he kept going. "He's made fools outta us we won't live down."

Kelly caught Ruthie's arm as she started to run toward her buggy. "Johnny's all right now. It worked."

"What about me?" Ruthie said, near tears. "The whole town watching!" Ruthie was scrubbing her mouth with a handkerchief.

That was the moment, in the dusty street, when Kelly was inspired again. "Forget the town, Ruthie. All you need is a good man to take hold and carry the troubles."

Ruthie looked at him with suspicion. Kelly's grin was spreading. "What man?" Ruthie asked, still suspicious.

Kelly thought fleetingly of the high hills—but he was looking at Ruthie. The empty hills, he thought without regret at all, the empty, lonely hills. He tilted his hat again, because this was the way he suddenly felt. "I'll drive you home and tell you all about him," Kelly said.

Some of Ruthie's suspicion drained away, but she had known Kelly a long time. "I have to stop at the Radwicks' and help with the new baby," Ruthie remembered, watching him.

Kelly's grin held. "I was thinking we ought to," he said—and he had known Ruthie a long time, also. Ruthie was smiling faintly, almost secretively, as she let Kelly help her into the buggy and, following her, take the reins.

Night Ride

Peter Dawson is the *nom de plume* used by Jonathan Hurff Glidden. He lived most of his adult life in New Mexico. In his career as a Western writer, he published sixteen Western novels and over one hundred and twenty Western novelettes and short stories for the magazine market. From the beginning, he was a dedicated craftsman who revised and polished his fiction until it shone as a fine gem. His Peter Dawson novels are noted for their adept plotting, interesting and well-developed characters, their authentically researched historical backgrounds, and his stylistic flair. His first novel, THE CRIMSON HORSESHOE, won the Dodd, Mead Prize as the best Western of the year 1941 and ran serially in Street & Smith's *Western Story* prior to book publication. During the Second World War, Glidden served with the U.S. Strategic and Tactical Air Force in the United Kingdom. Later in 1950 he served for a time as Assistant to Chief of Station in Germany. After the war, his novels were frequently serialized in *The Saturday Evening Post*. One of Jon Glidden's finest techniques was his ability after the fashion of Dickens and Tolstoy to tell his stories via a series of dramatic vignettes which focus on a wide assortment of different characters, all tending to develop their own lives, situations, and predicaments, while at the same time propelling the general story forward. DARK RIDERS OF DOOM (Five Star Westerns, 1996), RATTLESNAKE MESA (Five Star Westerns, 1997), GHOST BRAND OF THE WISHBONES (Five Star Westerns, 1998), and ANGEL PEAK (Five Star Westerns, 1999) are his most recent books. The story that follows was written just before Jon Glidden left for military service but for some reason was not sent on to his agent at the time for sale to the magazine market.

★ ★ ★ ★ ★

At sixty-two, Sheriff Clint Benbow was a sound sleeper. It was several seconds before the earth-felt *clomp* of the explosion brought him fully awake, several more before he attached any significance to the shouts from down the street and the snow-deadened footfalls of a man running past the jail office door.

His boots came down off the desk. He reached for his shell belt and straightened stiffly from the swivel chair. His gnarled hands awkwardly cinched the gun about his waist and, going out the door, fumbled sheepskin and Stetson down from the peg on the wall. Outside, he squinted against the sharp sting of flying snow, putting one arm in the coat and reaching back for the other sleeve as he trudged down the walk toward the wind-muted sound of raised voices. As he came abreast the alleyway flanking the jail, a stocky figure stepped out of it, the weight of the gun left his thigh, and a harsh voice said: "Reach, old-timer!"

Benbow's arms were pinned. The gun jabbed his small paunch, and there came a second sharp command: "Quiet, and you won't get hurt! You're takin' me out of here!"

"Like hell," Benbow drawled, but all the same moved across the walk under the prod of the gun, now at his spine. He had a brief glimpse of the stranger's hard, blocky face. Predatory eyes, a slate-gray, burned into his blue ones with an intensity that told him to be careful.

Two horses, a gray and a black, down-headed and with

rumps to the flying smother of snow, stood at the hitch rail immediately above. Benbow was pushed toward the rail.

The stranger said tersely: "You take the gray."

The gray, a gaunt mare, was the poorer animal. Things were coming a little straighter to Benbow now that the biting cold had brought him fully awake. More shouts carried up against the wind. As he climbed onto the gray, he saw the stranger swing a bulging burlap sack onto the saddle ahead of him. It clinked as it struck. Benbow knew then that the bank had been robbed.

They were wheeling out into the street when, suddenly, two men appeared out of the obscurity along the walk. One stopped at sight of them, called—"Hey, Clint, you can't. . . ."—when the flat explosion of the stranger's gun cut him short. Both men dived for the cover of the jail doorway as the stranger crowded his pony into Benbow's, snarling: "Ride, damn it!"

At the edge of town, Benbow pulled the gray down out of her run, asking: "Where to?"

"This is Cienega, ain't it?"

"You tellin' me or askin' me?"

"And it's twenty miles across to Pinetop, ain't it?"

"By road, yes."

"Forget the road. Get goin' You're takin' me there."

"They'll think of Pinetop," Benbow stated deliberately.

"Let 'em think. The lines are down." The gun in the stranger's hand rocked slightly, demanding haste, as Benbow grimly remembered that the telephone lines were always down in a storm like this.

He spoke to the mare and began the business of covering ground. He rode with stooped shoulders hunched, chin nudging the fold of his sheepskin collar. Three miles beyond the town he swung abruptly away from the trail, and immediately they were climbing a rolling piñon-studded reach of ground, the horses slogging stifle-deep in the snow along the wind-drifted bottoms. The mare had a bad habit of shying at each looming tree or bush that moved in out of the white darkness. It was bitterly cold, and this was work for Benbow.

Once the stranger said: "Shake a leg!"

"Want to trade places?" Benbow asked acidly, and held his steady pace.

They rode a cañon, skirting rimy chokeberry and scrub-oak thickets. For a while the wind let up. The gray was less willing now. They came up onto the flats, and the wind, in their faces, punished them with its icy blast riding off the peaks.

They found temporary relief in crossing a narrow spur of second-growth timber. It was there the stranger asked: "What does your watch say?"

Benbow stopped, unbuckled his coat, and took out his watch. He lit a match, and its flare was caught and reflected in the burnished silver of his sheriff's badge. He said— "Three-twenty."—and looked up as the stranger all at once laughed. "What's eatin' you?"

The laugh became prolonged, raucous. When the stranger got his breath, he answered: "That thing you're wearin'."

"What thing?" Benbow asked quietly.

"That badge. They said the law down here didn't cast much of a shadow. Wait'll I tell 'em how right they were!" Once more the stranger gave way to an uncontrollable fit of laughter. "Think you can hold out for another two hours, Pop?"

"I think so." Benbow appeared to be a shivering, tired, old man, his drooping and frosty mustache somehow symbolic of his utter misery. But in that moment there flared alive in his eyes a look younger than the other man's.

"Get me there by five, no later," the stranger said, and motioned Benbow to go on.

There was, Benbow knew, a night freight due through Pinetop at five. Two hours later it would cross the state line. The stranger obviously intended hopping the freight out.

When they rode out of the timber, the wind was at their backs. Benbow said: "Wind's changed. Want to go on alone?"

"Not on your life, Pop. You're stayin' with me."

From then on it was harder for Benbow to urge the gray on. The black, too, was tiring. Presently the gray went down, and it took them both to get her on her feet again. The stranger was beating his gloved hands each time he had the chance to let go the reins.

Finally Benbow said, as though to himself—"Ought to be somewhere close now."—and wiped the snow from his grizzled brows, peering ahead into the darkness along a down-sloping fall of drifted open ground. He started down it, wondering how much farther the gray would carry him.

Twenty minutes later a light shone dimly through the fog of snow. Two more came into sight behind it. Benbow stopped and slid from the saddle, afraid that the gray was going down again. He said: "There's your town. Think your jughead can make it from here on?"

"Mine? What about yours? You're comin' along, Pop. You stay with me till the train leaves." The stranger's right hand, thrust deeply into his pocket, moved significantly. "And be good or I'll use this."

Benbow said—"I'll walk."—and started on.

Within a hundred yards they were walking a drifted street running between rows of weathered frame houses.

The stranger came alongside Benbow, saying: "We'll get rid of these nags."

They left the horses tied to a picket fence in front of a two-story turreted house and footed their way to the middle of the street again, the stranger lagging a step and warning: "Remember this gun in my pocket. Head right for the station."

He was carrying the burlap sack by the neck in his left hand, leaning a little that way under its weight.

They crossed the intersection of two streets and were approaching a lighted restaurant, the only building showing lights along the block, when a long-overcoated man wearing a bearskin cap came out its door. He stood regarding them curiously as they drew abreast of him, and Benbow called: " 'Mornin', John."

Beside Benbow, the stranger's voice grated—"You asked for it!"—and Benbow replied hastily, in a low voice: "He'd think it funny if I didn't speak up." The man on the walk made no answer, and they went on.

There was a light in the station. Benbow said: "God, how good a stove will feel!"

At the station doorway he stomped the snow from his boots and led the way in, the stranger a stride behind.

Benbow stood a moment relishing the welcome draft of heat that struck him in the face. The agent peered out through his wicketed window as the door slammed but didn't catch. He stared curiously at Benbow, began— "Where . . . ?"—when Benbow cut him short with: "How soon's the train due, Fred?"

The agent's stare was a puzzled one. "Due? She's been gone forty minutes."

The stranger, standing to one side of Benbow, said querulously: "What's wrong with your timetable? It says the train's due through Pinetop at five."

"Pinetop? Sure. . . ." The agent was interrupted by the opening of the door behind Benbow.

The stranger and Benbow turned as a man outfitted in a long overcoat and a bearskin cap and mittens shoved the door shut. He stood looking at Benbow as he unbuckled his coat. He stood stiffly, left arm hugging his side. At length he said: "You been out in this, Clint?"

Benbow nodded. "All night. Bitter, ain't it?"

The stranger, seemingly satisfied at this casual exchange of words, turned back to the ticket window. "Well, how about it? Where's the train?"

The agent had a peculiar, wary look on his face. He glanced toward the man at the door, then at Benbow, and caught the slow nod of Benbow's head. He said: "Mister, that timetable's right. The train's due at Pinetop at five. But this ain't Pinetop. It's Cienega."

The stranger stiffened, wheeled on Benbow as Benbow said sharply: "Don't shoot him unless you have to, John."

The stranger turned further to look into the barrels of the shotgun at the shoulder of the man at the door. His right hand lifted from his pocket, empty.

Wild Challenge

Robert Easton was born in San Francisco, California. In one way or another all of his work has been centered on the history and people of the American West. His first great critical and popular success was THE HAPPY MAN (1943), a portrait of California ranch life in the late 1930s. *The New York Times Book Review* said of it—"Good writing of a kind that is difficult and rare."—and *The New Yorker* stated that it has "a clear narrative style and a sure sense of authenticity." Easton went on to write MAX BRAND: THE BIG "WESTERNER" (1970), a biography of Frederick Faust, and recently with his wife, Jane Faust Easton, edited THE COLLECTED STORIES OF MAX BRAND (1994). After three decades of research, his epic Saga of California began with THIS PROMISED LAND (1982), spanning the years 1769-1850, and is continued in POWER AND GLORY (1989). Since THE HAPPY MAN there can be no doubt of Robert Easton's commitment to the American West as both an idea and as a definite and distinct place. Beyond this, in all of his work he has been guided by his belief in what he once described as a writer's concern for "the living word—the one that captures the essential truth of what he is trying to say—and that is what I have tried to put down." His most recent novel is the third volume of his Saga of California, BLOOD AND MONEY (Five Star Westerns, 1998), providing a panoramic view of California during the Civil War. The characters, Porfirio and Shorm, who figure in this story, are also to be found in "The Legend of Shorm," contained in Robert Easton's recently published short story collection, TO FIND A PLACE (Five Star Westerns, 1999). LOVE AND DESTINY, the next volume in his Saga of California, will be appearing in 2001.

★ ★ ★ ★ ★

Shorm looked at it with expectation. The wildest country left in the West was what they had said. Civilization spreading to the water had missed it, there at the very end. Cattle that escaped from early settlers had bred wild here for generations. The last bull of the black Spanish strain brought by Cortés to the New World ruled there like a king, or like the fictional whale Moby Dick, because the ropes he had gone off trailing, the horses and men he had torn up, the scars and victories and prodigious feats attributed to him were legend. Equally legendary was the man who owned him yet never laid a brand on him. Don Porfirio de la Vega y Calderón. He cherished the bull like the wife and children he never had had. He delighted in its exploits as in those of a son. And in the confusion of its enemies, the old and impoverished *ranchero* took comfort.

He received Shorm as they had said he would: ironic, yet kind.

"So the fame of the Santa Rita bull has reached Texas? I am honored. But get down, come in. While you are living, you shall be my guest. And what is that you have brought with you?"

"That's my catch dog," said Shorm. "Come here, Mutt."

Mutt jumped out of the pickup truck and came wagging his tail.

"What does he catch?" asked Porfirio. "Chickens?"

Mutt was a white-haired, thin-skinned bull terrier that caught wild cattle by the head as lobo wolves used to do but was gentle till he tasted blood.

"We heard you had a bull around here," said Shorm, "that could stand catching."

"He never yet has stood for it, though you are both welcome to try . . . at your own risk."

The ranch dogs had come prowling around, watching their chance with Mutt. There was a flurry of dog flesh, a snapping, snarling pinwheel of it, Mutt at the hub, and then there was just one dog standing alone, Mutt, while the rest slunk away all cut to pieces, Mutt wagging his tail after them.

"Pity he's so mild-mannered," drawled Shorm. "If he was *mean*, we might get something done."

Porfirio gave a snort. Next to his bull, he thought most of his dogs. "Tomorrow will be another day, eh, as the old proverb says? But now it is evening and time for hospitality, such as my poor house affords."

They went into the *hacienda*. Shorm already had noted the run-down corrals, the barn with the sagging ridgepole, the brush encroaching down the mountainside, but, when he saw the inside of the ranch house, he knew that hard times, indeed, had come upon this grandee of Spain, descendant of *conquistadores,* who had once owned the whole valley of the Santa Rita.

A massive black wood table and two or three chairs, an old painting over the fireplace, that was all the furnishing. The three-foot-thick adobe walls already had caught the gloom of night.

Porfirio lit a kerosene lamp, walked to the fireplace with it, and looked into a crock that simmered there without any visible sign of being on coals. "Beans," he said, "*frijoles bravos.* And I remember when a man went all day in the hills on a dish of these, and came home leading his wild bulls alone, black ones, Spanish ones, not these silly red cattle that rode into the country in railroad cars like bankers, that bawl like babies when they are hungry."

"Seems like they don't make men right any more, nor cattle neither," said Shorn.

"But you're too young to remember."

"That's why I like to listen."

"Then I will tell you," said Porfirio, sitting down at the table and pouring wine from a demijohn, "of the first time I met the bull. He was a yearling then. I found him bogged to the brisket in the quicksand of the upper river. . . ." He poured two glasses, clicked, and they drank, Shorm at a gulp. "The mission wine?" protested Porfirio. "The wine of Andalusia! You must sip . . . you must *pass the aroma* . . . like this." He passed his hand over his face and head, as if the aroma were passing from his nostrils through his brain.

Shorm, flushing, refilled and drank again more slowly. "So you had the bull where you wanted him, at the very beginning?" he asked.

"Oh, yes."

"What happened?"

"I roped him out and let him go."

"Why did you do that?"

"Because I had never seen an animal with such a promise," said Porfirio.

He continued his routine with an explanation of the painting over the fireplace. Don Quixote, the delightful madman who in a modern day and age insisted on behaving like a knight of old.

"Think I'll just call you Don Quixote," Shorm joked.

Porfirio told about the bell rope in the corner of the room that in days gone by proclaimed the arrival of Boston ships.

"Them Yankees never did quit coming," said Shorm.

"We learned something about that, too."

After supper they went onto the verandah, in the moonlight, where Mutt had been waiting, ringed at a respectable distance by the other dogs. Porfirio said—"Listen, now!"— and then they heard the wildest sound God ever made and put in the throat of a living creature, the call of the wild bull, twice wild in coming from an animal once tame.

It was on the ridge right above them. Mutt was gone for it in a flash.

"You had better call him back," Porfirio said.

"He can take care of himself. What's the matter with your dogs?" They had bristled and stirred but had not moved.

"They are sensible," Porfirio said.

So all of them waited and listened together while the moon got up above the ranges and the call of the wild cattle got up with it, a high trumpet rising, growing, becoming a chorus, as if the whole wild universe were gathering out there to lay a challenge to things tame and human. Or maybe it was a triumphal chorus.

Mutt did not come back. After an hour, Porfirio said: "I'm sorry about that dog. You should have called him."

"He'll be all right," Shorm said. "Ever see a wheel go 'round with a rag tied to it? That's Mutt and a wild bull."

"Sometimes a wheel crushes."

"In the high country of New Mexico," said Shorm, "gravity helped him. He broke their necks sometimes. That is to say, they broke their own."

"In the morning, then?"

"In the morning."

"Your room is the door, there," said Porfirio, pointing to one that opened off the verandah. "I hope this music does not keep you awake. The wild cattle are celebrating to-night."

On the bedside table Shorm found a bowl of gold coins, placed there as in old days so the guest in need might help himself. He read the dates—1850, 1830, 1800—while the wild cattle raised their song of celebration.

In the morning the trail was plain to see in the dust at the barnyard gate. A set of tracks the size of soup plates. Mutt's paw marks in them.

"Ready to go look for your dog?" asked Porfirio.

Porfirio gave Shorm his pick of the remuda, and he had chosen a black gelding without any white on him at all.

"Black is the indestructible color," Porfirio said, and produced a black stallion for himself, and they followed the tracks up the cañon of the Santa Rita which entered the mountains a short distance from the ranch house.

"You understand you're on your own?" Porfirio said, all at once.

"The insurance companies gave me up long ago as a bad risk."

"But with a saddle like that. . . ." Porfirio shook his head.

Shorm's rig was the low-cut, flat-horned, double-cinched Southwest model. Porfirio's was high-cut, high-horned, single cinched in the style of old California.

"And that rope . . . ?" said Porfirio.

Shorm's was twenty-five feet of Manila hemp spliced hard and fast to his saddle horn. Porfirio's was eighty feet of braided rawhide, carried free. He was a dally man, taking wraps at the horn when he caught something.

Around a bend in the cañon they surprised a half-grown coyote. While Shorm was still racing to get within throwing distance, Porfirio's loop shot past and collected the coyote.

"That's how we did it in old days," he said, putting ear-marks on the animal with his pocketknife and turning it loose. "Eat all the rabbits and gophers you can!" he said. "Except that in old days it was grizzly bears."

A rattler buzzed at them out of a sage bush. Before Porfirio could unlimber his riata, Shorm's little rope had turned into a whip and its knot had found the snake's head again and again. "We have quite a few of those down in our country," he explained. "Man needs a short length of rope to defend himself."

They followed the tracks up into the high country at the base of the wild cattle range, and there, under the pine summits, they found the remains of Mutt, a white rag stamped into the hillside. The buzzards were coming for it.

"I am sorry," Porfirio said.

"Nothing to be sorry about," said Shorm. "It's one of the chances. One of the chances of living is dying, isn't it, Porfirio?"

"Many years after I pulled the bull from the quicksand," Porfirio said, "he trapped me in a blind cañon, and we fought all through the twilight of one summer's day. Till my latigos broke and I pitched with the saddle to the ground. There he could have finished me. But he stood and he looked and he faded away in the brush."

"If you had been using a double-cinched saddle like mine, it wouldn't have happened," said Shorm.

"But how too bad, if it had not happened."

Shorm looked up, but Porfirio was examining something high above them on the slope. "Brush tips moving on a windless day, see there . . . there it goes." It was a shadow in the undergrowth, no more. It was a sound stranger than any, the midnight rallying cry of the wild cattle raised at noon. Eerie, triumphant, it sounded and resounded through the countryside, as though up there on the mountain was a monster trumpeter.

"Proud of what he's done," said Shorm.

"Wouldn't you be," said Porfirio, "if it was the other way around?"

Shorm demanded with a little exasperation: "Say, Don Quixote, whose side are you really on, mankind's or the animal's?"

"Neither," said Porfirio. "I just hate to see you come all this way and have nothing to show for it. And I feel very sorry about the dog. I tried to warn you, however."

Returning down the cañon at evening, they found a band of cattle moving ahead of them, as gentle cattle will, thinking they are being driven, until sometimes you have to gallop and head them or they will move clear out of the country. Porfirio and Shorm were doing this when a man rode from the willows and blocked the way. Four other riders joined him.

"Where do you think you're taking those cattle?" he said to Shorm.

"Why, nowhere," said Shorm, a good deal surprised at first, but gathering himself quickly at the tone of the fellow's voice, he added: "And what would it be if I were?"

"Just this. Them cattle don't belong in nowhere. They belong to me."

Shorm looked around at Porfirio, but the rancher sat his saddle with bowed head, saying nothing. Something in his attitude made Shorm hot against the men who surrounded them.

"Let me get this . . . ," he began.

"You working for the Mexican?"

"Mister, I don't know your nationality, but I don't like it."

"I can tell you don't, and it makes me cry. Just keep this in mind. Rafe Watkins and his friends don't appreciate having their stock monkeyed with. Next time they might not like it at all."

He galloped off with the others to head the herd.

Shorm could have sworn the animals had the Three Christian Crosses of Cortés, Porfirio's brand, but in the twilight he couldn't be sure any more than he could be sure what had governed Porfirio's silence during the interview with Rafe Watkins.

"Nice neighbors you have around here."

"We have fun together sometimes."

"What do you mean by that?"

"Did you ever see a man get roped from his saddle and dragged?"

Shorm shook his head.

"We . . . my family . . . had owned the land always. We felt it unnecessary to file claim under the Yankee law."

"Well, they left you the house and the barnyard."

"And the wild cattle range. It might have been worse."

"You let them squat on you?"

"The law is on their side."

"Porfirio," Shorm burst out, "you've got reason not to like Americans, haven't you?"

"Just as you have not to like black Spanish bulls?"

"You've never had a son, a family, anyone to stick up for you?"

"A son would, indeed, be a comfort. There are some who claim my paternity. None whom I claimed."

And Shorm had to laugh. All the way home he felt as if something were following them through the high undergrowth of the cañon wall, as if Porfirio had a shadow up there, somebody to stick up for him. And when the moon rose again, the wild cattle song rose with it.

"We have ridden all day on a dish of *frijoles*," said Shorm, "but we have not come home leading our black bull. Tomorrow, Porfirio?"

"Perhaps."

"I got that dog when he was a pup. I got him from a fellow who ran a livery stable. This fellow wanted Mutt to grow up to be a mean, one-man dog, so he used to give the kids a nickel every time they kicked him, to make him mean. Well, it didn't cost me no nickel, and it wasn't the dog I kicked. Mutt and I've come a long way together. I don't believe I can leave here without settling for him."

"It's you or the bull . . . one or the other?"

"Yes, sir. With your permission."

"Nothing else will satisfy?"

"What else could there be?"

The old man shrugged. "Who knows?"

For a long time that night Shorm lay awake, waiting for the bull to call, but it was as if the rascal knew and were making preparations of his own. He did not call.

The moon was down when they started to ride, daylight still hours away. Shorm followed Porfirio's figure when he could see it, faint music jingling in the dark, the spurs, the *conchos*, the silver-mounted bridle reins. For all his experience, he never could have found his way back along that trail.

At dawn they came out onto a high point and saw wild cattle on a burn across a draw. Wild cattle like the new green shoots of a burn. On this one, the fire had run up to the ridge top and been cut off by the wind as by a knife, leaving a bare side hill. The cattle on it were no bigger than miniatures in the distance and faint light. Yet one seemed bigger than the others.

"He'll take cover at sunrise," Porfirio whispered. "If you want him, rim around and get between him and the brush."

Shorm did so, climbing toward the pines that marked the top of the peak, feeling his heart beat just a trifle faster than it should, and that of his horse the same, against the calf of his leg.

The wind was from the east at dawn, and, since the cattle lay that way, Shorm was able to slip up undetected till he stood at the top of the burn. He saw Porfirio on the high point opposite. He hoped to run the bull into the cañon that lay between and deal with him there on more level ground with trees as snubbing posts. A thousand-pound horse tied to a two-thousand-pound bull on a forty-five degree slope is not the pleasantest connection.

But he met him face to face as he rode out of the brush. He was leading his band to cover. His head went up with a start; the sunrise caught with a flash on both white horns; the nostrils blew a snort of wind as if to blow Shorm off the face of the earth. For a second they confronted each other, man and beast, so close that Shorm could see the red insides of his nostrils working as the breath passed in and out and the amber brown eyeballs with their jet slits.

The bull made a run for the brush. Shorm headed him. He turned without offering to fight. It was as if he hesitated to make that first move. Shorm, too. His rope was out, but he did not use it. They fenced back and forth across the ridge top. The bull wanted the high ground; he wanted the brush desperately. But when he saw he could not have them without that fatal move, he turned and plunged into the cañon. Shorm pitched after. Reluctance left him as his blood got heated. He followed closely lest the bull play 'possum in some brush patch and lie hidden while the chase went tearing by.

A commotion told Porfirio on his high point something of this sort was happening. He could not see through the treetops that bunched thickly as cabbages along the cañon floor, but he heard a sound like rifle fire that was a crackling of branches, nothing then but silence, then the cry.

It was not the cry a man makes after cattle, or that cattle make after a man, or that any sort of animal gives rise to. It was the one and only cry of a man after another man.

A voice came clearly: "Get 'im, Rafe."

Porfirio pitched down the mountain like an avalanche. At the bottom he could see nothing because of the undergrowth, but, stopping to listen, he could hear a heavy, breathing sound of whirling ropes.

He burst full speed into the clearing and saw Shorm surrounded by the squatters, five of them, trying to snare him from the saddle with their lassoes, and he holding them off with his, by the threat of it, never letting it meet theirs, and he collapsed, but whirling and darting it in every direction like a sword. He was grinning as a man in a fight should. But he could not have held out longer. Rafe Watkins was building a loop that would end matters while the others closed from every side. Then Porfirio hit them.

His riata went hissing like a rattler straight for Rafe, all eighty feet of it, alive and very angry. Rafe ducked. The rope sailed over. But snatching it back, Porfirio left a red welt rising on Rafe's face, a burn as painful as if hot iron had seared.

"For a friend's sake, Rafe!" Porfirio cried out.

"Save your breath, my friend," said Rafe. "You'll need it when I personally drag you from here to the river."

"I believe you marked that maverick," said Shorm.

"Had you but a longer rope. . . ." Porfirio grinned. They were fighting side by side.

"Beats bull hunting," Shorm managed breath to say, as he danced his pony out of a figure-eight loop that would have trussed them both. "Swear these boys are starting to play hard."

"We are not yet through. But, *compadre,* this is as it was in olden days. With the hot blood, ye-e-e-es."—and Porfirio swung his great rope around his head with a sound like a scythe. In open country it would have been more than a match for the squatters' shorter loops. In the close work of the brush they had the advantage. They caught Porfirio. Quicker than the noose could tighten, he flung his head against his upraised arm, and the noose slid off his leather wristlet as off a tapered peg, taking his hat, and his riata.

"That's what you get for being a dally man," Shorm kidded him. "Tie hard and fast and it never would have happened!"

His own little string of a rope that spliced firm to the horn was now doubled for use as a whip. Shorm went in lashing. He nearly cut somebody in half.

"Beat it while you can, Porfirio! I'll come when I've taught these boys their manners!" He went so close they overreached him with their throws. His pony, wild from the spurs, sprang among them so that Porfirio had time to start away. And just as he started, from a nest of green-white manzanita, he flushed out a shape, all but stepped on it, a monster apparition with bone-bright horns, that burst out of the ground and charged into the group surrounding Shorm.

They had hemmed him against the bank. The bull scattered them as a hawk does quail, every which way, hot after all of them. He wasn't one bull, he was five, and he left no doubt what those five intended to do. He passed so close that Shorm could have touched him, but he went by and after the others.

For a long time, the crashing and swearing could be heard going off across the hillside. Then there was a horse's scream, and the listeners knew a bone-bright horn had reddened at the tip.

"I never seen the like of it from here to the Gulf Coast!" cried Shorm. "He had me hemmed against the bank. Did you see it? He could have mashed me all to jelly there."

Porfirio merely nodded.

"Why, I could have punched him with my bare hand!" Shorm put his hand out and looked at it; then began to laugh; then extended it to Porfirio. "I thank you, Don Quixote."

"And what for?"

"Your bull. He took my life away and gave it back, all in a moment's passing. I've got it now with his permission."

"And are you satisfied?"

"I am."

"Is the matter settled, then?"

"The account is paid in full."

"Then it is you, my son, who are to be congratulated."

Don Porfirio never would admit to anything except that Shorm's little string of a lariat might be useful at times, and so it proved in years to come.

Day of the Dedication

Cliff Farrell was born in Zanesville, Ohio, where earlier Zane Grey had been born. Following graduation from high school, Farrell became a newspaper reporter. Over the next decade he worked his way west by means of a string of newspaper jobs and for thirty-one years was employed, mostly as sports editor, for the *Los Angeles Examiner*. He would later claim that he began writing for pulp magazines because he grew bored with journalism. His first Western stories were written for *Cowboy Stories* in 1926, and his byline was A. Clifford Farrell. By 1928 this byline was abbreviated to Cliff Farrell, and this it remained for the rest of his career. In 1933 Farrell was invited to contribute a story for the first issue of *Dime Western*. He soon became a regular contributor to this magazine and to *Star Western* as well, later contributing to *The Saturday Evening Post* and *Collier's*. In all, Farrell wrote nearly six hundred stories for the magazine market. Increasingly his stories began to focus on characters in historical situations and the problems faced by those characters. FOLLOW THE NEW GRASS (1954) was Farrell's first Western novel, a story concerned with a desperate battle over grazing rights in the Cheyenne Indian reserve. It was followed by WEST WITH THE MISSOURI (1955), an exciting story of riverboats, gamblers, and gunmen. FORT DECEPTION (1960), RIDE THE WILD COUNTRY (1963), THE RENEGADE (1970), and THE DEVIL'S PLAYGROUND (1976) are among the best of Farrell's later Western novels. DESPERATE JOURNEY (Five Star Westerns, 1999) is a first collection of Cliff Farrell's

Western short stories selected and edited by R. E. Briney. The story that follows was the last one Cliff Farrell wrote.

★ ★ ★ ★ ★

This was Elisha Potter's ninetieth birthday, and he was in the worst fix of his life. This was the day in 1960 that they were going to dedicate the Pioneer Day statue to him. He was trying to get up the courage to tell them it was all a mistake and that he hadn't been exactly what they seemed to believe. Either that or resign himself to spending the rest of his days afraid to meet that knowing look in young Johnny Kemp's eyes—which could mean a long time yet because Elisha Potter expected to be around for quite a spell. He was as spry as a squirrel and not much bigger. He was exceedingly keen of mind, as anyone who tried to get the best of him soon found out. As Johnny Kemp had.

Elisha Potter, commonly known as 'Lish, sat sweating it out in his room in the rambling house in which he had lived the greater part of his life in Millersburg. It was less than an hour before time for the parade to start, and the morning in late August was turning hot and sultry. He could hear a steady rumble from all over the house. The Potter clan, down to the great-grandchildren, had gathered for this occasion when the head of the family was to be honored. He could look out into the maple-shaded town square where the statue stood, shrouded in canvas and bunting, awaiting the unveiling. That gawshawful statue! That falsehood in bronze. Why had he ever let it go this far? He uttered a dismal groan.

A hand tapped the door. "Father! Are you all right?" It was Clarice, his daughter-in-law.

"Of course, I'm all right!" 'Lish snapped.

Clarice came bustling in. She was firm-voiced, firm-bodied, and energetic. Her graying hair was dyed a blue shade. She was the widow of 'Lish's youngest son. Clarice had raised five children, was head of the Women's Club, and had a hand in most every civic activity that went on in Millersburg. She was accompanied by Penny, her last un-married daughter. Clarice was a little afraid of 'Lish, but she knew that Penny could handle him. Penny was 'Lish's favorite granddaughter.

It was Clarice who was mainly responsible for 'Lish's pre-dicament, although it was that affable man, Winfield Church, who had first said that they ought to put up a monument to a person like 'Lish. Clarice had done the rest. She had orga-nized the Pioneer Day committee and had seen to it that the fund-raising campaign for the statue was a success.

"You ought to get into your shirt and collar, Father," Clarice admonished. "The committee will be here any minute."

"Maybe I don't aim to wear any gol-danged collar an' shirt on a day like this," 'Lish snorted. "It's goin' to be a scorcher."

"Now wouldn't you look pretty, sitting up there in front of all those people in your undershirt?"

"Maybe I won't wear even an undershirt," 'Lish said darkly.

"Now, Father, please behave!" Clarice sighed. "I just can't have anything happen to upset things at the last minute."

Someone downstairs called that Clarice was wanted to settle come crisis. She gave Penny an appealing look as she left.

Penny confronted 'Lish. Her blue eyes were determined.

He saw that he was in for trouble with her, but not about the shirt and collar. Penny was nineteen and growing lovelier every day. She had tawny golden hair caught in a pony tail, a small nose, a few freckles, a peach-blown glow in her cheeks, and a figure that was definitely fetching.

"Johnny Kemp just phoned, saying he wants to talk to you before the ceremonies," she said. "Alone. He's on his way here."

Johnny Kemp was the last person 'Lish wanted to see at the moment, Johnny and his knowing look. "I can't waste time on that dude today," he said.

"What have you got against Johnny, Elisha Potter?" Penny demanded. "Why do you act like he's got leprosy or something every time he comes to this house?"

"What'm I supposed to do?" 'Lish snorted. "Bake a cake for every young whippersnapper who wants to hold hands with you?"

"When Johnny's around, you act positively impossible. All that snorting and glaring and grumbling under your breath. It isn't fair. It hurts Johnny."

"Hurts him!" 'Lish jeered. "That big walrus? You couldn't get through his hide with a buffalo gun."

Penny's eyes flashed fire. "Walrus is he? Is it because he's a law officer that you don't like him?"

'Lish grasped at this straw. All he wanted was to end the inquisition. "I never had much use for badge-toters. Not since a time at a trail town called. . . ."

"At least not since last week when they began giving you tickets for crossing Pawnee Street against the new traffic light down at the corner," Penny said.

"They don't need a traffic light there," 'Lish howled. "All wasted money. I told Mayor Ote Crane so before they put it in."

"Well, Johnny had nothing to do with it," she said. "He's not a traffic cop. He's in charge of fraud and bunko prevention. Even though he's only twenty-seven years old and in a small town like Millersburg, he's already attracting attention. Just the other day he received a letter from J. Edgar Hoover, head of the FBI, commending him. Chief Haskell told me that Johnny is the brightest. . . ."

"I've heard all this stuff," 'Lish sniffed. "That's all anybody hears from you. Johnny Kemp this, and Johnny Kemp that."

"What *is* the trouble between you and Johnny?"

"Has he said there was trouble?" 'Lish asked apprehensively.

"So there is something!" she declared triumphantly.

The sound of a car pulling up at the curb drew her to the window. "Here's Johnny now!" she exclaimed. She hurried downstairs, the glow brighter within her.

'Lish slumped down, his chin on his cane. She was in love with Johnny Kemp, and only he stood in their way.

From somewhere in the town the booming of a bass drum could be heard. That would be the high school band, marching to the parade assembly. 'Lish's time for a decision was very short. He glared accusingly at the veiled statue. He had seen the cussed thing when it was finished. It was supposed to look like him as he had been when he came up the trail with a herd of longhorns back in '87. 'Lish had been seventeen at the time, and trail-driving was in its sunset. Kansas was nothing but farms and fences, and they'd had to swing far west into the dry sandhills of Colorado. Even so, it was touch and go, getting through the settled land into Nebraska. They put the cattle on trains at Ogallala.

That had been 'Lish's only drive. After he was paid off by the trail boss, he took a job on a farm in Nebraska and soon homesteaded on what was now an important part of the Millersburg business section. George Kemp had done the same. Both had prospered and had helped populate the land. Millersburg was now the center of a county that flowed with milk and honey. George Kemp, who was a year older than 'Lish, had not quite made it to ninety. He had died two years previously. He was Johnny Kemp's grandfather.

The face on the statue may have some slight resemblance to 'Lish when he had been seventeen. Clarice had furnished the designer with a tintype of 'Lish, taken when he was a young man. But there any likeness ended. The statue depicted a chap-clad cowboy in a ten-gallon hat who was crouching in the classic pose of a gun-fanner. He was in the act of firing a six-shooter. The bronze teeth were bared; the metallic eyes had a fierce aspect. The truth was that 'Lish had never worn chaps or a ten-gallon hat. In addition to being beyond his means, such attire was impractical for trailing cattle at twelve miles a day over hot, open country. 'Lish had been arrayed in denim jeans, a cotton shirt, dog-eared boots, and a round felt hat. Worse yet, he had never fired a six-shooter more than three or four times in his life. The concussions always scared him. He detested violent noise. He didn't like guns, but he had kept that a deep secret all his life. Only George Kemp had known.

The foreman on the trail drive had compelled 'Lish to carry a pistol so that he could signal for help in case he got lost. 'Lish's father had given him the pistol. The foreman had not been aware that 'Lish never kept the gun loaded. The pistol now hung on the wall of 'Lish's room. It was a Frontier Model Colt, and he had kept it as a relic of his days as a drover. Its wooden grip was battered, for he had found it useful for pounding coffee beans or driving picket pins. Otherwise, it was in good condition for he had kept it carefully cleaned and oiled. The gun had proved to be a great conversation piece when he had visitors. "What exciting times you must have gone through when you were a cowboy, Mister Potter," was the usual reaction.

This was how 'Lish had gotten into the present fix. He was a kindly man who hated to disappoint people. They expected yarns, and he had accommodated them. He hadn't actually meant to draw the long bow, but he had kept adding a few details with the telling and retelling—and maybe inventing some new episodes. He admitted it. He had got in the habit of telling it scary. People seemed to want to be impressed. 'Lish had even let his hair grow long, and had cultivated a drooping white mustache and a goatee. Sadly he realized he had even got to talking like the cowboys on television.

A hand tapped the door. "It's Johnny Kemp," the arrival said. "I'd like to speak to you, Mister Potter."

Suddenly it dawned on 'Lish what this meant. His beard began to jut belligerently. Johnny Kemp was older than Penny by nearly eight years, and 'Lish knew danged well that all he'd been waiting for was for her to grow up. They'd known each other all their lives, for their families had been as close as piecrusts. Penny was now grown up.

Johnny entered. He closed the door carefully. He looked a lot like his grandfather. George Kemp had been big and brawny with good dark eyes and hair.

"What's on your mind?" 'Lish growled. "This is my busy day."

Johnny had that look in his eyes. "It's about this dedication, Mister Potter," he said, lowering his voice.

Wrathfully, 'Lish decided he had guessed right. Johnny Kemp knew 'Lish's history on the trail. His grandfather had told him, no doubt, and he was going to use that knowledge. 'Lish tried to bluster it out. "What'n Tophet are you drivin' at?" he growled.

"It might not turn out like it's supposed to," Johnny said.

'Lish had a notion to whack Johnny over the head with his cane. The brazen rascal! It *was* to be blackmail. "You can't bulldoze me, you schemin' horned toad," he hissed, keeping his own voice down, for Penny likely was in the hall trying to eavesdrop.

Johnny stared. "What's that, Mister Potter?"

'Lish waved the cane. "If you're figurin' on marryin' my granddaughter, go ahead an' marry her, but don't expect me to like it."

Johnny went crimson, then white. "Penny doesn't want to do anything against your wishes," he said. "It seems to me that you're taking too serious a view of something that doesn't really matter."

"If you think you're goin' to weasel your way into the family with my consent, so you can hang around, laughin' up your sleeve at me an' holdin' a club over my head, you're saddlin' the wrong bronc'," 'Lish fumed.

"Club over your head? Why . . . ?"

"I know your grandpap told you all about me," 'Lish snarled. "George Kemp never could keep his yap shut. He told you about the night of the big storm below the Aricakaree, too, didn't he?"

Johnny drew a resigned sigh. "Yes," he said.

'Lish glowered at Johnny. He was recalling the big storm, and the lightning and thunder. Even after all these years he cringed a little. He had always been deathly afraid of thunder. The herd had been bedded in open country south of the Aricakaree headwaters. 'Lish and George Kemp had drawn the last trick before dawn on night guard. It was the hour when the spirit was mighty low. 'Lish had never seen a blacker night. It had been suffocatingly hot. The cattle had got to their feet on the bedground and were standing tense and nervous. The heat generated by twenty-five hundred head of longhorns had been like the steamy breath from a jungle.

He and George, afraid to speak for fear of touching off an explosion in the herd, had huddled their horses close together. There had been no stars. The only speck of light had been the lantern on the tilted pole of the chuck wagon, half a mile away. 'Lish had never felt so utterly alone. He had been homesick all the way up from Texas, and he was wishing more than ever that he was back home, helping with the cotton and the corn. He had heard the cattle stir. St. Elmo's fire had glowed on the tips of the horns of the twenty-five hundred animals. That cold phenomenon gave no light. It was like being stuffed in a black box with a pack of ghostly fireflies.

'Lish had said in a thin voice: "Get rid of everything metal, George. Metal attracts lightning. Get away from your horse. Its shoes are of iron."

George had never been afraid of noise. "I don't want to throw away anything," he had said uneasily. "Things like that cost money."

It had hit then. The storm. The herd stampeded. Lightning burned the sky to ruins and blazed across the earth. Fireballs rolled on the prairie. The thunder was a din that stunned the mind. The cattle scattered to all the winds and were vanishing phantoms in the white glare.

'Lish had abandoned his horse and threw his pistol and spurs as far away as possible. He hurled away four silver dollars and a gold piece, for they were metal, also, and he wasn't taking any chances. These were the last of his material possessions. He had run then, blindly, until George overtook him and roped him to earth like a leppie calf for the branding. Beside himself with fear, 'Lish had smashed a fist into George's face. George's lip had split. Blood had spurted. George's skin had turned a greenish hue, and he keeled over in a heap, knocked out cold. 'Lish had never realized he packed such a wallop.

George had revived, but kept drifting back into a daze. Eventually he came out of it and seemed all right. The storm rolled on eastward, and the stars came out. They rounded up the cattle the next day and proceeded on their way. They arrived at the shipping pens in Ogallala in due time.

But after the night of the big storm George Kemp always had that odd look in his eyes. And now Johnny Kemp had that same look and was trying to club 'Lish into approving his marrying Penny as the price of his silence. 'Lish couldn't swallow that. Even though it meant humiliation to the Potter clan, he was going out there and tell them that all this stuff about gunfighting and wild Indians and rustlers had been spun out of whole cloth and that he had been just a young greenhorn, afraid of his shadow all the way up the trail.

"All right, Johnny," he said. "I know what you're up to."

"You mean you know about it?" Johnny seemed amazed.

"I'm going to beat you to the draw," 'Lish said grimly.

"Now hold on, Mister Potter," Johnny said, worried. "We want to handle this without any shooting if possible."

"Shootin'?" 'Lish heard his voice squeak a trifle.

Johnny eyed him. "Maybe we're not talking about the same thing. I came here as a police officer to tell you that the ceremonies are being used as a cover for a bank robbery."

"Bank rob . . . ?" 'Lish's voice failed completely.

"Just what do you know about this man, Winfield Church?" Johnny asked.

"Winfield Church?" 'Lish gurgled. "Say, you don't mean he's a crook. He didn't act like one. He seemed like a real nice *hombre*. Clarice had him to the house for dinner a couple of times. He was on the fund-raising committee for the statue."

"I got his fingerprints off a highball glass after one of the dinner parties," Johnny said. "Penny gave me the glass. The FBI checked the prints in their files. That put me hep to the whole thing."

"What whole thing?"

"Winfield Church, which isn't his real name, was the one who put the bug in the head of people around here to hold this Pioneer Day celebration. No reflection on you, of course, Mister Potter. Church showed up in Millersburg about four months ago. He posed as an investment expert, who planned to open an office here. He even gave a talk at the Women's Club on stocks and bonds. That's how he got acquainted with Penny's mother. He's a glib one. He was, in fact, casing the town. He's the brains for his mob."

"Mob?"

"They're pointed at Security Savings," Johnny said. "I'm sure the job is to be pulled during the parade."

He saw 'Lish's stunned look. "What started me investigating Winfield Church," he explained, "was that I recalled reading about some big scores that had been made in towns like this one during parades."

"Scores?"

"Successful crimes," Johnny said. "I spent a lot of hours thumbing through files. I had help from the FBI. We found it. A year ago a bank was robbed at a town in Oregon during a parade that was held to honor a citizen. They got away with nearly two hundred thousand. A clean job. Everybody was watching the parade, with only two cashiers in the cages. A year before that the same thing was pulled at a town in Ohio. And that one netted them a quarter of a million."

'Lish was listening, dumbfounded as Johnny went on. "We have a similar situation today. Banks don't stay open in many places on Saturday mornings. Just agricultural centers like Millersburg. It's the end of the harvest, with plenty of money moving around and the banks loaded to take care of demand. In the cases in Ohio and Oregon the promoter of the celebrations had dropped out of sight and was suspected of complicity. The descriptions fitted our Winfield Church, barring allowances for dye jobs on the hair, a mustache, and glasses. The fingerprints did the rest. Church, under other names, did time in his younger days in Texas and Illinois for fraud and armed robbery."

"Sufferin' horned toads," 'Lish moaned.

"We put a tail on Church," Johnny said. "There are three others in the mob. They drifted into town during the past ten days. They've cased the bank thoroughly. We've identified them. All have criminal records. They'll be armed and dangerous."

'Lish brightened. "Then the cussed dedication's off?"

Johnny shook his head. "On the contrary. We want everything to go through as arranged so as not to arouse their suspicion. The chief told me to inform you in advance of what was in the wind. He's got the criminal squad staked out in and around the bank along with some FBI men. I've been ordered to sit with you in the speaker's stand."

"I know danged well why you'll be up there," 'Lish growled. It was plain enough to him. Johnny wasn't taking any chances on him making a fool of himself if any shooting started like he had done the night of the big thunder storm.

"I'm fully aware that you know," Johnny said glumly. "I'll be safe up there."

Cars were again pulling up at the curb. The committee had arrived. A bomb exploded in the sky, causing 'Lish to jump.

"Them danged things!" he mumbled.

The bomb was the signal for the parade to start. 'Lish hadn't had a chance to make up his mind as to what to do.

Clarice came bursting in, followed by the committee. "Father!" Clarice moaned. "You aren't ready! Your shirt . . . !"

"That's all right, Missus Potter," said one of the committee. "We brought along the proper outfit for the occasion."

They swarmed upon 'Lish. He was jammed into a shirt in spite of his resistance and blistering language.

"I stuff my own shirt in my pants, dang you people!" he bawled at one point in the proceedings. "There's females present."

He glimpsed himself in a mirror. He stared, appalled. Instead of his customary sedate white shirt and starched collar, he was arrayed in a gaudy, double-breasted, checkered cowboy shirt and a vest of spotted calfskin. They were buckling chaps on his legs—huge, yellow, batwing monstrosities. A holster carrying his own Frontier Model Colt was belted on him at a rakish angle.

"How romantic you look, Father!" Clarice exclaimed.

"We've got to hustle," Johnny said. "The parade's starting."

Before 'Lish could frame a roaring protest, he was on his way, gripped by the strong hands of the committee.

"Get me outen these durned dude ranch duds!" he raged.

"Good Lord, don't gum up things now, Mister Potter," Johnny pleaded in his ear. "Any delay might spoil the stakeout."

'Lish found himself in a decorated automobile that circled the park square to the speaker's stand. He was practically carried up the steps to the place of honor. Breathless, he stared up Pawnee Street. The parade was on its way. The color bearers were less than a block away, followed by the high school band that was led by a trio of bare-legged girls twirling batons.

Back of the band 'Lish could see half a dozen bunting-draped cars that evidently bore leading citizens. The first machine—a huge, open car—contained Mayor Ote Crane and two other dignitaries, all wearing silk hats.

'Lish remembered his own gaudy attire and felt naked. Someone clapped a hat on his head. It was a cream-colored ten-galloner and sizes too big. It almost blinded him. He pushed it back and gazed wildly around, seeking an avenue of escape. There was none.

The band broke into "Stars and Stripes Forever" as it passed the Security Savings Bank. The brass and the drums were in full voice when the shooting started. The muffled reports came from the interior of the bank. The band quit playing abruptly, and its members scattered like ants. So did the spectators on the sidewalks.

Three men raced from the bank. One fell and lay in the street. The other two, brandishing pistols, ran to the gleaming car carrying the mayor. One dragged the chauffeur from his seat and leaped back of the wheel. The other vaulted into the rear seat. Two of the silk-hatted dignitaries made undignified escapes by diving overside into the street, but the bandit grabbed Mayor Ote Crane and held him in the car, using him as a shield.

Officers, who had been on the stakeout, appeared from the bank, weapons poised, but they did not dare fire for fear of hitting the mayor. The car, a gearshift job from a past era that was used only for parades and ceremonials, was not built for a fast getaway. Furthermore, it had four forward speeds, a feature with which the desperado was unfamiliar. The engine issued a thunderous roar, but the machine itself built up momentum with elephantine deliberation. It came lumbering down Pawnee Street, for there was no side street for escape from that thoroughfare until it had passed by the length of the park square where stood the speaker's stand—and 'Lish.

"Duck, Mister Potter!" Johnny shouted.

'Lish froze and could not move. Johnny had a revolver drawn. 'Lish understood what was in Johnny's mind. From this higher elevation he would be in a position to fire almost directly down at the driver with little risk of hitting the mayor, once the car came abreast.

The car was still more than a hundred feet away when the bandits spotted Johnny. Both began shooting at him, the driver grasping the steering wheel with one hand while he used an automatic. Johnny could not return the fire because at that angle the mayor was still in danger.

Johnny staggered. The pistol was torn violently from his hand. It fell on a chair, then rolled to the platform floor at 'Lish's feet. 'Lish realized that a bullet had glanced from it.

Johnny didn't seem to be wounded, but he bore a shocked expression. He bent dazedly, trying to retrieve the gun. His fingers evidently had been numbed by the impact, for he merely groped helplessly. On a wild impulse, 'Lish snatched up Johnny's gun. It didn't seem to be damaged. It was of modern make, but its operation was essentially the same as his Frontier Model, except that it had double action.

The car was careening near. 'Lish, now that it was done, regretted that he had picked up the weapon. He was more afraid of it than of the bandits. Still, he had to do something. He just couldn't stand there in his fancy cowboy attire. Something brushed his face and jerked at the brim of the big hat. He felt another twitch at the hat. Both of the bandits had sighted him, standing at the platform railing with the pistol in his hand, and had turned their fire upon him.

'Lish used both hands in an attempt to hold Johnny's pistol steady. Even then, it wavered. He didn't want to take any chance on hitting Ote Crane, so he aimed at the long hood of the car as it came abreast, hoping to put it out of commission by placing a bullet in some vital spot in the engine. He squeezed the trigger, shutting his eyes at the last moment and wishing he could shut his ears, also. The concussion and the recoil left him all quivering inside. He tried to steady the gun and fire again, but he was unable to pull the trigger. He didn't have the strength.

A second shot wasn't needed. The car swerved toward the speaker's platform. It tore a corner support from the structure, leaped over the curb, and smashed solidly into the trunk of a venerable maple tree. It came to a stop with broken glass falling.

The impact hurled the driver against the wheel. He sagged back, dazed. His comrade and also Mayor Ote Crane were pitched headlong against a seatback. The mayor came up on top, a trifle dazed of expression, but in possession of the bandit's automatic. Ote Crane, 'Lish recalled, had been quite a football player for state college in his younger days.

The platform tilted a trifle on the broken support, but remained upright. 'Lish recovered his equilibrium. Officers who had been pursuing the car on foot arrived and seized Ote Crane's prisoner. The one in the front seat revived and found himself in handcuffs.

'Lish saw that the rim of the big, old-fashioned wooden steering wheel of the car was broken. A bullet had struck it, evidently near the point where the bandit had been grasping it. Lish had aimed at the hood but had missed that ample target by a wide margin, but his shot had found another vulnerable point. He knew now why the car had swerved out of control.

'Lish recovered more than his equilibrium. The power of speech returned. He glared down at the captives, hoping that his eyes had a steely quality. He gave them the full effect of the big hat, the hair vest and checkered shirt, and the long gray hair and drooping mustache. "Stand quiet you yella-livered skunks!" he thundered. "Else I might notch right plumb center on you the next time and give you a dose of lead pizen."

Startled, he realized that blood was dripping from his chin. He discovered that he had been nicked across the cheekbone either by a bullet or by a fragment from the ricochet off Johnny's pistol. However, it wasn't more than a scratch, although it was bleeding liberally. He also found two bullet holes in the brim of the big hat. He remembered the twitching of the hat when the bandits had been shooting at him. He again froze a little inside. But he soon got over that.

Johnny Kemp was looking at him. There was a greenish hue on Johnny's face. That bilious color deepened. He tried to sit in one of the chairs. He missed the chair and slumped in a heap on the floor. All brawny six feet of him lay there, out as cold as his grandfather had been that night of the big storm when 'Lish, in a frenzy, had split George's lip and George had gone down.

Penny came rushing up. "Johnny's dead!" she screamed. "He's been shot!" She knelt, weeping, over the recumbent form.

"He's not dead," 'Lish snorted. "Nor shot. It must be the heat that got him."

But he knew it hadn't been the heat. He was remembering that Johnny's grandfather had shown that greenish hue around the mouth that night. And it came to him that he'd seen George Kemp turn a trifle green and bilious on two or three other occasions during their many years of association. He had thought it had been a freak of the lightning glare that night, and hadn't given it much attention at all on the other occasions. But now he had discovered the real reason for that look he had seen in Johnny's eyes. And the look that had been in George's eyes all those years. 'Lish had misinterpreted. It hadn't been a *knowing* look. Nor amused. It had been hopeful. Hopeful that 'Lish would keep certain knowledge to himself. 'Lish had never mentioned the events of the night of the big storm to George. Nor had George. 'Lish realized now that both of them had their own reasons for keeping quiet.

Johnny revived. By that time 'Lish's slight injury had been dressed with court plaster, and he was receiving the congratulations of the admiring citizens of Millersburg.

'Lish took it modestly. "Why, any old waddie would have done the same thing," he declared. " 'Twasn't much of a trick to bust that steerin' wheel with a slug. I recollect a time down Tascosa way when some galoots tried to stick up a stage just as our outfit showed up. We smoked them jaspers up aplenty."

★ ★ ★ ★ ★

Afterward, Johnny found a chance to speak to 'Lish alone. "Well, now you know why I'm on the bunko detail instead of with the criminal squad," Johnny said sadly. "Like my grandfather, the sight of blood is not for me. I always just keel over."

'Lish slapped him on the back. "We all have our weaknesses, son," he said. "It's nothing to fret about."

Johnny could only stare for a moment. "But I thought you figured I wasn't quite the right kind of a man. . . ."

"You inherited it from George, and he was a mighty good pard," 'Lish said. "A man to ride the river with. You an' Penny will make a mighty pert couple. I'll dance a jig at the weddin'."

Johnny acted like he still couldn't believe it. When 'Lish last saw him, he had a dazed look on his face, but he was holding hands with Penny, and she was glowing.

The parade re-formed. The band marched past with the bass drum booming. 'Lish jammed the hat tightly over his ears, for a bass drum always made him worry about thunder.

After the speeches had been made and the statue unveiled, he was asked to say a few words. He complied.

"I mind a time down Abilene way when I was ridin' for the X I T outfit an'. . . ."

"Give-A-Damn" Jones

Bill Pronzini was born in Petaluma, California. His earliest Western fiction was published under his own name and a variety of pseudonyms in *Zane Grey Western Magazine*. Among his most notable Western novels are STARVATION CAMP (1984), set during the days of the Yukon gold rush, THE LAST DAYS OF HORSE-SHY HALLORAN (1987), concerned with the humorous adventures of an inept road agent, and FIREWIND (1989), the harrowing story of an evacuation from the timber country in northern California during a fire storm. He is also the editor of several excellent single-author Western story collections, including UNDER THE BURNING SUN: WESTERN STORIES (Five Star Westerns, 1997) by H. A. DeRosso, RENEGADE RIVER: WESTERN STORIES (Five Star Westerns, 1998) by Giff Cheshire, RIDERS OF THE SHADOWLANDS: WESTERN STORIES (Five Star Westerns, 1999) by H. A. DeRosso, and HEADING WEST: WESTERN STORIES by Noel M. Loomis (Five Star Westerns, 2000). He has the extraordinary and rare ability to know a good Western story when he reads one, and he has written several fine Western stories himself, collected in ALL THE LONG YEARS: WESTERN STORIES by Bill Pronzini (Five Star Westerns, 2001). He is married to author Marcia Muller, and they make their home in Petaluma, California.

★ ★ ★ ★ ★

The most admirable man I've ever known?

Gentlemen, that is a question that should require considerable thought and reflection. In my nearly seven decades of life I have traveled from one end of the country to the other, north and south of our borders and twice across the Atlantic Ocean. I have shaken hands with statesmen, been entertained by royalty, drunk brandy and smoked cigars with two sitting Presidents of these United States. I have known many celebrated and respected newspaper editors and publishers, among them my own father, the redoubtable William Satterlee. And I have spent hours in the company of famous authors, artists, philanthropists, and titans of commerce. The answer to your question should not roll easily off what one member of the fourth estate has seen fit to call "the golden tongue of Senator R. W. Satterlee." But the fact is, my answer requires not five seconds of brain cudgeling.

The most estimable and significant man of my acquaintance was a tramp printer named "Give-a-Damn" Jones.

No, no, I'm not pulling your legs. "Give-a-Damn" was the moniker bestowed upon him by his wandering brethren; his given name was Artemus. Artemus Jones. A tramp printer is what he was, in fact and in spirit, and proud of it.

Most of you are too young to recall the days when itinerant typesetters, a noble and misunderstood breed, were a vital element in the publishing of newspapers large and small. If you have read my resumé, you know that I myself was one of that adventurous fraternity in my early youth. Yet the tale of why I chose such a vagabond's trade is not nearly as well known as it should be. Nor, I dare say, is Artemus Jones and the rôle he played in the destiny of the man who stands before you. I have been remiss in publicly according him the credit he deserves. But no more, gentlemen. No more.

Make yourselves comfortable and I'll tell you why I place a traveling printer above any other man in my life.

It was the summer of 1883, two years after my father purchased the Bear Paw *Banner* and moved our family to that eastern Montana town from Salt Lake City. Bear Paw was generally a peaceful place, but in the spring of that year trouble had sprung up between nearby cattle ranchers and a group of German and Scandinavian farmers who had come west from Wisconsin and settled in the region. The farmers weren't squatters, mind you. The land they claimed was theirs free and clear. The cattlemen, however, had used it for beef graze for a generation and more, and considered the farmers an invasion force bent on using up precious water and destroying prime grassland. Feelings ran high on both sides, with most of Bear Paw siding with the Cattlemen's Association and its leader, Colonel Elijah Greathouse, owner of the sprawling Square G. Fistfights, fence-cutting, arson, two shooting scrapes, and one near lynching came of the disagreement, and there was as much name-calling and finger-pointing that spring and summer as you'll find on the floor of the United States Senate in session.

I was a mere lad of fifteen, but as interested as any full-grown adult in these volatile goings-on. My father, a man of strong opinions and iron will, had taken up the cause of the immigrant farmers and penned several fiery editorials defending their rights and denouncing the injustices perpetrated against them by their Bear Paw neighbors. As a result, the *Banner*'s plate-glass front window had been shattered by a rock one night, and the local job printer who had done our typesetting was intimidated by the cattlemen's interests into closing up shop and moving to Helena. William Satterlee had little choice but to set type himself, with my inexperienced help, except on those occasions when a tramp printer happened to stop off in our town.

In the three months before Artemus Jones arrived, an equal number of hand-peggers were hired. None lasted more than three days, and the only one who paid no attention to the uneasy climate was an old man of at least eighty years named Charlie Weems. He was completely toothless, though he chewed tobacco and could ring a spittoon at twenty yards with unerring accuracy; and he had but one eye, claiming to have lost the other in the explosion of a Queen Anne musket not long after the War of 1812. He drank forty-rod whiskey from a seemingly bottomless flask, could recite the names and addresses of most houses of ill repute in the Western states and territories, cussed a blue streak while he worked, and set type faster than any man I have seen before or since. He boasted to me that he had never spent more than three days in any town, and he was true to his word where Bear Paw was concerned. There one day, gone the next, riding the rods or the blind baggage or tucked away in a boxcar on the Great Northern's east- or westbound night freight.

Another freight train, the tramp's favored form of transportation, brought Artemus Jones into our midst. I was alone in the *Banner* office when he walked in on a Tuesday morning. He was a lean, wiry man twice my age and a little more, with drooping, tobacco-stained mustaches and eyes a brighter blue than a Kansas cornflower. He wore a disreputable linen duster and carried a bindle wrapped in a bandanna handkerchief. Prepossessing? Not a bit. Yet despite an air of hard-bitten toughness, he was soft-spoken and polite and gave the impression of having more to him than met the eye. I sensed his profession even before he approached with the breed's standard opener: "How's work?" And after only a short while in his company, I sensed, too, that he was no ordinary man.

"Available," I said. "You'll be welcome. We go to press tomorrow night and circulate Thursday morning."

"Standard union wages?"

"Yes, sir. Twenty-five cents a thousand ems."

His blue eyes took my measure. "Young to be the owner of a territorial newspaper, aren't you?"

"William Satterlee is the owner. My father."

"William Satterlee, eh? I believe I've heard the name. And you'd be William, Junior?"

"No, sir. I go by R.W."

He barked a laugh. "You'll go places, then. Men with initials instead of given names always do. My name is Jones, Artemus Jones."

" 'Give-a-Damn' Jones?"

"So I've been called. How do you know the name?"

"We had a printer several weeks ago named Charlie Weems. He mentioned you."

"Toothless Charlie's still above ground, is he? I'm glad to hear it, even if he is an unrepentant old liar and sinner."

"He didn't say how you came by the moniker, Mister Jones."

"Nor will I." Short and sharp, as if he were embarrassed by the explanation. "I prefer to be called Artemus. Your father on the premises?"

"Off hunting news. He'll be back before long."

"Well, let's have a look at your shop while we wait."

I took him into the composing room and stood by while he eyed our cranky old hand press, stone table, type frame, and cases. He opened upper- and lower-case drawers and nodded approvingly at the selection of Revier, nonpareil, and agate. Another approving nod followed his examination of the previous week's issue from a leftover bundle.

"This is tolerable good for a jim-crow sheet," he said—jim-crow being printer's slang for small-town. "Your father's been in the game a while, I take it."

"Two years in Bear Paw. Before that five years in Salt Lake, and before that stints in Sacramento and San Francisco, where I was born."

"I like working for a man who knows his business," Jones said. "Heard of the 'Perch of the Devil,' have you, R.W.?"

"Yes, sir!" I said. It was what Butte was called in those days. The copper mines there ran twenty-four hours, and the air was so poisonous thick with sulphur and arsenic fumes and smoke from roasting ores and smelter stacks that no vegetation was left anywhere in or near the town. This fact, plus its location on a steep hillside overlooking a bare butte, plus its reputation as the most wide-open camp in all of Montana had brought it the name. "Is that where you last worked?"

"It is."

"I've heard that on windless days, the smoke is so heavy over Butte it blots the sky and lamps have to be lit at midday."

"True, and then some."

"Which paper were you on? The *Miner* or the *Inter-Mountain*?"

"A. J. Davis's shop. Another man who knows his business."

I was impressed. A. J. Davis was editor and publisher of the *Inter-Mountain*, and reputed to be a stickler for hiring only the best among the typographers and reporters who applied. No "blacksmiths" for him!

"I was there a month," Jones said. "Wages cut above scale, but that wasn't the reason."

"No. What was?"

"Free beer on tap."

He went on to explain that above the *Inter-Mountain*'s offices was a saloon whose beer pipes happened to run through a corner of the composing room. One of the home-guard printers had devised a cleverly hidden plug for the pipe, all unknown to the saloonkeepers. Thus the printers had a constant supply of free suds whenever they felt thirsty.

Jones owned a storehouse of such anecdotes, and, when he was in a proper mood, he would regale me with one after another. He was also a fount of opinions, quotations, professional gossip, place descriptions, and capsule biographies of men and women he had known in his travels. He had been a roadster and gay cat, as young tramp printers were called in that era, since the age of fourteen and had crossed and re-crossed the country half a dozen times. Yet he was reticent about his family background and personal life. He became rude and profane on the few occasions when I attempted to draw him out. And while it was plain that he shared his breed's liking for alcohol and ladies of easy virtue, he did no drinking on the job and was unfailingly courtly to women of every stripe.

He had worked for more than a few of the legends of newspapering, among them Joseph Pulitzer on the St. Louis *Post-Dispatch*, Edward Rosewater, the fighting editor of the Omaha *Bee*, and the beaver-hatted old firebrand, J. West Goodwin, of the Sedalia *Bazoo*. For a time he had traveled with "Hi-Ass" Hull, considered the king of the tramp printers for his union organizing work, whose nickname was derived from a Northwest Indian word meaning "tall man." For another period he'd run with the band of roaming typographers known as the Missouri River Pirates, who frequented the towns along the Missouri River between St. Louis and Sioux City. He had met Jesse James when the outlaw was living in St. Joseph under his Tom Howard alias, two days before the dirty little coward, Bob Ford, fired a .45 slug into Jesse's back. Others whose paths he'd crossed were Bat Masterson, Texas Jack Omahundro, the poet Walt Whitman, himself a tramp printer in New Orleans, and the acid-tongued San Francisco writer, Ambrose Bierce.

Artemus Jones had no formal education, but he was an erudite man. By his own estimate he had read two thousand books, the Bible more than once, and the entire works of Shakespeare. He could quote verbatim passages from the Book and the Bard two and three pages long. Poetry, too, everything from Lord Byron to bawdy limericks. And he conversed knowledgeably on politics, philosophy, art, music, what-have-you.

Now it may seem to you gentlemen that time has clouded my memory, led me to paint you a romanticized picture of this man Jones. You may even be thinking he was a blowhard, a dissembler, or both. I assure you, none of that is the case. My memory of Jones is as clear as spring water. He was exactly as I've described him, and within his province a wholly truthful and honorable man.

Well, then. My father put Jones to work, and an expert typographer he was. He handled planer, mallet, rule, and shooting stick as though he had been born with them in his hand, corrected misspellings without consulting a dictionary, plugged dutchmen in a pair of poorly spaced ads, and generally made the publication of that week's issue an easier task than usual. My father was pleased, and I confess I was in awe. I clung to Jones almost as tightly as his galluses, asking questions, begging more stories, listening with rapt attention to his every word.

William Satterlee's front-page editorial that week was particularly inflammatory—written, in Jones's considered opinion, with a pen dipped in snake venom. There had been another shooting shortly before Jones's arrival, of a farmer who had dared to stray onto Colonel Greathouse's land after a runaway horse. The horse had been shot dead and the settler severely wounded by two Square G fence riders. Sheriff Buckley ruled the shooting justifiable. My father damned Buckley, not for the first time, as an incompetent dullard in the moral, if not actual, pay of the Cattlemen's Association, and he demanded prosecution for murder not only of the two cowhands but of their employer, whom he called, among other things, a cowardly Napoléonic tyrant.

Now Elijah Greathouse was a proud man with a fearsome temper. He had been a brevet colonel with C Company of the Tenth Kansas Volunteers during the War Between the States, and, although he was rumored to have been roundly disliked as a bully by the soldiers under his command, he was boastful of his war record and his military background. The "cowardly Napoléonic tyrant" label infuriated him more than anything else my father had called him in print. The day after the issue appeared, he stormed into the *Banner* office with his foreman, a troublemaker and alleged gun artist named Kinch, and confronted William Satterlee.

"You retract that statement," he bellowed, "or by God you'll suffer the consequences."

My father was unruffled. "I don't respond to threats, Colonel."

"You'd damn' well better respond to this one. I mean what I say, editor. Write one more vicious lie about me and you'll pay dear, in one type of coin or another."

"You've made yourself clear. Before witnesses, I might add." Both Jones and I were standing in the composing room doorway, where Greathouse and Kinch could plainly see us. Not that either of them seemed to take much notice. "Now I'll thank you and your cow nurse to get off my property."

Blood-rush turned Kinch's face the color of port wine. He stepped forward and poked my father in the chest with his forefinger. "Cow nurse, am I? Call me that again, you son-of-a-bitch, and you'll find out what else I am."

"I know what else you are," William Satterlee said meaningfully. "Get out before I summon that buffoon of a sheriff and have you arrested for harassment and public profanity."

The two cattlemen left, glaring and grumbling. Jones said to my father: "You've made bad enemies in those two, Mister Satterlee. I've seen their stripe before. Push them too far and one or both will act on their threats."

But my father was a stubborn man, and he had put blinders on where Greathouse and his foreman were concerned. "Humbug," he said. "Knaves, fools, and blowhards, the pair. I've nothing to fear from the likes of them."

Artemus Jones said no more. I held my tongue as well, though I was more than a little worried. No one had ever won an argument with my father when his back was up. Whenever I or anyone else tried, it served only to strengthen his conviction that he was in the right.

The next week passed swiftly. To my considerable pleasure, Jones stayed on in Bear Paw. He had built a stake, he said, working for A. J. Davis in Butte, and after the copper camp's rough and rowdy ways he was content to linger a while in calmer surroundings before moving on. He took a room at Ma Stinson's Travelers' Rest, a combination hotel and boardinghouse near the Great Northern dépôt that catered to railroad men, drummers, and transients. When he wasn't working, he spent most of his time at the Free and Easy Saloon, which had the best free lunch in Bear Paw. I suspect he also visited Tillie Johnson's parlor house, though I never dared to ask him.

In the composing room I watched his every move while he sat on the tall printer's stool, clad in his leather apron, and picked up the types and assembled them in the composing sticks. He showed great patience in answering the thousand and one questions I asked him about his trade and his travels. Prior to his coming, I had been uncertain of my future goals, though naturally I was tempted to follow my father's ink-stained profession. Before that week was out, I had decided unequivocally that an itinerant printer was what I wanted to be.

Jones neither encouraged nor discouraged me. His was a world of new vistas and high adventure, true, but it was also a lonely life, and a sometimes perilous one. I would have to be willing to take the bad with the good, he said, the hardships along with the ease and freedom of the open road. I allowed as how I could and would, and urged him to take me along when wanderlust claimed him again. He refused. Since his days with the Missouri River Pirates, he had traveled alone and preferred it that way. Besides, neither he nor anyone else could teach me the tricks of his trade—a man learned for himself and by himself. Some weren't cut out for the life and quit sooner or later for tamer, settled pursuits. Why, he had done some reporting here and there and been told by editors that he showed promise, and one day he might just take up that line himself. But when I pressed him, he admitted it was much more likely he'd remain an itinerant typographer until he was too old and infirm to ride the rails. Chances were, he said with a shrug, he would die in a strange town and be buried without a marker in a potter's field grave.

Well, this dissuaded me not at all. If anything, it strengthened my resolve to become a gay cat, to see and do the things and meet the people Jones had. By the end of the week I was making plans to leave Bear Paw on my sixteenth birthday. Plans that I may or may not have carried through, boyish as they were, if the events of that Saturday night had not taken place.

On Wednesday, fuel had been added to the strong feelings between cattlemen and farmers, in the form of a fire of dubious origin that claimed both the barn and house belonging to a homesteading family named Jansen. No one was seriously injured, though Jansen suffered burns in trying to save his livestock. It so happened the farmer's land bordered Colonel Greathouse's south pasture, and there had been a dispute between Jansen and Greathouse over water rights. My father took this to mean that the colonel was guilty of ordering the burnings. His front-page editorial was even more vitriolic than the previous week's, accusing the cattle baron outright and damning him as a savage oppressor who would commit any heinous crime to achieve his purposes.

I was helping Jones with the page layouts when William Satterlee came in with the editorial. Jones, while I peered over his shoulder, read it through in silence. Then he said: "Are you sure you want this to run as it stands, Mister Satterlee?"

My father was in an abrasive mood. "Don't ask foolish questions. And don't change so much as a comma when you set it."

"It's certain to provoke Colonel Greathouse."

"That doesn't concern me. What concerns me is his despicable behavior toward the settlers. If I don't take him to task for it, who will?"

"Father," I said, "suppose he does more this time than make idle threats? Suppose he comes after you?"

"He doesn't dare."

"Hadn't you better carry a sidearm just in case? Or keep a shotgun by your desk?"

"You know how I feel about weapons and violence. I'll not be reduced to the tactics of men like Greathouse and Kinch, nor will I be intimidated by those tactics. I write the truth, and the truth is the only weapon I want or need." With these noble, if improvident, words, he stalked back into the office.

"Artemus," I said, "I think he's wrong, and I'm afraid for him. If he won't take up a sidearm, maybe I should. . . ."

Jones fixed me with a sharp eye. "How much practice have you had with a hand gun?"

"Not much, but I know how to shoot one."

"Graveyards are full of men who knew how to shoot guns, or thought they did. Lads your age, too."

"Do you own a pistol?" I asked.

"No."

"But don't you need one on the road, for protection?"

"Some think so. I'm not one of them. I've seen the results of too many gunfights. Your father's right to want to avoid violence if he can."

"But what if he can't? What if he has gone too far this time?"

"There's not much use," Jones said, "in crying fire before you see the flames."

I took his meaning well enough, but I didn't much care

for it. I'd expected more of him than a tepid homily. That was all I was to get, however. Twice more I broached the subject that day, and both times he changed it, the last by launching into "The Girl with the Blue Velvet Band" in a rusty baritone. After that, I left him alone and fretted in private.

When the *Banner* appeared on Thursday, it caused the anticipated stir. Men and even a few women flowed in and out of the newspaper office, some to praise my father and more to berate him loudly. None of the visitors was Colonel Elijah Greathouse, his foreman, or anyone else off the Square G. And what few threats were flung at William Satterlee were mild and seemed mostly wind.

Neither Greathouse nor any of his men showed on Friday, or on Saturday. My relief was tempered by the knowledge that the colonel could be a devious cuss. He might well be plotting a more subtle form of revenge, I thought, and I said as much to my father. He scoffed at the notion. William Satterlee was a brave and principled man, but his self-righteousness, his unshakable faith in his beliefs, at times made him his own worst enemy. In this case, as matters soon developed, it nearly cost him his life.

It was his custom to work late at the *Banner* most evenings, even on weekends. He would come home to take supper with my mother and me, then return to the office until eight or nine o'clock. Some evenings I joined him, but my mother did not care for my being out of a Saturday night. It was when cowhands rode in off the nearby ranches to let off steam, the saloons and parlor houses did a boisterous business, and now and then arguments were settled with pistols and knives. Farmers came to town then, too, and, with feelings running as high was they were, there were confrontations virtually every Saturday.

Time passed slowly, and, when my father had yet to come

home by nine o'clock, I grew fearful enough to slip out through my bedroom window and hurry the few blocks to Main Street. From the hurdy-gurdy section near the railroad yards I could hear piano music and the shouts and laughter of revelers. But in the business district it was quiet, the street empty. Dark, as well, for the night was cloudy and moonless.

Lamplight shaped the *Banner*'s front window. Except for a flickery gas street lamp, it was the only light on the block. Or it was until I neared the building, passing by the alley that ran along its north side. Then, of a sudden, a different kind of light bloomed bright and smoky from the rear, and a faint crackling sound reached my ears.

Fire!

Heedlessly I plunged into the alley. It was our back wall that had been set ablaze, and, as I ran, Artemus Jones's words jolted into my mind: *There's not much use in crying fire until you see the flames.* I opened my mouth to cry it then, thinking to alert my father inside, but the shout was stillborn in my throat. For another cry sounded in that instant—the voice of William Satterlee, already alerted and coming through the rear door.

A scant few minutes later, as I ran clear of the alley, there was the bang of a pistol shot.

In the bright fire-glow I saw my father stagger and fall. I saw the other man clearly, too—Kinch, a smoking six-shooter in one hand and a tin of kerosene in the other. An anguished bellow burst from my throat. I stumbled and nearly fell myself. Kinch spun toward me, and, as I regained my balance, I saw his arm raise and his weapon level. I have no doubt he would have shot me dead within another two or three heartbeats. His face was twisted unnaturally, his eyes wild in the firelight.

It was Artemus Jones who saved my life.

He came lunging through the door, his arm upraised, a short, blunt object jutting from his closed fist, and shouted—"Kinch! Not the boy, Kinch, *me!*"—in a thunderous voice. No man could have ignored the savage menace in that cry. Kinch swung away from me as Jones charged him. The pistol banged again. Jones's left arm jerked, but the bullet's impact neither stopped nor slowed his rush. He flailed downward with what was clutched in his right hand—a printer's mallet, I realized in the instant before it connected with Kinch's head. The sound of wood colliding with flesh and bone was audible even above the crackling of the flames. The Square G foreman went down all of a piece, with no buckling of his legs—dead before his body settled into the grass.

Jones dropped the mallet and knelt beside my father. "He's still alive!" he called as I started toward home. "Run and fetch a doctor, R.W. Quick!"

I turned and ran. Other men were drawing near on Main Street, summoned by the gunshots. I was aware of lantern light and raised voices as I raced upstreet to Dr. Ferris's house. It took what seemed eons to rouse him from his bed and into his clothes, lead him back to the newspaper building. The flames had been mostly extinguished by then, a dozen men having formed a bucket brigade and others wielding burlap sacks from the feed and grain store. So intent was I on my father's motionless body, it was not until the next day that I learned the fire damage had been confined to a charred wall and portion of the roof.

Jones was again on one knee beside him, his left arm loose and dripping blood. In spite of his wound he had brought out a cushion to prop up William Satterlee's head and a blanket to cover him. The bullet had entered my father's chest, but its path had missed any vital organs. When

I heard Dr. Ferris say—"I don't believe it's a mortal wound."—my limbs went jellied with relief.

The rest of that night is a blur in my memory. I recall a long vigil with my mother at the doctor's house, and at some point a brief conversation with Artemus Jones. The damage to his arm was minor, requiring no more than an application of carbolic salve and a bandage. He had no difficulty in using it.

When I thanked him, belatedly, for saving my life, he said in gruff tones: "You shouldn't have been there. And there shouldn't have been any gun play."

"What do you mean?"

"Your father was on his way to the privy when he heard Kinch outside . . . he was already through the door before I could react. Else I'd have been the first one out."

"Then you'd have been shot instead."

"Maybe not. I can throw a mallet as well as swing one."

It took a short while for the significance of this to sink in. "You had no reason to be at the office so late tonight," I said then, "unless you were as worried as I was. On guard even if my father wasn't."

Jones shrugged and made no reply.

"But why?" I asked. "It wasn't your trouble."

"I had my reasons."

"You might have been killed. . . ."

"I might have," he said, "but I wasn't. Some chores are worth doing, R.W., for your own sake as well as others'."

I understood that, and something else then, too. I understood why he was called "Give-a-Damn" Jones.

As serious as William Satterlee's wound was, he was conscious and out of danger by sunup. My mother and I went to church to give thanks, and, when we returned to the doctor's, we found a surprise visitor—Colonel Elijah Greathouse. News of the shooting, attempted arson, and Kinch's demise had been delivered to him by another of his cow-hands, and he had come to town, he said stiffly, for only one reason. To tell Sheriff Buckley and now my father that Kinch had acted on his own, in this case and in the burning of the Jansen homestead. Despite William Satterlee's public opinion, he neither ordered nor sanctioned senseless violence. Greathouse swore to this with his hand on a Bible he produced from his coat pocket. Afterward, he turned on his heel and walked out.

Admitting to mistakes in judgment was never easy for my father, but no man lying flat on his back with a punctured chest can be as cocksure as when healthy and standing tall. He offered a brief, grudging apology to Jones and me, and, when the sheriff came to see him, he made no attempt to bring charges against Colonel Greathouse. Later, after his recovery, he softened his editorial stance considerably. Still later, when a harsh winter forced an uneasy alliance between ranchers and farmers, he ceased taking sides altogether. There were no more clashes between him and the colonel. They never spoke to each other again.

Artemus Jones did not leave Bear Paw immediately, as I'd been afraid he would. He stayed for three more weeks, while my father slowly mended. To everyone's surprise, Jones volunteered to act as both the *Banner*'s editor and typesetter during the convalescence. I was delighted when William Satterlee, a newspaperman above all else, agreed. He seemed to take it for granted that Jones was momentarily motivated, but I knew better.

Jones and I worked tirelessly during those three weeks. In addition to his other duties he wrote most of the news copy and a pair of editorials on brotherhood and Christian charity. If his style was rough-edged, it was also sincere, forthright, and offensive to no one. And for good measure, he made sure that in none of the issues he edited was there a single typographical or grammatical error, unplugged dutchman, pied line, or widow.

By the middle of the third week my father was well enough to return to his desk and pen that week's editorial, in which his praise of Jones was, for him, lavish. Upon reading it, Artemus refused to do the setting and argued in vain against its publication. William Satterlee won the argument, as he always did when hale and hearty, but it was I who set the type. My father also paid Jones, in addition to his printer's wages, a bonus of twenty-five dollars for his editorial work. Jones took the money with no particular reluctance and, in the tramp's typically profligate fashion, spent most, if not all, of it over the next two days at the Free and Easy and Tillie Johnson's.

The day after that, Saturday, he packed his bundle and hopped one of the Great Northern's night freights for parts unknown.

He said nothing to my father or me about moving on. He was not a man for good byes, any more than a man for praise or conceit or sentiment. There one day, gone the next. True to himself, his calling, and his principles in every way.

Well, gentlemen, there you have it, in sum and without embellishment. Why Artemus Jones is the most admirable man I have ever known.

Did we meet again? To my everlasting regret, we did not. I left Bear Paw myself shortly after my sixteenth birthday, and for the next six years I followed the adventurous trail of the itinerant printer across the width and breadth of the country. I encountered men who knew Jones and spoke highly of him, and twice I arrived in cities—Joplin, Missouri, and Spokane, Washington—a few short days after he'd been there and traveled on. But not once, despite my best efforts, did our roaming paths cross.

As many of you know, I left the wanderer's life in 1890, to take the position of police reporter on the Baltimore *Sun*. Newspapering was as much in my blood as printer's ink, but that was not the only reason I settled down. The day of the tramp typographer was drawing to a close. The mechanical age was upon us, and a new-fangled machine in which matrices ran down channels and were assembled to cast a whole line of type at one time—the Linotype, of course—had come into widespread use. Some of the old hand-peggers reluctantly learned the new device and became home-guards in various cities and towns. Others threw out their stick and rule, gave up their union cards, and took the same route as I or embarked on different careers entirely. Only a few hung on to the very end of their days taking catch-as-catch-can typesetting jobs, living hand-to-mouth on the open road.

It is my belief that Artemus Jones was among that last, ever-dwindling group. If he is still above ground, he is an old man, as old as toothless Weems and doubtless as feisty, and still hand-pegging in some backwater shop. More likely he has gone on to his reward, having fulfilled his own prophecy of death in a strange town and burial in an unmarked potter's field grave.

Were it ever in my power to determine his final resting place, I would erect upon it a marble stone engraved with his name and the words: "He gave a damn about his fellowman." That was the credo he lived by, gentlemen—and it is the credo I adopted for myself. Where I have succeeded in following it, the credit is largely his. And where I have failed, the failings are R. W. Satterlee's alone.

The Last Ride of Gunplay Maxwell

Stephen Overholser was born in Bend, Oregon, the middle son of Western author, Wayne D. Overholser. Convinced, in his words, that "there was more to learn outside of school than inside," he left Colorado State College in his senior year. He was drafted and served in the U.S. Army in Vietnam. Following his discharge, he launched his career as a writer, publishing three short stories in *Zane Grey Western Magazine*. On a research visit to the University of Wyoming at Laramie, he came across an account of a shocking incident that preceded the Johnson County War in Wyoming in 1892. It was this incident that became the inspiration for his first novel, A HANGING AT SWEETWATER (1974), which received the Spur Award from the Western Writers of America. MOLLY AND THE CONFIDENCE MAN (1975) followed, the first in a series of books about Molly Owens, a clever, resourceful, and tough undercover operative working for a fictional detective agency in the Old West. Stephen Overholser's latest novels are DARK EMBERS AT DAWN (Five Star Westerns, 1998) and COLD WIND (Five Star Westerns, 2000), the latter an extraordinary story filled with especially memorable and remarkable characters. Stephen Overholser with his wife and family makes his home in Boulder, Colorado.

★ ★ ★ ★ ★

On the one-hundredth anniversary of Boulder's great flood, a historian lecturing at the University of Colorado cited entries from the Schnorebus diary and read a Boulder *Herald* article dated May 16, 1894. The newspaper article was a colorful account of a coyote that had lost all caution. Old and mangy, too slow to hunt for a living, the pointy-nosed thief rifled garbage cans in Boulder's residential alleys. Cats fled, treed until they figured out the coyote was no threat. Town dogs tried their darnedest to run him off, according to the newspaper account. But even though slowed by age and limping on a hind leg likely gnawed out of the jaws of a trap, he put up one snarling-fierce fight after another, and earned a place. This, despite the fact that, when he lifted his leg, he staggered and hopped, spraying every tree and fence post in range.

Bedraggled and bony, the coyote survived that winter followed by a hot summer, and acted like he owned those alleys. He put on weight. His coat took on a luster. Then came autumn, a season of warm days and cool nights, a season of evening porch-sitting amid the fragrance of burning leaves, a season when the coyote did not slink into town. Folks debated his fate, divided over the question of whether he was dead or had returned to the wild.

This coyote story was cited as a sort of historical bookmark to the author's primary research, an account of the last years of "Gunplay" Maxwell. The complete version is found in BOULDER COUNTY HIGHLIGHTS, a volume gracing the shelves of good folks who study then-and-now photographs and chuckle over events that were hardly viewed with humor at the time. Men, women, and children from that era would be truly horrified to learn a street in Boulder was later named after Maxwell.

The outlaw first camped on the bank of Boulder Creek downstream from the current site of the high school. Hungry, he followed railroad tracks along Water Street into town. (Water Street was re-named Cañon Boulevard after the rails were pulled up and city fathers determined

Boulder needed a "boulevard" to enter post-World War II modernity, an era unsuited for trains rumbling into the heart of town.)

In the historian's account, the words used to describe that mangy coyote were brought to bear on old Gunplay as well. For he was a wreck of a man, a graybeard who swamped saloons as a means to an end, that end being passed-out drunk with vomit caked to his shirt front, snoring open-mouthed in an alley while oblivious to the pain of stones thrown by boys detoured on their route to the schoolhouse.

The Temperance Union raised a howl, offering the man a choice between two evils—reform or get out—but Gunplay, like the coyote, was cornered and cross, snarling-fierce in his refusals. Lawmen steered clear of the stand-off, preferring to let the thing work itself out with no disruption of revenues from Boulder's saloon district.

The subject of taxation carried the historian off on a tangent. In those days businesses averaged $124.00 in city taxes while saloons and dance halls paid $280.00 *per annum,* and illegal "houses" in the red-light district were "fined" on the first of the month, adding some $613.00 to city coffers. Every month. Lawmen stepped carefully in this section of town.

Returning to the subject of his research, the historian noted the reprobate's nickname did not arrive with him. It caught up later when a retired prison guard from Canon City passed through town and recognized him.

"Oh, yeah, that's Gunplay Maxwell," he had observed.

"Gunplay?" Boulderites had repeated with a collective rolling of their eyes.

The historian explained: "It was claimed that he rode stirrup to stirrup with Butch Cassidy when the Wild Bunch galloped outta Hole-in-the-Wall, Wyoming, Hanksville, Utah, and To-Hell-You-Ride, Colorado to hold up banks and knock over trains . . . robbing the robber barons, as Butch used to say. Truth is, the criminal element feared Gunplay Maxwell more than Pinkertons or Joe Lefors, or any other lawman who ever put a posse on the Outlaw Trail."

"Feared him. How so?" he was asked.

"Let me put it like this. If there was any possible way in hell for things to go wrong . . . well, Gunplay was there to make it happen."

The historian repeated the commonly held belief that Maxwell had been too clumsy to get himself arrested, that after years of unsuccessfully dynamiting bank safes and blowing apart baggage cars he staggered away from burning buildings and de-railed trains with befuddled lawmen wondering what the hell was going on. With his hearing damaged and one eye dimmed by flying débris, Maxwell was reduced to stealing unbranded calves and raiding back yard chicken coops just to survive.

He had been apprehended by accident. Alone after being shunned by self-respecting outlaws, his plan was to rob Bernard Lawrence Mercantile in Pueblo, Colorado, where he was convinced he had been overcharged in his purchase of a cream-colored Stetson and flat out cheated on a pair of silver spurs that were actually nickel-plated. The store was next door to a false-fronted building recently remodeled for use by the county sheriff, and Gunplay wandered into the wrong place, revolver drawn.

Six slugs from a double-action Colt had sent lawmen diving as Gunplay realized his error and backed out, gun empty. The rowel in the shank of one of those shiny spurs got wedged in a gap between two planks in the boardwalk, and like a coyote in a trap Gunplay went down, ass over tea cup, his hat rolling out into the street where it was trampled by a passing freight wagon's team of eight oxen.

He was accused of endangerment, mayhem, and numerous robberies. The jury had deliberated long enough to have their dinners paid by the county in the old Vail Hotel dining room. Found guilty, he was promptly sentenced.

On the first day of his incarceration in Canon City's stony lonely, the prison kitchen burned while the new inmate peeled Colorado potatoes. Gutted by a grease fire, it was, and during a week of gagging over low-bid box lunches the prisoners came to know who resided among them. Stories abound, but to sum them all up, if anything else could go wrong for a man in prison, it did. By the time the desperado had served eight of his sentence of ten years, guards and inmates alike not only favored parole, they demanded it.

Gunplay did not disagree with the views of dues-paying members of Boulder's Temperance Union. He surprised folks with his claim that prison life had set him on that dead-end road named Alcohol. He was not a drinking man until he was sent up to repay his debt to society. Eight years of quaffing fermented potato juice had ruined him proper. The only authenticated quotation from the mouth of Mr. Maxwell treats that very subject: "Not a man nor any woman should drink spirits, not a-tall, for it is the road to ruin I have traveled, and that is a fact."

And, in fact, it was that expression of remorse that inspired Willard Schnorebus to offer him a job. Actually, it was his wife who inspired him after she penned that quotation in her diary. Something of a pioneer in the rehabilitation of the criminal mind, Alma Schnorebus was secretary of the Temperance Union and managed to convince her husband and a long line of doubters that providing Mr. Maxwell gainful employment would steer him away from his life of crime and alcoholic debauchery. This particular employment, however, would seem to place temptation under the ex-convict's twitching nose. Willard Schnorebus owned the Blue Columbine Mill at the mouth of Boulder Cañon, and personally delivered the monthly payroll. Mr. Maxwell would ride shotgun.

More or less. In truth, Mr. Maxwell rode a big black-nosed mule behind the spring wagon, and both chambers of the double-barreled .12-gauge in the crook of his arm were empty. Folks would wonder long afterward, though, if the aging outlaw himself had been loaded on the rain-soaked day of the Schnorebus payroll robbery.

In that crime Willard Schnorebus was clubbed, found hours later belly down on the muddy road with his company's strongbox open and overturned. Ever since the Silver Panic of '93, when bank loans were called in and mortgages foreclosed, jittery millworkers were paid in eagles and double eagles, and those gold coins were gone. Gunplay Maxwell was gone, too. When the mill owner regained his senses, he had no memory of what had happened to him since his breakfast of three fried eggs, two links of sausage, and a wad of oatmeal, his morning repast for all thirty-nine years of his marriage, as noted in Alma's diary.

Heavy rains and run-off from a spring snowfall sent Boulder Creek out of its banks, and west of town mule tracks led into mud beside rushing waters. Some folks believed Gunplay Maxwell was dead, his body washed far downstream, while others theorized he had merely gone somewhere else to drink like a king, and here again the historian invited comparison between the man and the coyote.

The difference was that a muddied and bedraggled

Gunplay Maxwell slunk into Boulder a day after the flood that washed out Water Street. He claimed he had been overpowered by a gang of road agents, that he had attempted to fend them off with swings of that long-barreled shotgun, but one misguided cut had laid out his employer like a pole-axed steer. While Gunplay tended to Mr. Schnorebus, the robbers made off with the gold coins stuffed into two pairs of saddlebags. They forded the rising creek with Gunplay in pursuit and by then armed with the revolver formerly carried by Mr. Schnorebus.

Aboard the mule, Gunplay crossed the creek just before the Sixth Street bridge went out, and took up the chase. The payroll was heavy, slowing the thieves' escape. Gunplay got the drop on them in a grove of rain-dripping cottonwoods where they had halted to divide the loot. Alma Schnorebus believed one of them now recognized Gunplay Maxwell waving a revolver as he charged them, and the name alone struck fear into their hearts. Others said it was the threat of a posse that sent them into flight, leaving their plunder behind.

On his way back to Boulder, however, Gunplay had been followed, the robbers mere shadows in the fading light of a wet evening. One had a rifle that he fired from a distance to no effect. The thieves must have realized that far-off roar was a churning flood destroying everything in its path, and Gunplay Maxwell was alone and cornered. Outgunned, he could not survive a shoot-out, and to ford the raging river he would have to abandon the gold, or drown.

According to Gunplay's account, as penned in pages between the pressed flowers of Alma's diary, he secured the bulging saddlebags and urged that mule into troubled waters. The robbers looked on in disbelief. Give this strong animal his head, Gunplay had figured, and he will instinctively swim to safety. Hip-deep in muddy waters choked with rolling tree branches, wagon parts, and animal remains, the mule was swept off his hoofs. Gunplay slid off the saddle and grabbed his tail. Man and beast were carried downstream with great violence, but the mule kept his nose up and struggled across the raging flood waters, at last dragging his rider through the mud on the other side.

Such was the account recorded in a fine, feminine hand, diary entries that seemed to confirm Alma's belief in the good character of a reformed man. The fact that one set of saddlebags, half the payroll, was missing, and the last man to see it departed Boulder soon afterward, gave rise to a variety of accusations. These theories, none confirmed, centered on the notion that the outlaw had figured out a way to commit a crime and escape prosecution—simply invent a gang of robbers, lay claim to a heroic ride, and return half the loot to a grateful employer.

"But for all that was known then and now," the historian concluded, "Gunplay Maxwell made his last ride, and, like the coyote, no one in Boulder saw him again."

A later report, unconfirmed also, placed Gunplay in San Francisco, California, as late as April of 1906, where he was believed to be one of those residents photographed in the middle of Market Street amid smoking ruins—the aftermath of the great earthquake.

Ruby's Cape

Born and raised near Pittsburgh, Pennsylvania, Jane Candia Coleman majored in creative writing at the University of Pittsburgh but stopped writing after graduation in 1960 because she knew she "hadn't lived enough, thought enough, to write anything of interest." Her life changed dramatically when she abandoned the East for the West in 1986, and her creativity came truly into its own. THE VOICES OF DOVES (1988) was written soon after she moved to Tucson. It was followed by a book of poetry, NO ROOF BUT SKY (1990). Her short story, "Lou" in *Louis L'Amour Western Magazine* (3/94), won the Spur Award from the Western Writers of America as did her later short story, "Are You Coming Back, Phin Montana?" in *Louis L'Amour Western Magazine* (1/96). She has also won three Western Heritage Awards from the National Cowboy Hall of Fame. DOC HOLLIDAY'S WOMAN (1995) was her first novel and one of vivid and extraordinary power. The highly acclaimed MOVING ON: STORIES OF THE WEST (Five Star Westerns, 1997) is a short story collection that includes her prize-winning stories and one that can be read and reread with pleasure. It can be said that a story by Jane Candia Coleman embodies the essence of what is finest in the Western story, intimations of hope, vulnerability, and courage, while she plummets to the depths of her characters, conjuring moods and imagery with the consummate artistry of an accomplished poet. Her most recent books are I, PEARL HART (Five Star Westerns, 1998) and THE O'KEEFE EMPIRE (Five Star Westerns, 1999), followed by DOC HOLLIDAY'S GONE (Five Star Westerns, 2000).

★ ★ ★ ★ ★

She had been wearing the cape when he met her in the bar in Delphi. It was patterned like an afghan, crocheted in great squares of outrageous colors, and her head with its raggedy, dyed red hair poked up from the center like the heart of a sunflower.

The day was hot and dusty, one of those Arizona-in-July days that made him think of water and peer at the sky for signs of rain. He was hauling a load of hay and stopped in for a beer before going home. The place was empty except for the bartender, an ex-cowboy bent nearly double from injuries, and the woman in the corner, wrapped in color like a squaw.

"Mind if I sit?" he asked her.

She blinked and gathered the cape around her throat. "I was just going."

"Ain't it kind of hot for that?" He gestured at the bright wool.

She stared at him as if trying to see better in the dark. "I don't know. I guess," she said finally. "But it's pretty. Isn't it pretty?"

"It sure is," he said. "Care for a beer? On me?"

She shrugged. "My name's Ruby Finn. My car broke down. The man at the garage said he'd take a look."

"Then you ain't going anywhere for a while." He tipped his hat and felt the sweat on his forehead. "Earl Dingley. I'm caretaker up at Wilson's racing stables. How about that beer?"

She nodded once, and he took that to mean yes. Then she said: "Now I do love horses. Mules, too. I'm from Missouri a long time back."

He got up and went to the bar, came back with two cans, and snapped the tabs. "Never been there. Been pretty near every place else, though." Raising a can he said: "Here's to travel."

"It's not what it's cracked up to be," she told him. "Travel, I mean. My last husband traveled. Had his own rig and took me with him all over. For a while, anyhow." Then she ducked her head as if she'd said too much and didn't know how to take it back. The cape rippled as she moved, its squares of orange, yellow, and purple startling, like planted fields seen from the air.

As a kid in Kansas, he'd worked for a crop-dusting outfit. One Fourth of July the boss had taken him up in the old Stearman, and, although his stomach wobbled and his vision blurred, he could still remember his amazement, how the ground looked like something he could pick up and move around, as if earth and everything on it were merely toys, stick figures, at the mercy of someone, something. He worked there four years, until his mother died, and there was no longer a place he called home. He hit the road and headed West without plans or ambition, only the desire to get out and get by as best he could.

Sure, he knew about travel, the little towns on the High Plains blowing away in the wind, the inhabitants, their faces frozen in some other time or place, as hopeless as he himself had become. He'd gotten married in one of those towns—to a little woman nearly as lost as he was, and, when she died, he moved on the way he always did, leaving the past behind.

"You want me to take a look at your car?" he asked. "Leo's OK, but, like I said, he's slow."

She fooled with the beer can, turning it around with her small fingers. "Don't go to any trouble. You got things to do." A smile shivered across her face and disappeared. "Maybe I should get a horse like those pioneers. I keep thinking what it was like back then. All this country and them in wagons never knowing where they'd end up. Or how."

"Some didn't make it."

"That's what scares me." It was a whisper, a thread of sound, no more.

"You made it this far," he said, draining the can. "That's something. And long as you're in town, you ought to come see the horses. I'll show you around." And then he was surprised at his offer, at the words that had come out without any forethought. "Got to go," he said then. "Got a load of hay on the truck. Horses eat."

"Nice talking to you." She looked past him toward the door that opened onto a square of brilliant sunlight.

"You bet."

He drove home, unloaded the hay, fed the horses, and showered before sitting down to the chili he'd had cooking in the crockpot. He filled a bowl for the dog, Blue Duck, who crouched at his feet and ate noisily. When he finished, he left the plates in the sink, flicked on the TV, and fell asleep without turning it off.

He never would have thought about her again except that, on the following Sunday, she knocked on his door. She was wearing jeans and a blouse made out of some shiny red material. The color clashed with her hair. Her shoes were sandals, cracked, dusted over, not made for walking.

"I came to see the horses," she said, looking up at him dubiously as if she'd misunderstood and done the wrong thing. "I walked," she added. "It's farther than I thought."

He thought she was a damned fool—five miles without a hat in the middle of summer. "Better come in out of the sun," he said.

She looked around the trailer while he looked at her. She wasn't as young as he'd thought, maybe late forties. Her small face had a webbing of fine lines, and one cheek was faintly off-center as if it had been broken and healed wrong. Her nose was badly sunburned.

"You married?" she asked suddenly, as if she already knew the answer from her inspection—the dishes in the sink, the straw and grass that dropped off Blue Duck's coat and lay on the carpet, in the corners with the dust.

"I was." He grinned at her. "Four times. None of them worth a damn except the first, and she up and died." Come to think of it, this woman reminded him of her with her sunken cheeks and the helpless chin of a kitten. "They used to call me 'Shipwreck,'" he added. "Everything breaks on me."

"Can I use your bathroom?"

He nodded and pointed the way, wondering why conversation with her was so difficult. Maybe she was deaf. Or maybe she just didn't want to answer questions, didn't give a damn what he thought.

When she came back, he noticed that she had washed her face and slicked down her hair. It lay flat along her head, making her seem vulnerable. He felt he could see her bones.

"I can wash those if you want," she said, pointing at the dishes.

"Naw. Let's go look at the horses." He was uncomfortable with her in the small room. He didn't make passes at strange women, and these days those he sought out were younger, livelier, less inclined to be serious about anything or to have any expectations, an attitude that suited him.

His life had been like a jigsaw puzzle, a thousand pieces scattered behind him—jobs, women, good luck and bad, mostly bad. He could laugh at himself and his nickname, but it was true. Things broke on him, he could never say why. But his work here was peaceful with a sense of order.

Horses had to be fed, put on the hot-walker to exercise, their stalls cleaned every day without fail, and he liked that. No surprises. A man got to where he couldn't handle surprises—or much conversation, either.

He opened the door. "Come on, Blue," he said to the dog that was sniffing Ruby's hand.

"Come on, pretty thing," she said, and followed him out.

"Not too many horses here right now," he said. "They're mostly at the track."

But there were, it seemed, enough to satisfy her. She stroked their noses, made little sounds through the railings and over the stall doors, and seemed to have forgotten him completely.

Then she said: "I sure do miss the country. I been living on the road. Cities. Truck stops. You get absent-minded in cities, you know?"

He shook his head.

"You forget what day it is. What time of year. That kind of thing. You get . . . ," she frowned. "You get lost."

He knew about being lost. "Out here's different," he told her.

She looked around at the bowl of the valley, the yellow grass, the ring of mountains. "All this space." She stretched out her arms that were skinny but muscular, as if she were used to hard work.

"After a while you get so it don't bother you," he said. "You don't even notice it."

"That's not what I meant."

He looked at her, puzzled.

"I meant there's nobody crowding you. Telling you. There's just the days, and you can count on them. I been pushed around till I don't know what. But no more." She lifted her chin and looked at him, as if daring him to contradict her. She had yellow eyes like a cat's, and in the sunlight the pupils nearly disappeared. Looking into them was like looking at fields of grass that had no boundaries.

"I know what that feels like," he said after a minute. He did, too. His last wife had pushed at him, nagged at him until he felt he was slowly dying, the breath leaking out along with his strength. He walked out one day and left her in the house, hitched a ride all the way here, and found a job—and the pup, Blue Duck, abandoned on the highway. Now he lived in a kind of silence, performed his duties with only the dog and the horses for company, and liked it that way.

"Want a beer?" he asked.

She grinned, her face shattering into a thousand crevices. "I thought you'd never ask."

They drank a few, sitting on the stoop and watching thunderclouds build down in Mexico. After a while she got up, went inside, and washed the dishes.

"Can't stand a dirty sink," she said. "You mind?"

He shook his head. He hated washing dishes.

She stayed for dinner, the heated-over chili, and washed up again, and then he drove her home, Blue Duck riding in the back of the truck, his tail waving like a flag.

She had found herself a little house in the village, two rooms and a falling down porch behind a cluster of abandoned sheds.

"You shouldn't be here by yourself," he told her. "This close to the border, you never know who's going to come calling."

"Nice of you to worry, but don't," she said.

"I could lend you Blue. He's a good watch dog."

"You'd be lost without that dog. Thanks for a nice day." Then she shut the door.

He stood on the porch for a minute. It was overrun by a

honeysuckle vine, and the fragrance lay like a weight in the evening air. It unsettled him, or maybe she did, making pronouncements, taking charge, and her as little as a gnat.

"I wouldn't be lost alone, either," he said to himself. Thinking about it, he felt that he'd been alone most of his life whether or not he'd had company. He wondered if she saw a weakness in him, a defect overlooked by everyone else, even himself, and was laughing at him from behind those yellow eyes.

When he got home, he looked at himself in the mirror over the bathroom sink, but all he saw was the leathery face he'd seen for years behind the soap spots on the glass, in the dim light of the one bulb that hadn't burned out.

The next evening after the horses were fed, he threw his tools in the truck and went down to fix the loose floor boards on her porch. The door was open, showing the rooms empty except for what looked like a pile of laundry on a chair, a newspaper open on the table. Her absence annoyed him. She could at least be here when he came.

He sat on the steps a while waiting, watching the mountains change colors in the sunset. Still she didn't return. He got his tools then and nailed down the worst of the boards, hitting his thumb in the process and cursing. Likely he'd loose his thumbnail now, and for what? She'd never even know he'd been here.

You could never figure women. They slipped past somehow, like dreams, while you were busy doing a job that couldn't wait, and, when you did look, they were miles ahead of you, or gone altogether, or changed into some other person you didn't know.

He saw her latching the rusted gate. She was wearing her cape, and her arms emerged from its folds, fragile and white like crippled wings.

"Thought I'd nail down these boards," he said, gesturing with his good thumb.

"I was out," she answered, rather foolishly it seemed to him.

She came and sat on the step, arranging the folds of wool so that she was nearly hidden, only her hands, clasping her knees, visible. Then she looked at the mountains, drinking them in with her eyes, her body leaning slightly in their direction as if she were magnetized and at any second would drift off, leaving him alone.

"I got to get back," he said.

"I guess."

"You won't trip now."

"Mmm-mmm." It was an agreeable sound that meant, he decided, exactly nothing, a sound of dismissal as if she didn't care whether or not she tripped, whether or not he existed.

He didn't know what to make of her, swathed in the colors of sunset, or of himself, shuffling his feet in the dust like a kid. "You sure are an aggravating woman," he said to her. "I never knew a one like you."

She turned her head. Her eyes twinkled as if she enjoyed the attention. "Me?" she asked.

"You. I come down to help you out, and what do you do? You just sit there like a stone, no thanks, no nothing. It ain't nice."

"Sorry." She wrapped her arms tighter around her knees. "What did you want me to do?"

"I don't know." He didn't, either, and that was the trouble. She left it up to him to connect the dots of her person, and he wasn't equal to the task.

He stuck his hands in his pockets. "See you around," he said, and backed off down the path. The last he saw, she was still sitting, arms around herself, her face a pale circle in the twilight.

On payday he cashed his check, did his grocery shopping, got his hair cut, then headed for the Delphi bar. He didn't feel like dropping his money on the Mexican girls across the line, or visiting Melody who was street-smart and had a path beat to her door by every cowboy for fifty miles. He was thinking, instead, about Ruby as he'd last seen her, huddled in the dark. He turned off the highway and pulled up outside her gate.

Her door was open to catch the breeze, and through the screen he saw her standing by the sink, peeling potatoes with total concentration. As he watched, he felt a stirring in him, not of the body but of memory, hunger for feelings overlooked in the rush of his youth, the shiftlessness of his adulthood. Standing there, she reminded him of his childhood, of his mother and aunts, the women pictured in the magazines— good women, nurturing, like saints or madonnas, protected from harm by a kind of golden halo that surrounded them.

He swallowed hard. "Hey," he said.

She looked up. "Door's open."

He scraped his boots on the porch and took off his hat. "Want to go dancing?" he asked, surprising himself once again.

Her eyebrows rose. "Me? Go dancing?"

"Why not?"

"I don't know. Maybe I forgot how. It's been years."

"Then it's time. Forget those potatoes. Let's go."

She weighed one in her palm, let the other hand come up empty. "OK," she said. "Give me a minute."

She got drunk later, more on air than on beer it seemed to him, but he wasn't exactly sober, either. When they danced, she was as light as a butterfly and as many-colored, and she laughed, spinning over the floor as if she couldn't stop.

"Let's get married," he said to her in mid-flight, cutting off her laughter as if he'd had a knife. Her mouth stayed open, showing missing teeth.

"That's crazy," she said.

"Yes or no. None of those words that don't mean nothing. I'm tired of it."

She stood back from him and folded her arms like a butterfly come to rest. After a minute she said shyly, her voice hardly audible: "We do get along, you and me."

She told him she'd been married twice and had two children by her first husband, a salesman who'd abandoned them when the children were babies. Desperate, she'd left them at her sister's farm and took a job as a waitress in town. She had been young, even pretty. She showed him a picture of herself standing on the porch of the farm house wearing white slacks and a striped top. Her hair was long and yellow and blowing across her face.

"You wouldn't know it was me, would you?" she asked.

He peered at it. "Well, I would," he said, more to please her than out of truth.

"I had some good times, I can tell you." She handed him another photo from the album she kept in a suitcase under the bed. "There's my kids. Carrie's married now. Got a little girl. Tom . . . ," she stopped, and her shoulders rose and fell. "Tom's always in trouble. There's a wildness in him."

"Maybe he'll grow out of it," Earl said. "Kids do."

"I wish we could have him down here," she said, replacing the pictures. "Not that it would do any good."

"I guess we could," he said half-heartedly. He was too

old to have kids around, particularly troublesome ones. He'd seen enough trouble, been in enough himself.

"It wouldn't be right," she said.

She snapped the suitcase shut and locked it, putting the key in her pocket. It was an odd habit, but he wasn't bothered by her secrecy as much as by the way she kept to herself, planting and weeding the garden, canning when it began to produce and admiring the jars lined up on the pantry shelves, and seeming not to care whether he was around or not.

At first her silences baffled him. After a while, he found them comfortable and was startled when, if she drank too much as she often did, she began to laugh and talk without restraint in long, winding sentences that made even less sense than her usual cryptic responses. Sometimes she told bawdy stories about her youth and the men she'd known, stories he didn't want to hear.

"Just shut up about that," he told her once. "Just shut that drunk mouth of yours."

She'd kept silent for three days, refusing even to look at him. She reminded him of a dog, kicked, sullen, and he wondered how she had ever reminded him of the women of his childhood, those sturdy, selfless creatures who kept the home together and who now seemed set apart from the world and different from anyone else he had ever known, certainly from this woman he had made his wife.

She kept a different kind of distance, as if she were two people, or even three, and, although she was affectionate enough, never turning away or refusing him, there were times when she seemed a stranger, when her yellow eyes went elsewhere, leaving him behind.

"Are you happy?" he asked her once, reaching out for her mystery.

"Why shouldn't I be?"

"You never say. I just wondered."

She gave that little laugh, dust motes rising in the air. "If I wasn't, I'd leave. I did it before."

"That what you did to your ex?"

Her eyes went flat. "He beat me."

He couldn't picture anybody raising a hand against her, little as she was, but there was that sunken cheek and the missing teeth. "Son-of-a-bitch," he said.

"He was in the hospital. Cancer. I walked out and never looked back, but sometimes I wonder, maybe I should've stayed. Maybe something I did made him sick."

"He could've made you sick," he said. "He could've killed you. Ever think about it that way?"

"No. I try not to think about him at all. It's done."

That made sense. He tried not to think of his wives and usually succeeded. "Better that way," he said.

Except she hadn't said she was happy. As usual, she'd left him to fill in the blanks and slipped away by asking a question of her own. He went out to check the horses that nickered at his approach. When he laid a hand on their necks, they tossed their heads with pleasure, and he stayed in the barn a long time, talking to them as he talked to nothing and no one else.

When summer came again, they celebrated their anniversary. Earl took a weekend off, and they went into the city to a motel. Ruby bought a new blouse, striped white satin, and she wore it to dinner.

"Let's do this again," she said, bouncing a little in the booth. "Times like this, I forget the rest."

"That's done. I keep telling you," he said, annoyed and showing it. "Why keep harping on it?"

She sipped her drink, holding the glass between her teeth. "Sometimes I wake up and think I'm back there, and you're him. I think I did something wrong, and you'll make me pay for it. It scares me. It's like I'm having a nightmare, or I'm crazy or something."

He was supposed to be an adult, able to handle most situations, but with her he was always at a loss, not knowing the right words. "I'm not him, god dammit," he snapped. "If you think I am, then you *are* crazy." He looked down at his plate, away from the sorrow in her eyes.

Later, if he had to put his finger on when things changed, it would be that time, those words spoken that he didn't mean but couldn't take back.

She started getting up before dawn and going out on the stoop where she sat huddled in her cape, her lips moving, her eyes staring blankly at the mountains as if each day had to be celebrated with a prayer. After that, she worked in the garden on her hands and knees until it got hot, when she came in and shampooed the carpets, washed the curtains, painted the trim, and she did it fiercely until exhaustion stopped her.

"This house," she'd say. "This house," and click her tongue and toss down a can of beer like it was water.

She was drinking too much, even he knew that, although usually he could match her can for can. "Leave it be," he said finally. "And cut out drinking so much. You'll kill yourself."

She looked at him out of those inscrutable eyes. "Would you care?"

He didn't answer right away, trying to penetrate the murk that separated them and failing. "What do you think?" he said finally, using her own tactic.

"I don't know. I don't know anything any more." She

walked out and left him, went down to the pasture where the mares ran with their foals, and leaned on the fence, propping her chin in her hands.

After an hour, he followed. "You going to stand here all night?"

"I like to watch them. They're so right just doing what they do. Not like people at all."

"I don't get you," he said, meaning it.

She sighed, a rush of breath that shook her whole body. "I don't belong here," she said.

His frustration turned to anger. What she meant was that, as usual, he wasn't good enough, that he'd failed in some way he hadn't foreseen, in spite of good intentions. But then, part of his failure was her fault, always talking in some kind of code he was supposed to decipher. No wonder her ex had turned violent. He could feel it in himself, the frustration, the hope that a good slap would crack the wall she'd built around herself.

"You don't belong anywhere," he told her, the taste of bitterness twisting his mouth. "Don't feel you have to stay on my account."

He walked away, looked back once and saw her still leaning against the fence, her arms spread out on either side, and he had the uncomfortable feeling he was watching a kind of crucifixion, a taking in of pain he himself had caused.

When she came in, long after sunset, she went straight to the bedroom at the back of the trailer where she sometimes slept when she wanted to be alone.

"You're shutting me out," he said to her from the door. "It's not fair."

She was brushing her hair in front of the mirror. "You think anything's fair in this world?"

"We're married." He spoke to the image, to the yellow eyes that wavered in the glass.

"Don't I know it."

He moved toward her, taking pleasure in how she flinched away. "You're using me, is all," he said, putting his face close to hers. "You're like the rest of them, making a place for yourself, making yourself comfortable and shutting me out. I might as well live alone."

"Don't you know anything?" she cried. "I can't help anybody. Not you. Not me. Like I told you, I'm stuck somewhere, and I can't get out." She threw the brush at him. It glanced off his shoulder and fell to the floor.

He bent, picked it up, held it in his hand, and stared at the strands of red hair wrapped around the bristles. "Throwing things don't help," he said.

He was surprised to see her crumple against the bureau, folding in on herself like a flower, her head drooping on her neck so he could see the back of it—white, very thin.

"I guess the devil's got me," she said.

He put his hand on her neck beneath her hair and stood waiting for her to turn to him, to lift her face, give him an opening so that, somehow, he could help. When she didn't move, he went out and slammed the door behind him.

He made himself a sandwich for dinner and shared it with the dog, and then flicked on the television. He could hear Ruby moving around the back room, probably getting ready for bed. Alone. He felt guilt like a pain in his chest he couldn't shake. He'd tried to figure her, never raised a hand, turned over his pay, and trusted her to do right. He understood she'd been badly treated, so he'd held back, given her space to catch her breath, except she hadn't. She'd only gotten worse, and he couldn't shake the notion that, for lack of knowing what to do, he was at fault.

Shipwreck. The damn name fit. He drank a beer, then opened another. Alcohol helped, always had. When it came time for bed, he didn't bother to undress, just slipped off his boots and lay face down, his head in the pillow.

Sometime after midnight, Blue Duck began to howl and wouldn't quit, even when he threw one of his boots through the door.

"Shut up!" His voice came out harsh and cracked, and he stumbled over the strips of moonlight that came through the slats of the blinds.

"Go on! Git!" He shoved the dog out and went back to bed, his head pounding.

Outside, the dog howled again and was answered by a coyote hunting in the field. And then the night was silent except for the brushing of the branches of a pine tree against the trailer roof.

He found her in the morning, her blood spattering the walls like scarlet roses, her face peaceful in a way that he had never seen it. He hadn't heard the shot, hadn't heard anything, only Blue Duck's mournful howling.

The sheriff came, and a young deputy with eyes that reminded him of Ruby's—pale and accusing—and he answered their questions as best he could. No, he'd heard nothing. No, they hadn't quarreled. Not really. And he hadn't known about the pistol she kept in her suitcase. If he had, he'd have taken it from her, just to be on the safe side. A reason? He searched for words, shaking his head.

"All the time she talked riddles," he said. And he thought that life was a riddle, a will-o-the-wisp you couldn't hold, couldn't define, like Ruby's laughter, sometimes sad, sometimes bawdy, always fading away before he could learn its meaning.

He said—"She was my wife. We were married. I loved her."—and stared back into the accusing eyes with all the dignity he could summon, knowing he'd spoken the truth too late to make a difference.

They believed him. No fingerprints of his were on the pistol, no sign of domestic violence was found. What they had was obvious testimony—a woman, silent, tidying her nest, leaving her house spotless for those who came asking questions.

After the funeral he went back to the trailer and found that the neighbors had cleaned the walls, taken up the bedding and carpet, left only empty rooms and her cape hanging on its hook beside the door.

Sometimes now it moves in the wind and assumes the shape of Ruby's small body. Then Blue Duck growls, and Earl stops what he is doing and reaches out to touch the empty folds.

He does not know what he feels, or if he feels at all, although he peers through the window often, expecting to see her in the garden wrapped in light like the others—those women, real and imagined, who left their mark and moved on into memory.

He wonders if that is all there is to living—a mark to be made, found, marveled over—patterns plowed into earth, fossils trapped in stone, strands of bright wool woven into a multi-colored cape that moves with a life of its own. And he cannot decide if he himself has left any record anywhere at all.

His Personal Prisoner

Les Savage, Jr. was an extremely gifted writer who was born in Alhambra, California, but grew up in Los Angeles. His first published story was "Bullets and Bullwhips" accepted by the prestigious Street and Smith's *Western Story Magazine*. Almost ninety more magazine stories all set on the American frontier followed, many of them published in Fiction House magazines such as *Frontier Stories* and *Lariat Story Magazine* where Savage became a superstar with his name on many covers. His first novel, TREASURE OF THE BRASADA, appeared in 1947, the first of twenty-four published novels to appear in the next decade. Due to his preference for historical accuracy, Savage often ran into problems with book editors in the 1950s who were concerned about marriages between his protagonists and women of different races—a commonplace on the real frontier but not in much Western fiction in that decade. As a result of the censorship imposed on many of his works, only now have they been fully restored by returning to the author's original manuscripts.

Savage died young, at thirty-five, from complications arising out of hereditary diabetes and elevated cholesterol. However, his considerable legacy lives after him, there to reach a new generation of readers. His reputation as one of the finest authors of Western and frontier fiction continues and is winning new legions of admirers, both in the United States and abroad. His most recent books include COPPER BLUFFS (Circle V Westerns, 1995), THE LEGEND OF SEÑORITA SCORPION (Circle V Westerns 1996), and

THE RETURN OF SEÑORITA SCORPION (Circle V Westerns, 1997) as well as FIRE DANCE AT SPIDER ROCK (Five Star Westerns, 1995), MEDICINE WHEEL (Five Star Westerns, 1996), COFFIN GAP (Five Star Westerns, 1997), PHANTOMS IN THE NIGHT (Five Star Westerns, 1998), and THE BLOODY QUARTER (Five Star Westerns, 1999).

★ ★ ★ ★ ★

May 22, 1877
Montgomery, Alabama

To: Gen. Wm. Harding
      Austin, Texas

Located John Fenner here using alias John Steen. Have hint he is plan86ning Pensacola train robbery. Will try to pick him up before he leaves here. Please send requisition warrant at once.

E. Webb
State Troops

The rain made a dismal clatter on the red roof of the little clapboard station at Pensacola Junction. The rain beat a futile tattoo against the mat of saw palmettos that surrounded the building with their morbid tangle. The rain seemed to fill the black well of reluctance in Earl Webb till it threatened to overflow.

"Seems to me four train robbers is a lot for one man to handle, even a Texas Ranger," muttered the little stationkeeper. He ran a nervous hand through sandy hair tousled by the dozen times he had done the same thing since Webb arrived. "Why didn't you ask the sheriff at Pensacola to help?"

Webb started to answer sharply, with the tension in him. Then he closed his long, flat lips over the words. This stubborn, withdrawing habit of a lifetime must have helped to form the deep furrows in the weathered, roughened flesh of his jaw. It was connected, somehow, with the restraint under which his body seemed to suffer. It was a long, rangy body, heavy through the shoulders and narrow through the hips, made for movement and strife.

"I did ask the sheriff," he said, staring bleakly out the window. "General Harding was supposed to contact any local officers I needed for help. But Sheriff Granger said he hadn't gotten any word, and he couldn't help me unless I had a warrant."

The keeper's eyes grew luminous. "You ain't got a warrant?"

"I'd planned to catch John in Montgomery, and was having warrants and requisitions sent there. He jumped town. The station agent said a man answering his description had bought four round trips to Pensacola. This twelve-eleven carries the heaviest express shipment out of Pensacola. It's pretty plain what John plans."

"John," echoed the man wryly. "You'd think he was an old friend."

"Maybe he is."

"Huh?"

"I said maybe he is!"

"Well, you don't need to bite my head off." The stationkeeper puttered with his broom. "If he was your friend, why did they send you after him?"

The words blocked Webb's answer, for a moment, with a

flood of associations. *Your friend*. Thirty years. A lifetime. The dingy back yards of that little Texas town they'd played in as boys. The women they'd known. The horses they'd ridden. The countless things that swept up to blacken the reluctance already in him and make him wonder, if it came to pulling his gun, could he shoot?

Webb shook his head. "I guess the reason the general held off till now was because I knew John. But when John killed Casey Thomas, he had to be stopped. The general said my intimate knowledge of him made me the man for the job."

"Casey Thomas was an officer?"

"A ranger, guarding an express shipment John held up." Webb's body shifted restlessly. "What time you got?"

The keeper fished out an immense pocket watch. "Eleven twenty-three. She gets here in two minutes." He fumbled it back into his pocket, shaking his head. "You're crazy to do this without help. I sure wouldn't."

Webb shrugged, a bleak look chilling his gray eyes. "That's the rangers."

"I wouldn't do it even if I was a ranger," the keeper insisted. "One against four. More like something this Fenner would do. Wild. More like a gunman than an officer."

"I guess I always was a maverick." There was little humor in Webb's smile.

"You ought to have a posse. You ought to. . . ."

The whistle stopped him. It brought the old diamond-stacker into view down the track, cow-catcher gleaming wetly above the rails.

"You'd better stay inside," Webb told the keeper.

"Inside, hell! I'm going to be so far out in the glades I won't even hear the shots."

The broom clattered against the unpainted flooring, and the back door slammed behind his scuttling figure.

A grimy fireman swung off the grabirons and trotted toward the water tank. Then the link-and-pin couplings began to clang as the cars jarred together. A few heads made their blurred impression through closed windows on the first dull-red coach. The fourth window of the second coach was open, and the unmistakable profile gained focus in Webb's vision.

Webb heard the strained sound of his own breathing mingle with the squeal of handbrakes on the caboose. And again he found himself asking that question—could he shoot?—and it seemed to push the barrel of his Frontier against his belly, where the gun was stuck through his belt, until the chill of the steel was inside his very guts. For a moment, there was no will in him. Then, with a guttural sound, he walked out the door.

The rain made a kettle drum of his hat. He tugged the brim down over his eyes to keep Fenner from recognizing him. He reached for the grabirons and swung himself up the steps into the vestibule.

Nearest him, in the second seat on his right, there was a pair of men, one with greasy blue jowls and a cold cigar, sitting next to the open window, the other in shirt and galluses. Then John Fenner, beside another open window, alone in his seat. Two seats behind him was a derby-hatted man with a pasty face. At the rear, an elderly gentleman.

"You're under arrest, John," said Webb, stepping from the vestibule into the aisle. "Don't do it . . . !"

But the unbelievable, animal reactions had not left John Fenner. He seemed to be out of his seat before Webb finished the first word, sweeping his coat back off a holstered Colt. But the single-action hammer on the weapon caught in his suspenders as he yanked it free, hanging the gun up.

The man with the cigar had already let it drop from his mouth and was diving headfirst out the window. His partner was rising and going for a gun. Webb turned to strike him across the face with the barrel of his Frontier.

The man in the derby fired without standing up. This brought a stunning blow to Webb's leg, and he fell heavily across the aisle, his shoulders striking the seat. With this holding him up, he fired for the first time.

The bullet jerked the man in the derby against the back of his seat so hard it knocked his hat off. He remained that way a moment, mouth open in foolish surprise. Then he fell heavily forward and disappeared from view.

The man Webb had pistol-whipped was huddled over, holding his face, and Fenner was still struggling to get his gun unhooked from his suspenders, pulling his checkerboard pants halfway up his chest with every jerk. It must have reached him, at last, how useless it was now. He gave a final, bitter haul at the gun, then released it. The three-pound Colt sagged in his suspender. A rueful, twisted smile caught at his hard mouth.

"Damn it, Earl," he said, "I'll never wear galluses again!"

May 23, 1877
Greenville, Alabama

To: Gen. Wm. Harding
      Austin, Texas

Arrested Fenner on the Twenty-Second. Little trouble. Local officers took two into custody on suspicion of train robbery. Plan to be in Montgomery on Twenty-Fourth. Have you sent warrant and requisition there as I requested?

E. Webb
State Troops

The two of them stepped from the Greenville telegraph office into gummy heat. The wound in Webb's thigh was painful, but did not prevent his walking. He was using a cane, limping along behind Fenner.

"Same old Earl," grinned Fenner. "Same old cryptic, noble Earl. Little trouble. Why don't you tell them, just once, exactly how it was? How come you were all alone? The rumors I heard had every Texas Ranger in the force on my tail."

"Harding said he'd send me another man," muttered Webb. "Something held him up."

"Yeah, like it held Sheriff Granger up." Fenner's voice was acid. He turned his head to look at Webb. "So you don't have a warrant, Earl."

"Just keep ahead of me, John," said Webb.

"Sure, Earl, sure," chuckled Fenner throatily. He reached up for the grabiron and swung himself into the vestibule. He was built much like Webb, with the same animal drive to his narrow hips. His jet-black eyes, however, lacked the cool resoluteness that could fill Webb's gray ones. They flashed with unbridled little lights that seemed to come and go with a will of their own.

Cotton stuffing thrust its grimy white tufts from the moth holes in the horsehair covering of their seat. By the time they reached it, another man had boarded, holding a blue serge coat over one arm. He let the somnolent indifference of his eyes pass over Webb and Fenner before he sat down.

"You're taking a helluva chance, Earl," muttered Fenner. "My family's lived in this section of the state for generations. What if the sheriff at Whitney asks to see your warrant? You won't have any legal right in the world to hold me."

There was dogged withdrawal in the way Webb got out the panatela he had bought in the Greenville station, and carefully bit off the end. The car shuddered and lurched, and the train was under way, with the turpentine smell of stinkbrush in the air, and the red earth of open country sweeping into the square frames of the windows.

Fenner's brows lifted in a malicious speculation, till they formed satanic peaks above his glittering eyes. "Still a private, Earl?"

"The promotion didn't go through."

"The promotion!" Fenner's snort held disgust. "All the dirty work you've put in for them, you should have been the adjutant general by now. What the hell happened?"

Webb's voice was tight. "You know the rangers."

"I sure do. You'll never be anything but a private, Earl. They'll keep you pulling their chestnuts out of the fire till your fingers are all burned off."

Webb felt his teeth dig into the cigar. "Forget it."

"And you don't like it a bit. In fact, you don't like the rangers," insisted Fenner. "You think they's a lousy outfit and wonder why you ever got into them in the first place."

"I asked you to forget it, John."

"I can read you like a book, Earl. Why did you ever join the rangers? You weren't cut out for it. Dad was right when he called you a maverick. Remember the way he used to talk about you? What a precarious trail you walked, he said. The good solid ones, they never have a problem. They never steal plums from the corner grocery or beat up the mayor's kid in the livery stable or get kicked out of school for wrecking the furnace. They plod right through life, graduate from school, maybe even get a corner grocery of their own. It's the wild ones that have the temptations. Remember the way Dad talked? Every new fork they meet in the trail, it's a new battle. Not much odds between one turn or the other. An awful thin line between officer and road agent. One step the other way and you would have been riding with me instead of the rangers."

"Your dad always was sort of a philosopher, wasn't he, John?"

"Even when they hanged him." Fenner grinned. Then he leaned closer, his voice filling with that infectious confidence Webb knew so well. "Why not take that step, Earl? You're through with the rangers. I can see it in your face. Your hitch is up next month, isn't it? All right, make this your last job. There'd be half a dozen witnesses to tell how I knocked your wounded leg from under you and jumped out the window. Then, when your hitch is up, you could come back. I'd be waiting. There's big money here, for a man with your flair, Earl. You and me, just like the old days. We used to have some high-heel times.

For a moment that guttural, animal voice touched all the wild things in Webb. For a moment, the bitterness he had been trying to suppress welled up in him, and he could not help a kaleidoscopic memory of the grief, the pain, the disillusionment he had been handed. A dozen times. A hundred? Had they ever backed him up? Always it seemed like this. For what?

He stopped this with an intense effort. "That was before you shot Casey Thomas, John."

Fenner stared at him a moment, then all his false, quiet confidence was rent by the husky explosion of his voice. "All right. Do it the hard way. Crawl farther out on the limb and watch them saw it off behind you. You'll never make it to Montgomery. They'll gang up on you at every whistle stop. You'll ride to hell on your own shutter!"

Webb shoved his tall white Stetson down over his eyes to

shield them from the sun without cutting off his view, and slid down in the seat a little, trying to relax. He was glad it had been Fenner who broke. He did not think he could stand much more goading about the rangers.

Those link-and-pins began their staccato tocsin as the train slowed. A faded sign on the tarpaper roof of a whistle stop said Willow Junction. Three men seemed a lot of passengers to pick up at such a jerkwater stop. They were all tall, slovenly, loose-jointed men in homespun trousers and linsey shirts, filling the car with the sullen clatter of their uncouth feet, looking the seats over sourly.

"Hello, Cousin Anse," said the man with the serge coat over his arm, "going to the capital?"

Anse was the first to seat himself, spitting noisy tobacco juice out the window. "Nope. Winslow."

Fenner looked at them, smiled, and folded his arms to settle back against the seat.

North of Willow Junction the landscape turned the windows to a row of moving oils. Webb did not know for how long they passed herds of whitefaces fattening in Johnson grass beneath brilliant red-bud trees and immense Poland China hogs rooting through curing cover crops. But when the man who had boarded with them at Greenville started twisting into his serge coat, and the seat creaked raucously beneath Anse and another of the Willow Junction passengers, he knew they were pulling into Winslow.

There was the same red-roofed station with the white paint peeling like dried, browning crust off the clapboards of the wall. The crowd of men eddied like a nervous tide across the long plank platform, spilling off into the dirt at either end. Webb felt the eager tension fill Fenner's body beside him. He put his cane out into the aisle, waiting for the last jerking halt of the car.

"There he is," shouted someone from outside. "Hello, Cousin John."

"Hello, Cousin Rafe," called John "Looks like a regular fair."

"We come to take you off that damn' Texan's hands."

The man in the blue serge was starting to rise from his seat, and turning backward at the same time, and the Willow Junction passengers were already filling the car with their movements. Fenner's swift, sideward glance sought Webb's intent.

"Let it go, Earl," he said, seeing that cane canted out into the aisle. "There's too many of them. They'll hang your hide on the station if you try to stop it. You can't do anything now, Earl."

The car halted with a final, squawking thump, and Webb put his weight onto the cane and stood in the aisle. They were all alongside of the car now, boosting each other through open windows.

"Git his gun, Cousin Anse, and we'll ride him on a rail."

"Come on, John, climb through this here winder."

"Tell that Texas hog toler he's prodded his last razorback."

"That's enough!" shouted Webb.

Perhaps it was not so much the loud, flat tone of his voice, although it did carry to most of them, as it was the sight of what he had done, which held them. Those at the car's windows quit yelling, and two of them halted their movement with bellies across the sill, heads inside, the pressure giving their eyes the glassy protuberance of a frog's, as they stared at the ranger.

"What is it?" called someone from behind the first ranks outside.

"I've got my gun to John Fenner's head," Webb answered. "I want this car emptied before the train starts. If one of you lays a hand on him or me, I'm shooting John Fenner dead."

May 25, 1877
Montgomery, Alabama

To: Gen. Wm. Harding
Austin, Texas

Got here this a.m. Prisoner in jail. No papers whatever have arrived. What has happened? If I don't get them, I'm afraid there will be repeat of what happened at Winslow. Couple of Fenner's kin tried to take him off train. They didn't.

E. Webb
State Troops

After leaving the telegraph office, Webb had a doctor look at his leg. It had been giving him pain, and the doctor did not try to hide his concern at the infection. After dressing the wound, he advised Webb to stay off of it and see him again in a day or so. Webb agreed, and left, going to the lunch room across the street from the courthouse. Through the dusty, fly-specked front window, he could see the gleaming dome of the capitol up on Goat Hill, and the turgid expanse of the Alabama River flowing within a stone's throw of the business section, and the little frock-coated figure that hurried into view, climbing the courthouse steps, a briefcase under his arm.

Some premonition made Webb leave his greasy fried potatoes and cold eggs uneaten, and go across to the courthouse. Halfway down the hall to the cell block, Webb met them. Sheriff Benton, with raw beefsteaks for jowls, was herding the other two before his considerable paunch. The little man in the fustian halted momentarily in some dim confusion, tightening a bony elbow against his briefcase.

"I thought you were going to keep my prisoner locked up till I called for him," said Webb.

"Mister Meachum here is representing your prisoner." Sheriff Benton's voice substantiated the pompous quiver of his wattles. "He's brought a writ of *habeas corpus,* and Judge Collins says he'll honor it."

"Let's go up and see the judge," said Webb.

"Ranger," interposed the sheriff, "don't push this. . . ."

"Let's go up and see the judge."

The dust of cellared years dropped its glinting mantle over the half-filled bottle of Otard on the judge's desk. It must have taken a lifetime of cultivating this beverage to produce the fine, ruddy glow in the urbane flesh of the judge's face.

"I understand you're freeing my prisoner on a writ of *habeas corpus,*" Webb told him.

"*Ad subjiciendum.*" The judge's voice was as carefully blended as the Otard.

"What?" asked Webb.

"*Habeas corpus ad subjiciendum,*" repeated Judge Collins. "For inquiring into the lawfulness of the imprisonment you have imposed upon John Steen."

"John Fenner," corrected Webb.

"He says he is John Steen." The judge cleared his throat. "Can you produce a warrant?"

"It's on the way."

Collins adjusted his pince-nez. "If you'll give me the order, Sheriff, I'll sign it."

"Now, hold on, Judge." Webb took one limping step forward, putting his wallet and badge on the desk. "There's my commission in the rangers. Fenner is wanted on three counts of murder in Texas. You know as much about the case as I do, and you know this man is John Fenner."

"You're risking contempt, Mister . . . er . . ."—Collins reached for the wallet, flipped it open—"Private Earl Webb? Very well, Private Webb, all the court knows is that you are an officer of the law from another state, out of your properly organized jurisdiction, trying to hold a man prisoner without warrant or requisition."

"Collins?" Webb said deliberately. "Any relation of Ellis Collins who owns a farm out Birmingham way?"

It might have been the sunlight catching in the judge's eyes. "I can't say that I've heard of the man."

"John Fenner's cousin," said Webb.

The chair creaked sharply. One of the judge's fleshy hands caught the edge of the desk, whitened faintly at the knuckles with his grip. "I warned you about contempt, Webb," he said. "I could hold you for it, you know."

"I wish you'd wait a while, Judge," said Webb. "The necessary papers should be along shortly."

"You won't have a prisoner to use them on," said the judge, unfolding the release with a flourish. "I'm tired of all this paperwork. You have no authority for what you've done."

Fenner was close enough to Webb for his muttered words to be unintelligible to the others. "Let it go, Earl. If you fight it any further, they'll throw you in jail here for contempt of court and suspend you from the rangers for it when you get back home. Why stick your neck out for them any longer? They've let you down all along the line."

For a moment, with the inescapable logic of that insidious voice in his ears, the vague, tenebrous gods Webb had been clinging to so grimly for so long seemed to fade. How right John was! If he bucked Collins, the very service he was trying to uphold would turn around and kick him in the teeth for upholding it.

"There," said Collins, finishing his signature and blotting it. "You may conduct the prisoner out, Sheriff."

But Webb reached the desk before Sheriff Benton. He picked up the order and carefully tore it apart. Benton gasped and made an instinctive move with one hand toward his gun. The brush of Webb's elbow against the right side of his coat did not look particularly deliberate, but it pulled the garment aside enough to reveal of the butt of his Frontier, stuck through his belt. With his eyes drawn to that, Benton let reason take place of instinct.

"Oh, I wouldn't threaten a judge," said Webb. "But I will give you a promise. If I see any of you before I leave this town, you're liable to get a lump on your head that won't match your ears."

May 26, 1877
Jackson, Mississippi

To: Gen. Wm. Harding
    Austin, Texas

Plan arrive Austin the Twenty-Seventh with Fenner. Governor Price of Alabama issued warrants and requisition. It's all the way now.

E. Webb
State Troops

Evening was already staining the hills around Austin to

the color of ripe plums. It was the first glimpse Webb had of
the city, before they crossed the river, and then the glim-
mering row of lights marking Congress. Webb had gotten
very little sleep in four days. His face was a gaunt, drawn
mask of nervous tension, waiting for Fenner's bid. Fenner's
eyes had been full of the same rolling white mischief as in a
spooked horse for the last hundred miles. Webb felt the lift
of the other's frame as the train began to lose speed.

"Careful, John," he said.

"Sure, Earl, sure," chuckled Fenner, but that throaty
mockery was unconvincing. He turned to look at Webb.
"Tell me just one thing, Earl. Would you really have shot me
back there at Winslow if those hog tolers had tried to get
me free?"

"Yes, John." Webb met his gaze fully. "Right through the
head."

Webb turned to put his cane in the aisle for support. He
was leaning on it to slide his legs out when the coaches
started banging against one another with the stopping train.
This threw him off balance, and he had to twist out into the
aisle to keep from falling. He sensed Fenner's violent movement and tried to get on his feet.

Fenner kicked his wounded leg from beneath him. Going
down, Webb managed to get his gun out. But Fenner kicked
that from his hand. Webb heard it slide beneath the seat.
Fenner took a look in the direction of the sound, then
whirled to run.

Webb saw that he could not get the gun, either, as far
back under the seat as it was. He rolled to an elbow, lifted
the cane like a spear, and threw it hard. It must have had vicious force, striking the small of a man's back that way.
Fenner cried out, and his arms shot up as if he were spread-
eagled. His own impetus carried him on crashing into the

wall at the end of the vestibule. He slid to his knees, and Webb was on him before he could rise again. When the conductor came running down the aisle with his eyes as wide as they would open, he found Webb sprawled on top of Fenner with his cane held in both hands horizontally across Fenner's throat.

"Get my gun," Webb told the man. "Under the fifth seat on the right side."

They were on their feet by the time the little knot of shadowy figures filtered across the vague illumination of the station windows. Webb was surprised to see the adjutant general with the guards.

"I'm glad you brought your prisoner through, Lieutenant Webb," he said.

"*Lieutenant* Webb?"

General Harding smiled. "Anybody who couldn't read between the lines of those telegrams would be blind, Lieutenant. And anybody who did a job like that deserves a promotion." His face darkened. "I won't even try to apologize for the way things were held up. Red tape was a lot of it. I issued an order for those warrants a week ago. And I released Private Barrister last Thursday to meet you at Winslow. Somehow he got side-tracked. I've a sneaking suspicion part of it was due to the same men who've blocked your promotion before. They didn't think you were steady enough for the responsibility of a commission."

"You mean,"—Webb's voice was quiet—"they didn't think I'd bring John back, even if I could?"

The general made a vague, conciliatory gesture. "Now, Lieutenant. . . ."

"Forget it," Webb told him, smiling. "Maybe they weren't too far off. My record isn't exactly the most orthodox in the force. Maybe, even in your mind, this was sort of a test."

The general answered: "If it was, you came through with flying colors."

"Flying, hell," said Fenner disgustedly. "You just don't know how big a chance you were taking, General."

"Maybe it wasn't such a big chance, John," Webb murmured. "Maybe that line between you and me is wider than your dad thought."

Horse Tradin'

Rita Cleary was born in New York City. Some of her ancestors were pioneers in the frontier West. She earned a Bachelor's degree in French literature at Manhattanville College and a Master's degree in French at Harvard University. At an early age she learned to ride horses and today owns her own horse, a Thoroughbred mare. SORREL (1993) was her first Western novel and was voted a Spur finalist that year by the Western Writers of America. It was followed by GOLD TOWN (1996), a novel set in the mining camp of Varina, based closely on Virginia City, Montana, site of the largest placer gold strike in history. Always having had a profound interest in history and Western American history in particular, Rita Cleary is a member of the Lewis and Clark Trail Heritage Foundation, the Montana Historical Society, the Missouri Historical Society, and the New York Historical Society. She is married and the mother of three children, making her home in Oyster Bay, New York. RIVER WALK (Five Star Westerns, 2000) is the first volume in a saga concerned with the Lewis and Clark transcontinental expedition to the Pacific Ocean.

★ ★ ★ ★ ★

"That's a handsome stallion, Missus Claiborne. He'll pay Tom's note and then some."

"The note's not due until Friday, Mister Blaine." Mary

Claiborne squared her shoulders. "But you've a good eye for a horse."

Mary Claiborne's lithe form blocked the doorway of the sturdy log homestead. Mary was a tall woman, blonde, with sharp eyes and a voice melodious but firm.

Ned Blaine sat his horse like a statue outside the yard gate. It was a handsome bay, tall at the withers with the musculature and deep heart of a Thoroughbred. Ned Blaine was president of the Empire Bank and a powerful man. But he had one weakness—he was a sucker for a good horse.

Beyond the house, a rail fence separated a few rows of scraggly vegetables from the horse corrals and the wide prairie. Two children stood beside yellowed cornstalks, the larger holding a growling black dog by a rope collar. A baby cried from inside the house. The stallion pawed the ground near the corral gate.

Ned Blaine waited. He would not dismount uninvited.

Mary Claiborne squinted into the late afternoon sun at the back of Ned Blaine. "Did you come to admire my horse, Mister Blaine, or would you like a cup of coffee?"

"Coffee'd be welcome, Missus Claiborne." Ned Blaine flicked up his black coat tails and dismounted. "Is Tom home?" Tom Claiborne wasn't home, and Ned Blaine knew it.

"Tom took the three-year-olds to Larksburg for sale." Tom Claiborne took his three-year-olds to Larksburg this time every year. Tom was renowned throughout the state for breeding excellent horses. His mares dropped eight to ten foals every spring. He raised them, gentled them, green-broke them, and kept one or two of the best to train. The rest he usually delivered to Angus McGuiness in June of their third year, for sale. Angus gave Tom Claiborne $100.00 per horse on delivery, which was enough to retire any Claiborne borrowings left from the previous year. The rest went for small necessities. But Mary dreamed of the time when they could begin the year debt free.

Ned Blaine stroked his clean-shaven chin and twisted the ends of his reins around the gatepost. "Always selling stock to pay off the note."

Blaine's comment stung. Mary Claiborne stiffened. "Tom will be back, end of the week, before the note is due." There was an edge to Mary's voice, and it didn't soften when she directed the children: "Tim, mind Shag. Nancy, see that Mister Blaine's horse is watered." The boy tightened his grip on the dog but kept his eyes locked on the dapper form of the banker. The girl tugged the horse toward the watering trough.

Ned Blaine walked past the dog and stooped as he entered the dimness of the house. It was poor by the banker's standards and rudely furnished, but solid and warm as any house in Clay County. Checkered curtains fluttered at the windows. Crocheted mats softened the hard wooden seats of the chairs. The floor was swept, a jelly jar full of sunflowers graced the rough surface of the table, and the smell of freshly baked pie filled the air.

Mary lifted a red-cheeked baby from a crib and cradled him against her hip. With her free hand, she placed a cup and saucer in front of the banker and poured out a cup of thick black coffee.

"That's another mouth to feed since I saw you last year, Missus Claiborne." Ned Blaine indicated the baby. Beads of sweat rose on his neck. He was more comfortable in a barn around the horses or in the stark interior of his bank. Infants, mothers, so much domesticity made him nervous.

"This is Billy Claiborne, Mister Blaine, eight months old today. Give him another ten years and he'll be breaking the two-year-olds just like his dad."

Ned Blaine sipped his coffee and smacked his lips. "Now that's coffee that tastes like coffee." This was as close as Ned Blaine came to a compliment.

"Thank you Mister Blaine." She stood for a moment silently, the points of her mouth curled slightly upward. Neither Mary Claiborne nor Ned Blaine wanted to address the real reason he had come—Tom Claiborne owed the Empire Bank twelve hundred dollars.

"How many three-year-olds is Tom selling?"

"Eight."

Ned Blaine's head jerked up, eyes suddenly alert. "At one hundred dollars a horse? That's not enough to cover his note."

Mary Claiborne bit her lip. Carefully she set Billy Claiborne in his high chair. She handed him a spoon, but he proceeded to eat with his hands. She ignored the mess. "Prices are up this year, Mister Blaine." She nodded politely and smiled. "Angus himself tells us that you paid eight hundred dollars for that lovely mare you're riding just last November."

Ned Blaine ran a finger under his collar. "That eight hundred dollars was for a made horse, Missus Claiborne, gentled and schooled to bridle and leg, not some headstrong three-year-old."

"With good customers like yourself, Mister Blaine, Angus will be happy to advance us an extra fifty dollars per horse."

The cagey banker held his tongue, and Mary met him eye to eye. She continued: "Our yearlings are used to handling, and as finely bred, dare I say more finely bred, than your beautiful bay." She watched the banker closely. Again he didn't answer, but neither did he drop his eye. They stared stubbornly at each other like two bulls squaring off for a fight.

"There's apple pie to go with the coffee, Mister Blaine." Mary softened her tone.

At first, the banker did not react. His nose twitched, and a thin smile spread over his face. "I'd be grateful, Missus Claiborne."

Mary reached into the cupboard and drew out the pie. She sliced three pieces, one for Ned Blaine and one each for Tim and Nancy. The boy and girl came in quietly and took their seats.

Ned Blaine addressed the boy, Tim. "You old enough to handle that stallion, young man?"

The boy nodded politely. "Yes, sir."

"Tim is an able hand with a horse, Mister Blaine. He can groom and shoe." She watched the banker lift a shaggy eyebrow and added: "And he exercises the stock when Tom is away."

Ned Blaine turned his steel-blue eyes on the boy. "And I guess you're in charge here, the man about the house, when your pa is gone?"

The boy stared back as if there were any question who was in charge here when his pa was gone.

Mary Claiborne changed the subject. "Nancy is a handy little horsewoman, too. That stallion is gentlest with her, but we don't let her ride him. They're just best friends."

"Friends?" To the banker, it was a silly remark. Ned Blaine looked disdainfully toward the girl and wrinkled his nose. "You help your ma cook and sew or did your pa buy a half-pint side-saddle for you?" Clearly the banker thought a child's saddle was a notorious waste of money.

"I can ride astride, sir. My pa is teaching me."

Ned Blaine dropped his jaw. "Now that's something I'd like to see!"

"Come back tomorrow morning and you can watch us

all," Mary Claiborne said. "We start weaning tomorrow early. Work doesn't stop just because Tom is away. Some of the mares get angrier than that stallion when you try to take their foals away."

Weaning, separating the nursing foals from their mothers, pushing them out to pasture to feed for themselves, it was hard work. The mares never wanted to let go their offspring. Ned Blaine had finished his pie and drained his coffee. "Weaning," he hesitated while the idea settled in. His shaggy brows came together in a frown. "I'd like to see that." He pushed back his chair and got up, addressing the children: "Tim, Billy, girl, it was nice to meet you." He tipped his hat. "Ma'am, until tomorrow."

Tomorrow, Tuesday, the sun rose hot and dry, and Mary Claiborne rose with it. Tom Claiborne was a day overdue, but she didn't have time to miss him. She fed the children and nursed Billy, placed him in his crib with the black dog for guard, and ushered Tim and Nancy out to the barn.

She wore an old pair of Tom's overalls that she had taken in at the waist. Her blonde hair was tied with a string and piled under a broad-brimmed hat. Her brown arms were bare beneath rolled-up sleeves, and she wore lumberman's boots. They were tough clothes, barn clothes, the kind in which you mucked out stalls, the kind you only had to brush off when a playful colt dumped you in the dust. Little Nancy tagged along in a pair of her brother's hand-me-downs.

They pumped clean water and forked out hay. They curried and saddled and rode out to gather the nursing mares that trotted with foals at their sides. The horses crowded eagerly around water and grain. Mary Claiborne slipped a halter on a mare and led her into the corral. When her foal tried to follow, the children slammed shut the gate and chased it away.

That was when the fun started—the mare kicked, shrieked, and fussed in protest—and that was when Ned Blaine arrived. He stopped his bay at the same gatepost. He was not alone. The second man was dark and wore a faded blue shirt, worn and dusty leather chaps, and a high-crowned hat with a Montana crease. A black mustache drooped over his upper lip, and he rode a gray horse.

Mary Claiborne knew who he was, Josh Hammel, foreman of the Circle B, a fine and savvy horseman.

"Mister Blaine, come to see the ladies ride! Josh Hammel . . . how's that dun Tom sold you?" She had to shout, but there was still the ring of welcome in her voice. "There's coffee on the stove, Mister Blaine, but you ate the last of the apple pie yesterday. I'll be right with you."

Mary Claiborne led a second mare into the corral and shut the gate. The first mare would calm more easily with company.

Ned Blaine watched distractedly while Nancy and Tim drove the second foal away. They rode well, both of them, he had to admit, but there was another reason why he had brought Josh Hammel with him. He had one eye on the stallion pen.

The foreman watched with amusement and begrudging admiration. He folded his hands over the horn of his saddle, saw Tim and Nancy cut a good-looking foal away from its dam, and pronounced: "Rides better'n my gals . . . I should send them out here for lessons." He was a married man, and had two girls of his own.

Mary Claiborne held pride in her voice. "Your friend, Mister Blaine, doesn't believe we ladies do any hard work!"

Josh Hammel's next sentence startled Mary Claiborne

because he said it casually, with a smile beneath the black mustache, almost as an afterthought. "We just come by to see your stud, Mary." He was still watching Tim and Nancy.

Mary Claiborne stiffened. "No need, Josh. The stallion's not for sale. I got some good-looking foals."

Josh Hammel flashed a curious look at Ned Blaine.

Mary Claiborne's voice hardened with irritation. "I told you yesterday, Mister Blaine. You are welcome to my coffee and my cooking, or to watch us wean the foals, but you are not welcome to that horse, for trade, for repossession, or anything else. Tom and me, we bred him from a baby. He's the foundation of our herd."

Josh Hammel read the situation immediately. He turned on Ned Blaine. "I don't stay where I'm not welcome, Blaine. You take that stallion away, you put Tom Claiborne out of business." He moved his horse away.

"Hammel, come back here! I'm paying you to look over that horse."

"You heard the lady, Blaine! The horse is not for sale."

"He will be on Friday!"

Hammel was riding farther away. "You a fool, Blaine, or maybe you gone soft in the head? Ain't no horse worth twelve hundred dollars, and I know Claiborne. He'll be back." He stopped, turned his horse abruptly in the direction of Mary Claiborne, and softened his voice. "My advice, ma'am. You hold on to that stallion if you want to stay in the breedin' business. But that white-faced colt'd make you another fine stud in a few years." He pointed toward a handsome colt still at his mother's side. Finally he turned his black, soulful eyes on Mary. "If for some reason, Tom don't come back, ma'am, it's a good deal Ned's offering you . . . to cancel that note in exchange for a horse. Breedin' horses takes a man's kind of endurance."

Mary Claiborne choked back her anger. "Thank you Mister Hammel, but Tom will be back on Friday, with money enough to pay Mister Blaine. And now, gentlemen, I have work to do."

Josh Hammel apologized: "I didn't mean to offend, ma'am. Good day, ma'am." He jogged away.

But Ned Blaine sat his bay and stared at Mary Claiborne. He'd never met a woman quite like her. She was as attached to that stallion as she was to one of her children. His fingers tensed on the reins, and the bay backed a few steps.

He had always wanted that stallion, ever since Tom Claiborne had brought him and his dam all the way from Missouri. He'd finally hatched a scheme to get him while Tom was away. Tom would be delayed in Larksburg. One call last week to Layfayette Owen of the Denver Trust had insured that Angus McGuiness would not be in Larksburg when Tom arrived. He would be in Denver, covering a margin call for some of his own investments. Even if he returned in time, he would be far less willing to pay an extra fifty dollars for a three-year-old horse.

He watched Mary Claiborne and the girl-child whose name he could not remember. Mounted now, they cut two more foals away from their dams. Tim shut the gate on the angry mares. Mother and daughter drove the weanlings to the far range. Mother and daughter rode well with the fluid motion of natural-born riders, like the father, like any good cowhand. Ned Blaine looked with admiration and not a little disbelief.

Suddenly, the baby cried from inside the house. As if by instinct, Mary Claiborne whipped her horse up to the gate, dismounted, and ran inside. Blaine rode over to the children.

"What do you know about that stallion, Tim?" It was a brazen question, that of a grown man trying to outwit a young boy, to catch the boy between his own and his mother's interests. The boy didn't answer.

Mary Claiborne had come to the door with Billy Claiborne on one hip, mother and child framed in the rough wooden structure of the doorway. Ned Blaine felt a pang for the family he didn't have. "Don't you answer him, Tim Claiborne. A man who seeks the advantage of a boy deserves no respect. Mister Blaine, I repeat, that stallion is not for sale."

"Now Missus Claiborne. . . ." He sounded almost suppliant.

Mary set Billy gently behind the door and drew Tom Claiborne's shotgun from over the lintel. She stood the gun lightly against the door frame. "My son, Mister Blaine, is not for you to corrupt with your schemes." Her voice cracked like river ice in thaw. "Nor is my horse for you to buy. Good bye, Mister Blaine!"

Ned Blaine's mouth fell open, but no words came.

Mary Claiborne turned back into the house. Tim and Nancy slammed the gate on another mare and drove the white-faced weanling away. Speechless, Ned Blaine watched the handsome mare, nostrils flared, pawing and weaving back and forth at the gate, a superb animal, maybe worth the twelve hundred. He felt like that mare, frustrated, separated from the one object of desire. For a moment, he hesitated. Mares were many, but a good stallion . . . if only for the stud fees. He leaned his weight forward and rode away.

Ned Blaine couldn't wait until Friday to return. Mary Claiborne and Nancy were in the corrals, calming another nervous mare, when they spotted his bay jogging across the prairie. Like yesterday, he was not alone. A black figure loped at his side. Mary Claiborne recognized the sway-backed mare and the short, straight-legged rider in the flat planter's hat and black cutaway coat. His name was Crowell Washburn, and he cut a scrawny figure of angles and contrasts like the law he represented. He was circuit judge of Clay County. This time Ned Blaine had enlisted the law.

Mary shut the corral gate behind her and walked out to greet them. "Judge Washburn, what can I do for you?" She ignored Ned Blaine.

"Where's Tom? If the coffee's hot, I'll have a cup. Mister Blaine here says he has some business to discuss . . . that Tom owes him twelve hundred dollars."

"Tom does, but the money is due Friday, not today." She shot a suspicious glance at Ned Blaine, pushed a lock of blonde hair out of her eyes, and added: "Didn't Mister Blaine tell you Tom is not here? And I don't brew coffee when Tom is away."

The judge's voice whined as if he were instructing an ignorant child. "Now, Missus Claiborne, you mustn't upset yourself. Mister Blaine just wants to look over a horse of yours, check his teeth, his tendons, his feet, normal stuff if you're acquiring a horse."

Mary Claiborne answered sharply: "I know that, Judge, but Mister Blaine is not acquiring a horse." She squared her shoulders. "And he will be paid his twelve hundred." She hoped—she wished Tom would hurry.

Perched high in his voluminous saddle, the judge looked down on Mary Claiborne like King Solomon on his throne. "Missus Claiborne, Mister Blaine has offered to take your horse in lieu of the entire balance of this year's note, twelve hundred dollars. A horse would have to be made of gold to be worth that. You'd be a fool not to take it. Tom Claiborne never sold a nag for twelve hundred dollars in his life."

Mary Claiborne's poise snapped. "My horse is not a nag, Judge Claiborne. He is not some property for your court to partition. His blood runs in the veins of almost every foal on this ranch. He is the foundation of our stock, and the best stud in the state. Ned Blaine knows it. I know it. I regret you lack the same astute perception."

Strong words from a woman! The judge jerked his head back and frowned down on Mary Claiborne. But he turned on Ned Blaine. "I didn't come to be insulted, Blaine."

"Mary, be reasonable. Just let me have a look." Ned Blaine sounded almost repentant.

"Missus Claiborne . . ." She corrected the banker haughtily but sensed a thin empathy with him. Like Tom, like her, unlike Judge Washburn, at least Ned Blaine knew a good horse when he saw one. "You may admire my stallion all you like, Mister Blaine . . . from the back of your bay, with your seat planted deep in your saddle."

"I'll look him over for you, Ned." The judge started his mare in the direction of the stallion's pen. He was used to commanding proceedings, not cowering at rebuff.

"You ride your mare up to that gate, Crowell Washburn, and I don't guarantee your safety. Your mare's in season, or didn't you notice?" Mary Claiborne recited the danger, arms folded across her chest.

Judge Washburn pretended he hadn't heard and kicked his horse forward. When he neared the gate, the stallion leapt sideways, slamming his whole body into posts and gate, in an effort to get at the mare. The gateposts lurched but held. The mare jumped away, unseating Judge Washburn and leaving him hanging awkwardly, one knee bent around the slick fork of the saddle and clinging to the horn with both hands. The docile mare stood still until he righted himself.

"You crazy, Crowell!" Ned Blaine's temper flared. "That stallion hurts himself, nobody has a good stud . . . not Tom Claiborne, not me, not the bank." He gave a surly glance at Mary Claiborne. She was stifling a smile. "You'll see me again, Missus Claiborne!" He spat the words in anger. Signaling Judge Washburn, he reined his horse around savagely and galloped away.

Mary Claiborne grinned widely. Today's encounter had energized her. She checked to see that the stallion was not injured and posts and gate secure, walked back to the house, combed her hair, washed, and put on a skirt. Tom would be proud of her. He could arrive any time. He was two days overdue.

It was while she prepared dinner that her worries resurfaced. She knew she had treated the banker and the judge rudely. It was as if she had to speak louder, more sharply, for the men to take her seriously. Her hands shook as she sliced potatoes into a pan. She nicked her finger. Could she continue to keep the stallion out of Ned Blaine's hands? Should she even try, if Tom did not come? That awful possibility crept into her soul like an ugly worm. The potatoes sizzled in the fat. She grabbed the pan from the stove to keep them from burning.

Billy awoke suddenly at the sound of barking and clattering hoofs and started to cry. "Tom!" Mary's heart pounded, but Tom would not run horses like that. It was Tim and Nancy coming home at full gallop, horses lathered and breathing hard. Nancy was in the lead, and her brother followed on her heels, whooping and kicking lest his little sister get home first.

"Didn't Pa forbid you two to race! You both know better than to run them toward home. We're not training runaways." Mary Claiborne stopped herself—her voice still held the bite and sting of her encounter with Ned Blaine and of her nervous mind's imaginings. Tim hung his head down. Nancy, the winner, was jubilant. Neither was listening. "Walk those horses until they're powder dry."

Dinner was on the table, but Tim and Nancy would eat theirs cold. She went back to feed Billy, wringing her hands in her apron. While he suckled her breast, she swallowed a few bites of her own meal. They landed in her stomach like rocks in wet sand. Even if Tom were never to come back, she would not let Ned Blaine have the stallion. She would scrape and strain, bone and blood, to keep him. She would never pay stud fees to Ned Blaine and his bank. And Ned Blaine would be back tomorrow.

Tim and Nancy entered silently and began to eat. Satisfied, Billy sat propped on a pillow, watching his siblings.

Darkness descended. The children slept, but Mary Claiborne lay awake in the empty bed. Night was the time she missed Tom most.

But Ned Blaine did not come back tomorrow and neither did Tom Claiborne. All day Thursday, it rained. Mary Claiborne spent the entire day nursing, cleaning, cooking, feeding, and herding stock and watching the trail. Every sound of hoof, every flush of sage hen, made her heart stiffen its resolve to keep the stallion away from Ned Blaine or rejoice at the reunion with her husband. But no one came. They finished weaning. The mares began to calm, but they would have to be watched for the next few weeks, and their foals would have to be kept away. The handsome stallion pawed the earth in frustration. Big drops from heavy thunderclouds thumped into the earth.

When night fell, Mary summoned Tim and Nancy

around the table. "Children, your father is not home. It is up to us to keep that stallion out of Ned Blaine's hands."

Tim and Nancy listened with long, serious faces. Even Billy sat, quiet and immobile, on Nancy's lap.

Mary continued. "Tim, pack some food and your father's bedroll. Ride the red horse and lead the sorrel and black mares to Cooper's Cañon. Settle them in. Then take the stallion and keep him there. He'll want to stay with the mares. There's a brush corral and good water. And take Shag . . . he's good company, and he'll defend you. And don't come home until I say so."

Tim nodded gravely. He was young, and this was a man's responsibility. He left with the mares at sunup. The stallion was gone before breakfast.

At noon, Mary Claiborne spied a cloud of dust on the horizon. It came closer and shone red-brown on the dry prairie—a bay horse. It could only be Ned Blaine.

Mary Claiborne waited for him by the gatepost of the empty stallion pen, nervous hands plunged deeply into the pockets of Tom's overalls.

Ned Blaine rode up slowly. He stopped his horse and waited quietly. They glared at each other face to face. Finally the banker spoke. He did not humor, nor did he threaten. He spoke man to man.

"Did Tom come home Missus Claiborne?"

Mary Claiborne answered in a voice flat, emotionless: "No, Mister Blaine."

"Where's the stallion?"

"Gone away, Mister Blaine."

"And my twelve hundred dollars, Missus Claiborne?"

"Mister Blaine, you may take six of my mares, as collateral, until Tom comes home. You may bring your herders here and drive them wherever you intend. I trust you will keep them well-watered and fed. I would help you. I would go looking for Tom, but with Billy I cannot leave the ranch."

Ned Blaine nodded in silence. "You leave me little choice, Missus Claiborne."

Mary Claiborne did not answer. Her heart pounded like a hammer on an anvil. She wrung the corner of her apron into a tight knot. Ned Blaine turned his horse and rode away. He sent back two riders to herd the mares, but the mares would not be driven away from their foals. The herders cursed in frustration.

That was when Tom came home. Mary Claiborne was waiting at the gate. Her smile was radiant in spite of the tears that streaked her dusty face.

Even before he dismounted, he was shouting exultantly: "Fifteen hundred! Angus gave me a whole damn' fifteen hundred!"

A Question of Faith

Ray Hogan is an author who has inspired a loyal following over the years since he published his first Western novel, EX-MARSHAL, in 1956. Hogan was born in Willow Springs, Missouri, where his father was town marshal. At five the Hogan family moved to Albuquerque where Ray lived in the foothills of the Sandia and Manzano Mountains. His father was on the Albuquerque police force and, in later years, owned the Overland Hotel. It was while listening to his father and other old-timers tell tales from the past that Ray was inspired to recast these tales in fiction. From the beginning he did exhaustive research into the history and the people of the Old West and the walls of his study are lined with various firearms, spurs, pictures, books, and memorabilia, about all of which he can talk in dramatic detail. "I've attempted to capture the courage and bravery of those men and women that lived out West and the dangers and problems they had to overcome," Hogan once remarked. If his lawmen protagonists seem sometimes larger than life, it is because they are men of integrity, heroes who through grit of character and common sense are able to overcome the obstacles they encounter despite often overwhelming odds. This same grit of character can also be found in Hogan's heroines, and in THE VENGEANCE OF FORTUNA WEST (1983) Hogan wrote a gripping and totally believable account of a woman who takes up the badge and tracks the men who killed her lawman husband by ambush. Above all, what is most impressive about Hogan's Western novels is the consistent quality with which each is crafted, the compelling depth of his characters, and his ability to juxtapose the complexities of human conflict into narratives always as intensely interesting as they are emotionally involving. His latest books are SOLDIER IN BUCKSKIN (Five Star Westerns, 1996), LEGEND OF A BADMAN: A WESTERN QUINTET (Five Star Westerns, 1997), and GUNS OF FREEDOM: A WESTERN DUO (Five Star Westerns, 1999).

★ ★ ★ ★ ★

It was the time of war, the bloody, senseless conflict of ideologies now mercifully reeling toward its finish. New Mexico, having had its brief fling with shot and shell, hung suspended in neglected vacuum aware of the struggle only by reports from far distant battlefields or the occasional glimpse of a blue-uniformed patrol riding a remote trail. Mid July and the afternoon heat lay across the broad plains and choppy hills in a blistering haze. Overhead the sky was cobalt steel, and along its edges cloud mountains piled up in masses of jumbled, cotton batting to rim a breathlessly hot world in which nothing moved but vagrant dust-devils and the stagecoach bound for Rinconada.

Driver Luke Colegrove, the leather ribbons laced between his fingers sawing his arms back and forth as the double span of lathered blacks pressed against the harness, flung a sideward glance to Ed Drummond that day beside him on the box.

"Anything?"

Drummond again swept the savage terrain with his keen scrutiny. He shook his head, mopped at the sweat oozing freely from his weathered face. "Nope . . . nothin'." He waited a minute as the coach slowed around a curve, rocked precariously, righted itself, and plunged on. "You figure Cannon knowed what he was talkin' about? Never heard of Confederate guerrillas being this far west before."

Colegrove, an acid little man with hawk-like features and a straggling yellow mustache, said: "He knowed. Them guerrillas been stopping coaches all over the country, hunting them two women."

Drummond digested that in silence. Then: "Figure to tell the passengers? Bound to throw a powerful scare into them."

"They got a right to know. We get to Cook's, I'll speak my piece. You do some talking to that hostler. See if he's seen any signs of them. Was ten, maybe twelve in the bunch. Cannon wasn't for sure."

Thirty minutes later they rushed into Cook's Station, rolling the dust ahead of them in a great, yellow boil, and came to a sliding stop. The hostler trotted up with fresh horses and immediately began to make his change. Drummond, not relinquishing his rifle, turned to him. Luke Colegrove swung down, yanked open the coach door.

"Ten minutes, folks. Stretch your legs and get yourself a swallow of water." He wheeled away, entered the low roofed, adobe hut where further refreshments were to be had.

The passengers began to crawl stiffly from the cramped confines of the stage into the glaring sunlight. First, Mrs. Russell, a plump, gray woman, middle-aged and the wife of a territorial delegate. Next came her daughter, just turned seventeen. She was pretty, blue-eyed, and filling out her stylishly cut traveling suit to perfection. On their way to visit relatives in Silver City, it was said.

The third fare was a portly cattleman from Las Vegas, Armstrong by name. He was prone to much dozing and, when awake, fiddled constantly with a gold toothpick attached to a thin chain issuing from the top buttonhole of his checkered vest. He was a man who moved deliberately and with care, his ponderous bulk pressing the springs of the coach to basic level as he shifted to one side and emerged through the door.

The fourth fare was Dave Kirby, young, barely in his twenties in fact, with a rashness upon his features, a caged wildness glowing in his eyes. Handcuffs linked his wrists, and these glinted as sunlight touched the nickeled metal. His journey would end at Rinconada where he would stand trial for murder. He halted, leaned against the rear wheel of the vehicle in studied insolence as he awaited the tall lawman who followed close on his heels.

He was John Prince, marshal of Springville, in the process of delivering a prisoner. Lean of face, lank of body, a heavy personal trouble now lay upon him like a shroud, turning him taciturn and cold, and, when he placed his narrow glance on Dave Kirby, fresh anger stirred within him for he knew the outlaw was aware of that trouble. Kirby had been present during that hour before the stage departed Springville. He had witnessed the stormy scene, heard the bitter words that had passed between the tall lawman and his wife, Kate. Jealousy in a man is a pitiless scourge, forcing the worst to the surface—and the soul of John Prince had been laid bare before the outlaw.

Armstrong paused, stretched, yawned. The two women looked about uncertainly. Kirby caught the eye of the younger, smiled, his expression suddenly boyish.

"Water's inside, ma'am," he said, and nodded at the hut.

The girl thanked him and, with her mother, moved toward the sagging structure. At that moment Colegrove appeared, wiping at his mouth with the back of a hand. He glanced at Drummond, still in conversation with the hostler, halted, brushed his sweat-stained hat to the back of his head.

John Prince swore softly under his breath. He'd hoped to deliver Kirby and return quickly to Springville. The thought of Kate alone—with time on her hands—with Wilson Coyle subtly pressing his flattery and attentions upon her gouged into him like a saw-edged blade. He had not wanted to make the trip to Rinconada in the first place, but there'd been no choice. Now it appeared something was coming up that would keep him away even longer.

Resentment sharpened his tone. "Now, why . . . ?"

"Guerrillas," Colegrove spat. "Maybe part of Quantrell's bunch. Been stopping stages on this road last few days."

"Quantrell?" Armstrong echoed in frank disbelief. "This far west?"

The old driver shrugged. "Confederate guerrillas been spotted east of here. And in Texas. Just about everywhere, in fact."

There was a lengthy silence in the streaming sunlight broken only by the rattle of harness metal as the hostler worked at his chore.

John Prince said: "You carrying a money shipment?"

Colegrove wagged his head. "Only a smidgen of mail."

"Then why," Mrs. Russell said, dabbing at the patches of sweat on her face with a lace handkerchief, "would they want to bother us?"

Colegrove looked directly at the woman, his beaten features solemn. "Reckon it's you they're wanting, ma'am. You and your daughter."

Mrs. Russell caught at her breath. The handkerchief went to her lips to stifle a cry. Instantly Martha placed her arm around the older woman's shoulders. She stared at Colegrove.

"Why . . . why us?"

"Your daddy's a big man in this here country. Was I guessing, I'd say they figured to hold you for ransom."

"Maybe," Armstrong said. "Heard tell how Confederate guerrillas are always pulling raids to get women for. . . ."

"Forget it," Prince snapped. He swung his angry, impatient attention to the stagecoach driver. "Why the hell didn't you say something about this back at the fort? Could've asked for a cavalry escort."

Colegrove spat into the dust. "Didn't know about it. Just got the word at the last stop. Anyway," he added, glancing over the party, "I expect there's enough of us to give them an argument, if they try stopping us."

Prince allowed his jaundiced gaze to travel over the group. Enough—hell! Two women, an outlaw a man couldn't trust beyond arm's length, and a fat cow-nurse who'd likely curl up on the floor at the first shot. Only Drummond, the shotgun rider, might be relied upon for help—and, if the raiders were smart, they'd shoot him off the box at the start. Far as Colegrove was concerned, he could be counted out of it; he'd have his hands full with the team.

Mrs. Russell began to weep raggedly. Martha drew her closer, patting her on the arm gently.

Colegrove bit off a fresh chew of tobacco. "Right sorry I had to tell you about this, but I figured you ought to know. Now, everybody get aboard. Let's get moving."

Drummond came up at that point. "Pete says he ain't seen nobody around that maybe looks like guerrillas. Says he seen smoke west of here this mornin'."

Colegrove thought for a moment. "Could've been pilgrims. Or maybe 'Paches," he said, and started for the coach.

Armstrong hurried into the hut for his drink. The

women turned back, Mrs. Russell supported by her daughter. Dave Kirby stepped up quickly to assist, handing first the older woman and then Martha into the heat-trapped interior of the vehicle. Prince saw the girl touch the outlaw with her glance, expressing her thanks, and the thought—*Why will a woman always go for this kind?*—passed through his head. Shrugging then, he followed Kirby into the coach, settled himself on the forward seat next to the outlaw. A moment later Armstrong, puffing from the short sprint, took his place on the rear bench.

Colegrove shouted to the team, and they lunged forward, yanking the stage into forward motion with a violent rocking. Dust at once lifted between the opposed seats, began to rise and fall in a powdery cloud as the heat-charged air surged through the enclosure. In the road's deep ruts the coach crackled and popped and groaned from stress, those sounds blending gradually with Luke Colegrove's strident shouting.

Talk, desultory at best prior to the halt at Cook's Station, was now a dead issue, each passenger wrapped deeply in his own thoughts. John Prince was thinking of the past, of the seven years of married life with Kate who had grown more beautiful as time went by. Once he had been proud of her beauty, was vaguely complimented that she was the target for other men's eyes. Now it was a red-hot iron searing through his chest. How had that come to be? When had it begun?

Somewhere, sometime. . . . One day Kate and he were as any married couple, happy, content, insofar as means permitted, loving in a comfortable, satisfying way, and then the next there had been change. Their status had not altered, yet there was a difference between them, a sullen anger, a wariness and suspicion that fattened on the hours while they were apart.

Wilson Coyle, that old friend of bygone years, had much to do with it, Prince was sure. Not that he knew anything with certainty, it was simply—well, the way things looked, sounded—and in his profession he had learned to have little faith in mankind, and always expect the worst.

The heat increased. Armstrong removed his coat and hung it across the window sill, unbuttoned his straining vest. Mrs. Russell improvised a fan with her purse, waved persistently at her flushed face. She had recovered her composure, no longer wept but sat now perfectly quiet, her pale features frozen. Beside her Martha studied her fingertips, eyes downcast, dark lashes resting upon her cheeks. Once she looked up, placed her attention on John Prince.

"Will we get help at the next stop?"

"Not this side of Silver City," he snapped, the sharpness of his voice betraying the turmoil raging within him.

The girl colored, glanced away, chastened by his abruptness.

"Don't you mind the marshal none, ma'am," Kirby said in a light, mocking tone. "He plain don't like nobody. Not even hisself."

Prince shifted his bitter glance to the outlaw, but there was no change in his expression. He shrugged as the coach slammed on down the rutted road. Let the bastard talk. Let him run off at the mouth . . . his days were numbered. And far as he personally was concerned, it didn't matter what others thought. The whole human race could go to hell.

The shouts of Luke Colegrove lifted, and the coach began to pitch and sway with greater intensity. Armstrong thrust his head through the window, made his absent survey and murmured—"Coming into the hills."—and settled back. Prince glanced through the opening, saw the flat country swelling gradually into definite knolls that grew larger in the distance.

Outside the hard running of the horses was a steady drumming. The iron tires of the wheels screamed through the loose sand, clanged against rock, and the dust was an enveloping cloud racing with the coach. Luke's yells had become a constant sound, lashing at the horses as they began to climb a long grade. Frowning red buttes closed in on either side, and suddenly they were in a narrow channel.

Good place for an ambush, John Prince thought, and that induced him to sweep back the skirt of his coat, make his pistol more easily available. Martha Russell noted that and laid her questioning glance upon him. He merely shook his head, turned away.

The coach began to slow as the drag of the grade took its toll on the horses' speed. Colegrove's yells increased, well interspersed with profanity, but they were drawing near a crest as the diminishing height of the buttes indicated.

Suddenly they were on the summit, wheeling around a sharp bend and picking up speed. Unexpectedly they began to slow. Ed Drummond shouted something unintelligible. Immediately following there came the sharp, spiteful crack of his rifle. Prince stiffened, drew his weapon, and twisted about to peer through the window. A dozen yards or so ahead a scatter of riders milled about on the road, were blocking their passage.

"I'm going through 'em," Luke Colegrove yelled, and began to ply the whip. "Hang on!"

Prince threw a quick glance to Armstrong, was surprised to see the big man draw his long-barreled pistol, rest it upon the window sill. He looked then to the girl.

"Down on the floor . . . quick!"

She obeyed instantly. The lawman motioned Kirby to

her vacated spot. The outlaw complied hastily, and, when it was done, the girl was below them, protected by their legs, while Mrs. Russell was sandwiched securely between Armstrong on one side, Dave Kirby on the other. Prince thus had the rear seat to himself, enabling him to slide back and forth and watch both sides of the road.

Ed Drummond's rifle cracked again, and then became a continuing hammering as answering shots came from the road. The coach began to sway and reel, and dust became a choking, oppressive factor in breathing. Prince cast a calculating look at Mrs. Russell. She would be breaking down, going to pieces any moment now, and they'd have more problems. He ordered Kirby to look after her, keep her out of the way.

Reaching inside his coat he drew a second pistol, the one he'd taken off Dave Kirby and now evidence in the pending case, laid it on the seat. From a pocket he obtained a bandanna into which a handful of spare cartridges had been placed, dropped them beside Kirby's gun.

"Could give you a hand," the outlaw said, ducking his head at the weapon.

Prince shrugged. "No, thanks."

"My neck, too," Kirby said.

"But my responsibility," the lawman replied, and closed the subject.

Drummond's firing continued, and now Armstrong began to lay down his shots as they drew abreast the raiders. The acrid smell of powder smoke at once filled the coach, overriding the dust, and Colegrove's shouts began to mingle with others coming from the road. Bullets began to thud into the coach, dimpling the paneling. Armstrong jumped when one splintered the wood above his head.

They reeled through the cluster of waiting riders, two of

which were falling slowly from their saddles. A dark, whiskered man wearing a faded forage cap swerved in close, mouth open in a wild yell. Prince took deliberate aim, pressed off his shot. The man jolted, wilted, fell. Ed Drummond's rifle had gone silent, and, wondering about it, the lawman looked back. The guard was a crumpled bundle of dusty clothing in the road.

Prince swore silently. Armstrong . . . and him. That was it now. Another guerrilla hove into view alongside, lips curled into a grin as he aimed a bullet at the rancher. Prince fired at point-blank range. The raider threw up his arms, slid from his running horse.

Armstrong triggered his weapon with cool regularity, pausing only to reload. Prince guessed he'd figured him wrong . . . Mrs. Russell, too. She was a huddled, silent shape between the cattleman and Kirby. He glanced to the girl. Her face had paled, but, when she saw him looking, she smiled faintly.

Shots from the guerrillas had slackened. They were behind the coach now, on the road, regrouping. Colegrove's unexpected decision to barrel straight through them had caught them unawares, thrown them off balance. But it would be for only a few moments; already they were beginning to give chase.

Prince made a hasty calculation. Still a dozen or more in the raiding party. He and Armstrong could not hope to hold them off for long. He thrust his head through the window, looked beyond the wildly running team. A distance to the right he saw a low structure standing beside the road.

"That place . . . ?" he yelled at Colegrove. "What is it?"

"Baker's Ranch. Deserted. Not much."

"Pull in!" the lawman shouted above the hammering of the horses. "Fort up . . . our only chance!"

Colegrove bobbed his head in agreement. The team was running free on the downgrade, and brake blocks now began to whine, go silent, whine again as the old driver alternately applied and released them to control the swaying vehicle.

Back on the seat Prince faced the others. "We're pulling off, going to hole up in an old ranch house. Be ready to jump and run for it when I give the word."

He waited for reaction—some pointless protest from Mrs. Russell, a complaint from Armstrong, a note of despair from the girl. None came. Dave Kirby lifted his chained wrists.

"Take these off, Marshal . . . and give me my gun. I'll help."

Prince grunted. "Forget it. All you need do is run for the door of that house when I tell you."

He threw his glance back down the road. In the dust-filled distance he could see the dim outlines of the raiders pounding in pursuit. They were nearer than he expected. Abruptly the coach was rocking dangerously, and the brakes were a constant screaming as they wheeled from the main ruts. The vehicle skidded, tipped on two wheels, and for a breathless instant John Prince thought they would overturn, but the coach righted itself and plunged on.

"Get ready!"

Prince shouted his warning above the crackling of the wood, protesting the savage treatment. He looked through the window. The ranch house was just ahead. He turned then to the road. The guerrillas were curving in toward them, beginning to shoot again. Colegrove yelled something, and the coach began to slide, skidding close to the building.

"Now!" Prince cried and, flinging the door open, leaped

out. He dropped to one knee, began to fire at the oncoming horsemen, conscious of the other passengers streaming by him. Above, on the box, Colegrove had taken up Drummond's rifle, was giving him aid. He looked over his shoulder. The two women and Armstrong were already inside the adobe-walled hut. Kirby was standing in the doorway.

At once the lawman began to back toward the structure, shooting steadily with both pistols at the raiders. "Colegrove!" he yelled. "Come on . . . inside!"

Lead slugs were thudding into the thick wall behind him, into the wood of the coach, kicking up dust around his feet.

"Colegrove!" he shouted again.

He gained the doorway, saw then that Colegrove could not hear. The driver lay half off the coach seat, head hanging, a broad circle of red staining his shirt front. Prince took a long step. He felt the solid smash of a bullet as it drove into his thigh. It spun him around. Instantly he felt Kirby's hands grab him into the shadowy interior of the house. Angered, he shook off the outlaw, booted the door shut, and dropped the bar into place. In that identical instant he heard the pound of hoofs and a surge of yells as the riders thundered into the yard. It had been close.

He wheeled, ignoring pain, knowing exactly what must be done—the other door barricaded, the wooden shutters closed and secured. Surprise ran through him when he saw that Armstrong and the women had already performed those vital chores, and there was for John Prince a brief moment of wonder at his bitter judgment of his fellow passengers.

"You've been hit!" Mrs. Russell exclaimed, hurrying toward him.

"Nothing serious," the lawman snapped, and moved to

one of the front windows. He peered through a crack. "They'll be rushing us, but it won't be long till dark. If we can hold them off that long, like as not they'll give up and wait for morning."

Armstrong said—"Right."—in a business-like way. "I'll take the other door."

The house, a squat, one-room affair, evidently had been built for just such a critical moment except the owner would have had Indian attacks in mind. At each of the two doors and windows were small, round ports, blocked now by rags filled with sand. Prince pulled the bags away, looked again into the yard. The guerrillas had withdrawn fifty yards or so. They were in the process of bringing up a log they'd obtained from one of the decaying corrals.

"Armstrong," Prince called without turning. "They're aiming to ram the door, break it in. Get up here and cover this other port."

The cattleman crossed the room quickly, stationed himself at the small opening.

There was a sudden flurry of covering gunshots, the sound of bullets driving into the adobe bricks. A chorus of wild yells lifted, and then a half a dozen men supporting the log between them rushed for the door.

Cool, Prince said: "Take the lead man on the right. I'll handle the left. Don't miss.

He waited until the guerrillas were not more than ten paces away, fired. His target was a squat, dark-faced man wearing an ill-assorted uniform of both armies. The raider halted abruptly, fell. A step behind him the one singled out by Armstrong, hands clawing at his chest, was sinking to the ground. The remaining men, stalled by surprise, dropped the log and fled, evidently having overlooked the ports. Prince felled a third as they turned tail.

He was aware then of Mrs. Russell kneeling at his side. She had a strip of white cloth, probably ripped from her petticoat, draped across her shoulder and a knife in her hand. Deftly she slit the leg of his trousers.

"Never mind," he said, and tried to move away.

"Stand still," she replied sternly. "You're losing too much blood."

He looked down at her. Kate was like that. A little bossy when need be—and it mattered to her. Armstrong's voice caught his attention.

"Stopped 'em cold. Fact is, couple of them are pulling out."

Prince glanced through his port. "Going for the rest of their bunch, I suspect. Seems we're going to be encircled. Means they aim to pin us down for the night."

"Be dark soon," Armstrong commented.

Mrs. Russell, her job completed, stepped back. Prince shifted his weight to the injured member. It was paining considerably now, and getting stiff. It would be giving him hell later.

The acrid smoke was clearing from the room. Martha Russell turned to the cattleman. "When the stage doesn't arrive at the next station, will they send somebody to find out why?"

"Hard to say," the cattleman answered. "Only one stop between here and Silver City, and that's a team change. This run's a bit irregular. Not apt to start thinking about it until noon, maybe even later."

Prince was fingering the ammunition in the bandanna. He glanced to Armstrong. "How many bullets you got?"

There was a moment of silence. Then: "Four rounds. You?"

"Dozen or so. Don't think we can depend on that bunch

out there not making another try before morning. Best we stand watch at all four sides." He pivoted awkwardly, forgetting momentarily his injured leg, addressed Mrs. Russell. "You shoot a pistol?"

"A little . . . I'm not sure."

From the depths of their murky quarters Dave Kirby spoke up. "Better give me that gun, Marshal."

"We'll get along without your help," the lawman answered.

"I don't know about that," Armstrong broke in doubtfully. "Ought to have a man, good with a gun, helping. . . ."

"No prisoner of mine gets his hands on a weapon," Prince stated flatly. "I'll accept no help from one, either."

Mrs. Russell sighed audibly. "You're a foolish man. And one who's never learned the meaning of trust . . . or faith."

"You're figuring him right, ma'am," Kirby said, a thread of amusement in his voice. "He don't believe in nobody but himself . . . not even his own wife."

John Prince stiffened in the darkness. "That way a man never gets hurt," he said. "How about taking your stations?" He handed Kirby's gun to Mrs. Russell.

The minutes wore on, dragged into an hour, and night's chill settled over the room. Outside a half dozen small fires marked the positions of the raiders ringing the structure. Prince thought of Kate, wondered what she was doing at that moment. Immediately that sharp uneasiness began to gnaw at him. Was she with Wilson Coyle? Maybe with some other man he wasn't even aware of? And then another thought reached him. Perhaps it would all end here. Perhaps the raiders would settle the whole problem for him—for her.

"Got any ideas what you'll be doing come the morning?"

Dave Kirby asked, breaking the hush. "You got maybe fifteen bullets, Marshal. How long do you figure you can stand off that bunch?"

"Long enough."

"For what? They hit us from all four sides at once, and the ball will be over . . . for sure if they've got help coming."

Armstrong's voice showed interest. "You got something in mind?"

Kirby said: "Was I to get out of here and find me a horse, I could leg it for the next station, stir up a posse . . . maybe soldiers, even. They'd be here by sunrise."

"Could at that," Armstrong said. "Where'd you get a horse? Them raiders won't. . . ."

"Take one of the coach team. Still standing out there in front. What do you say, Marshal? Don't care nothing about myself, or you either, for that matter, but I sure hate to think of what'll happen to these ladies."

Prince sagged against the wall, taking the weight off his injured leg. "You'd try anything to keep from facing that judge in Rinconada," he said in a dry, sarcastic voice. "Well, you're not fooling me. Once you went through that door, you'd line out straight for Mexico."

"Figured you'd be thinking that," the outlaw said. "Only you're plumb wrong. I can make it past them ridgerunners out there. You got my word I'll be waiting at the station for you."

Prince shorted. "Your word? Forget it, mister. I wouldn't trust you. . . ." He stopped, feeling the hard circle of a gun's muzzle pressing into his ribs.

"I'm sorry," Mrs. Russell's voice, calm and confident, reached him. "I believe him. Make no mistake," she added quickly and prodded harder with the weapon as the lawman stirred. "I know enough about this weapon to pull the trigger . . . and this close I couldn't miss. At this moment I'm a desperate woman . . . a mother, and I'll do anything to keep my daughter from falling into the hands of those . . . those beasts out there. If Mister Kirby is willing to risk his life for us, I say we let him do so."

"You're a fool," Prince said in deep disgust. "He won't go for help. He's not interested in anything except a chance to get where the law can't touch him."

"I don't think so," the woman replied firmly. "Maybe it's your profession that's turned you hard . . . hard and bitter . . . and made you forget that there's usually some good in the worst of us."

"Usually, but not in this case," Prince said dryly. "Armstrong?"

"I agree with the lady," the cattleman said. "Our only chance."

"You saying you believe he'll do what he claims?"

"I'm willing to gamble on it. Comes a time, Marshal, when you've got to trust somebody. Man can't go forever depending on himself. It's a question of having faith."

"Faith!" John Prince echoed scornfully, his thoughts, oddly, swinging to Kate. There was no value in faith, no substance—just as there was none in trust. Believe in either and a man found only heartbreak and disillusionment. Had he not learned that the hard way? Perhaps he had no real proof concerning Kate, but the signs were all there—at least, what he considered indications. And true, she had denied them all, reproved him for his suspicions. But a man was a fool to ignore common logic.

"Just you stand easy," Armstrong's voice bored into his consciousness. "I'll be getting the keys for them handcuffs."

John Prince offered no resistance. He stood aside, watched them release Kirby, saw Mrs. Russell pass Kirby's gun to him, heard Armstrong murmur—"Good luck, boy."—and then his prisoner was slipping through the door opened only slightly. A heavy sigh escaped Prince. This was it. The end. He'd lost all . . . all.

The long night finally was over. The first flare of light began to spread across the plains, and the shadows took on form. The two women, pale and worn from their vigilance, turned from the window ports. Armstrong forsook the rear door, noting that the encirclement had been withdrawn from around the shack. He stooped, peered through one of the front openings.

"About twice as many of them out there now," he said wearily. "Seems they've rousted out the head man."

Leg paining him intensely, Prince turned, glanced through his port. A lean individual in a gray Confederate Army uniform was in the center of the guerrilla party. He appeared to be outlining a plan to his followers.

"Looks like the boy got away," Armstrong commented. "Lead team horse is gone, and there ain't no bodies except them three we cut down yesterday laying out there."

"He made it," Prince said. "Has that kind of luck. Right now I'd say he was halfway to the border." He paused, squinted into the glare. "Get yourself set. They're going to hit us. Don't waste no lead. We've only got. . . ."

His words broke off. Faintly, riding the cold, clear air of the early morning, the notes of a bugle carried to him. Prince, disbelief covering his face, turned to Armstrong, then to Mrs. Russell—to the girl. The thrilling sound grew louder, closer. Abruptly guns began to crackle.

There was a quick rush of pounding hoofs, and through the port Prince saw a line of blue-clad riders, some with sabers flashing, sweep into the yard. More gunfire crashed.

Two of the cavalrymen spilled from their horses; a half dozen guerrillas went down; others raced for their mounts. The line of blue swerved, gave chase.

"He did it!" Armstrong yelled happily, struggling with the bar that locked the door. "By heaven, the boy did it!"

John Prince shook his head. "Doubt that. Expect those soldiers were just riding by . . . happened to spot. . . ."

But the others were hurrying through the open door, smiling, laughing, grateful for their rescue, for the warming sun. The cavalry came into view again, a portion of it swinging on westward, a smaller detail cutting away, slanting toward the stranded stagecoach and its passengers. A waxed-mustached major with a round, sunburned face came in ahead of his men, slowed, his eyes on the coach team.

"Corporal Hayes!" he barked. "Catch up one of those stray mounts and hitch him into harness so these people can continue on their journey."

The officer moved in nearer to the house, halted. He saluted gravely, said: "Major Amos Allingham, at your service. We'll have you ready to move out in a few minutes. Pleased to see none of you has been seriously injured."

Allingham hesitated, looked over his shoulder where three of his yellowlegs were getting the coach ready. A smile pulled at his lips. "Want to thank you for dispatching that young cowboy to us. We've been hunting those guerrillas for weeks. Got them all . . . every last one of them."

Mrs. Russell, once again a woman, began to weep softly, sought comfort in her daughter's arms.

Armstrong took a deep breath. "Was close," he said. "That young cowboy . . . did he get through all right? Without getting hurt, I mean."

The officer smiled again. "Well, from here to where

we're bivouacked it's around twenty miles. He rode the whole distance bareback and at a fast clip. He'll find standing most comfortable for a few days. Otherwise, he's fine. And by the way, Marshal," he added, swiveling his attention to Prince, "said he was your prisoner. Soon as he gave me the information I needed, he put himself in my custody. You'll find him waiting in my tent."

John Prince stared at the officer. Somewhere, deep within his mind, a door opened, a wide door beyond which a pure white light shown brilliantly. He'd been wrong about Dave Kirby. There were others he'd been wrong about, too, most likely. And Kate . . . maybe he was wrong there. It was possible . . . no, probable. He could see that now. He'd been a fool, a great fool . . . and all that Mrs. Russell and Armstrong, the cattleman, had said he was.

He turned to them. There was a smile on his lips, the first they'd seen since he had boarded the stage. "I'm glad Kirby got through. Took a lot of sand, and, when he goes before the judge in Rinconada, like for you to be there with us. Maybe if we all speak up, tell what he did, we can help things along for him a bit."

"Count on me," Armstrong said fervently.

Mrs. Russell bobbed her head. "I'll speak to my husband. Perhaps he can do something."

Prince swung back to Allingham. "Our thanks to you, too, Major, for getting here when you did."

"My job, sir," the officer said, and started to pull away.

"One more thing," John Prince called after him. "You have a telegraph wire connection at your camp?"

Allingham nodded. "Hooked in temporarily with the main line."

"Good. Like to send my wife a message, tell her I'll be home shortly."

Eagles Over Crooked Creek

Max Brand is the best-known pen name of Frederick Faust. He wrote for a variety of audiences in many genres. Eighty motion pictures have been based on his work along with many radio and television programs. THE MAX BRAND COMPANION (Greenwood Press, 1996) edited by Jon Tuska and Vicki Piekarski provides a valuable guide to Faust's multitudinous fiction of all kinds as well as his life and times. Born in Seattle in 1892, orphaned early, Faust grew up in the rural San Joaquin Valley of California. At Berkeley he became a student rebel and one-man literary movement, contributing prodigiously to all campus publications. Denied a degree because of unconventional conduct, he embarked on a series of adventures culminating in New York City where, after a period of near starvation, he received simultaneous recognition as a serious poet and successful author of fiction. Later, he traveled widely, making his home in Florence, Italy, and, finally, in Los Angeles. Once the United States entered the Second World War, Faust abandoned his lucrative writing career and his work as a screenwriter to serve as a war correspondent with the infantry in Italy, despite his fifty-one years and a bad heart. He was killed during a night attack on a hilltop village held by the German army.

SIXTEEN IN NOME (Five Star Westerns, 1995) was the first Five Star Western, the first of more than a hundred volumes of Western stories by Faust that have not yet appeared in book form. Truly his work can be said to belong to all time, since he probably has more devoted readers today than even when he was alive, and his books have certainly contributed significantly to the commercial success of the Five Star Westerns. "Eagles Over Crooked Creek" was the last story Frederick Faust published in Street & Smith's *Western Story Magazine* for which he had once customarily written a million and a half words a year.

★ ★ ★ ★ ★

Two eagles were fighting at the head of the cañon, and the wind blew them and their screaming out over Crooked Creek, so that everyone looked up from the streets and some of the younger lads even took random shots at the pair. But the people were glad, really, to hear the screeching of the eagles, because it meant that winter definitely had left the mountains, and the spring was there to stay. Men thought of taking off flannel underwear; women thought of cleaning house. Young Chuck, coming up the trail into Crooked Creek for the first time in two years, proud of his seventeen years and his new horse, divided his mind between the eagles and the town itself. It seemed to have shrunk; the weight of the winter had pressed the buildings down and narrowed the streets. He was halfway into town before he saw anyone he knew, and that was old Ben Whalen, his uncle's partner. Ben stalked down the middle of the street, leading that ancient horse, Pepper, that still showed his name in the arch of his scrawny neck and the flattening of his ears, but Time was the permanent famine that roached his back and tucked up his belly. Old Ben Whalen was among men what Pepper was among horses, loose-kneed, gaunt, with the hanging flesh of his face tucked up at the corners of his eyes and his mouth.

"Hey, Ben!" called Chuck, and galloped his piebald up to the old man.

Pepper began to prance without going any faster. Ben Whalen sluiced himself around and squinted over his shoulder. "Don't go knockin' your dust over me, young feller," he said.

"Hey, Ben, don't you know me?"

"Why, you kind of appear like little Chuck," said Ben. "What you taken and done? Growed up?"

"I kind of been growing," admitted Chuck. "Where's Uncle Cal?"

"Yeah, you've taken and growed up on us," said Ben, as they reached the foot of the cañon where the road turned up among the rocks.

"Where's Uncle Cal?" repeated Chuck.

"No use you riding up this trail," answered Ben. "Cal always was a loon, and he's gone and spent the winter over by the Sugar Loaf. He got a dream that the Sugar Loaf was all veined up with gold, and he's gonna get at that gold as soon as things thaw out, so's to be ahead of the rush." Ben spat, then he laughed and smoothed his chin with his whole hand, a careful gesture that he inherited from the days when he wore a full beard. He repeated, as he turned up the cañon road: "There ain't any use you coming. You won't find Cal up there no more."

"I'll come anyway," said Chuck.

Ben stopped short, and Pepper bumped his nose on the shoulder of his master. "What for would you be such a damn' young fool?" asked Ben. "Cal ain't up there, and I ain't one for much company."

"I'd like to see the old shack anyways," said Chuck, and laughed.

Ben Whalen mounted Pepper and slumped into the

saddle. There was a jingling of tin cans from the pack that sat over the hips of the old horse.

"How's Pepper's sight?" asked Chuck. "Can he see pretty good now?"

"He can't see nothing no more," answered Ben. "Why else would I've been leading him through the street? But he knows the three miles of the cañon trail like it was wrote out on the palm of his hand."

"How old is Pepper?" asked Chuck.

"Don't be chatterin'," said Ben. "They don't raise up boys with no manners these days. They all keep squawkin' like them eagles up yonder."

So Chuck was quiet, unoffended because he knew Ben from of old. For that matter Uncle Cal was as silent as any sourdough, but for Chuck this trip was a return to something more than people. It was a voyage back into his childhood, where even mountains and rocks possess a living spirit that changes. And all the way up the cañon he watched with admiration how the old horse, Pepper, followed the sharp windings of the path that followed the twists and the leapings of the creek. There was never a misstep all the way. Only when they came to the head of the steep way, Pepper tried to veer off to the left instead of going straight on toward the shanty. Ben Whalen cursed the old gelding, and kicked him, and reined him the right way, but to the last step Pepper continued to sag to the left.

"Growed out of his good sense, the old fool," commented Ben, and began to unstrap the pack.

Chuck carried it into the shack in his strong young arms. It was the same flimsy structure, built of wide, warped boards with cracks through which the sunshine striped the floor with fuzzy yellow lines of light. The winter had blown through those crevices enough snow dust to paint the stove all over with a new coating of red rust, but there was little else in the single room that could take harm. More perishable stuff, of course, would be lodged in the small cellar through the winter.

"You tell me where, and I'll put things away," said Chuck.

"You take yourself off and leave me be," said Ben, leaning on his rifle and staring gloomily around him.

So Chuck went outside. Pepper was no longer standing in front of the shanty. He had gone off to the side, and there he hung his head and switched his ragged old tail at the flies that swarm thickest and bite deepest in the early spring. The grass stood up quite high in the place where Pepper was standing, and yet it was not for the grass that the gelding had gone there. He did not crop a blade of it, but hung his head as though he were tethered to a hitching rack.

Chuck sat down on the door sill. The little house was just the same, except that like everything else it had shrunk. The cañon, too, was narrower, and the walls no longer lifted so high, and the water roared neither so musically nor on so deep a note. It seemed to Chuck that, as one grows older, the world sifts away through the fingers, so what could remain inside the gaunt hands of old men like Ben or Uncle Cal? He turned and looked toward the great Sugar Loaf, frosted with blue and white toward the summit. Then he looked back down the cañon. It was not only smaller, but it was changed, for surely in the old days he had been able to look past more than two bends of the walls. There had been a rift, an outlet, and the eye was not stopped by the two joining sides of rock.

Chuck stood up and drifted to the side. The piebald, noisily ripping at the grass and jangling its bit, nevertheless followed him, and this warmed his heart. Now, as he passed to the right, Chuck saw that the cañon in fact opened a little. It was exciting. It was as though a door were swinging wide in his mind. He found the exact point from which, he could have sworn, he used to look down the narrows of the ravine. He could see past the second bend and caught a glimpse beyond the third, a narrow slot of blue sky that let the eye shoot onwards. That, as he remembered it, was exactly what he used to see from the threshold of the old shack.

He turned, bewildered, and saw that the shanty stood, in fact, well over to the right. But Pepper was exactly in line with him and that glimpse through the third bend of the ravine. There was something ghostly about it that brought a chill into his blood in spite of the strong mountain sunshine. He went up to Pepper, and the old horse jerked up his head and flattened his ears. He walked in front of Pepper. The ears and the pinched nostrils showed anger, but the filmy eyes showed nothing but the endless twilight within the mind. Stepping back, Chuck's foot sank into a hole. He looked down and saw, where the grass was beaten down, that the lips of the little depression made an exact square, like a posthole filled up. But no posts had ever stood near the old shack, none at all except the two of the hitching rack! An idea stranger than life or death made Chuck shuffle back and forth through the grass until he found, eight feet away, another square hole exactly like the first.

He took off his sombrero and rubbed the sweat from his face. The wind came off the mountains and blew his head cold, but the blood in his body was already well-iced. For here, where he stood, the hitching rack of the shanty once had been!

He moved back through that taller grass, still scuffing with his heels, and again he found a depression. It was not a narrow hole mouth, this time, but a long line. Still scuffing, he traced a depression inches deep that turned at four corners and outlined a space ten feet long.

"By the jumping thunder," said Chuck, "this is where the shack used to stand. Those were the postholes. This is the old cellar that's been filled in. . . ."

"What you doin' over there?" shouted Ben Whalen. "What's the matter with you, over there?" He stood in front of the shanty with his rifle at the ready. "Come here!" called Ben. "Come on over here! What you doin' there?"

Chuck looked with yearning toward the piebald horse that still followed at his heels, but he was not even tempted to jump for the saddle, because he could remember Ben Whalen's talent for putting bullet holes through tin cans flung as high as one pleased. If the grass had been a little taller, Chuck would have dropped into it and tried to disappear like a mole. Instead, he had to walk stiff-legged because his knees were rigid with terror toward the old man on the threshold of the cabin.

"What you doin' over there, anyway?" asked Ben Whalen.

"I dropped a coupla dimes outta my pocket," said Chuck. "I dropped 'em out when I pulled out my sack of Bull Durham. They went flip off into the grass, and I started kicking around in it to find 'em."

"Why for would you kick around in the grass if you wanted to find something?" asked Ben. "There ain't any sense in doing that. . . . I got an idea that you're a liar, Chuck, like your pa and your Uncle Cal and your grandpa all was liars before you!" He grew very angry. "You hear what I'm saying?" shouted Ben.

"Hey . . . don't swing that gun around," said Chuck. He threw up his hands in a gesture that was purely instinctive.

Then desperate fear tempted him, and he caught at the end of the rifle barrel.

"Will you? Will you?" screeched Ben Whalen. He jerked back on the gun. The front sight ripped halfway across the palm of Chuck before his grip held fast. He flung his other arm around Ben and hugged him close. It was like embracing a skeleton, and all the strength went out of Ben in a moment. His hands left his rifle. As Chuck jumped back from him, holding the rifle, old Ben simply leaned against the side of the door with a hand pressed to his side, panting. His mouth was open, sagging the lines of his face longer and longer.

"What's the matter with you, Chuck? You gone crazy or something?" asked Ben.

"I'm crazy enough to go and dig up that whole place!" shouted Chuck. "I'm crazy enough to dig clean to the bottom of the old cellar yonder, till I find out what you were coverin' up! I'm just crazy enough for that."

"What cellar?" asked old Ben.

"There! Right yonder where the house used to stand."

"What you mean, Chuck? Who'd take and move a house? Who'd have such a loony idea as that?"

"You took and done it yourself," said Chuck. "Post by post and plank by plank, you took and done it your own self. I'm gonna find why, if I have to dig right to the bottom of the cellar."

"Don't you do it, son," said Ben. "That ain't a cellar no more. That's a grave!"

A voice that Chuck never had heard before came out of his own throat: "Uncle Cal! It's Uncle Cal!" he was crying.

"Yeah. That's where he lies," said Ben. "Maybe you'll be wanting to take me back to town, Chuck?"

He mounted the blind horse, and, while Chuck rode behind with the rifle at a balance across the pommel of his saddle, Pepper went down the slope with his absurd prancing.

"It was Pepper that showed you the way, wasn't it?" asked Ben.

"Yeah. Pepper showed me."

"Dog-gone his old heart," said Ben. "I guess he's gunna outlive me, after all."

"Ben, will you tell me how it happened?" pleaded Chuck, looking with pity on that bent and narrow back.

"I dunno," said Ben. "I guess I've got kind of old and cranky."

He looked up where the two eagles, after giving up their battle for a time, had joined combat again in the middle of the sky. They seemed higher now, but their screaming came plainly to the ears of Chuck. Old Ben kept staring upwards while the blind horse carried him with careful feet down the trail.

Favorite Son

Cynthia Haseloff was born in Vernon, Texas and was named after Cynthia Ann Parker, perhaps the best-known of 19th-Century white female Indian captives. The history and legends of the West were part of her upbringing in Arkansas where her family settled shortly after she was born. She wrote her first novel, RIDE SOUTH! (1980), with the encouragement of her mother. Haseloff went on to write four more novels in the early 1980s. Two focused on unusual female protagonists. MARAUDER (1982), of the two, is Haseloff's most historical novel, and it is also quite possibly her finest book to that time. MARAUDER is available in a full-length audio edition from Chivers Audio, and her first five original paperback Western novels have now been reprinted in hardcover editions in Chivers' Gunsmoke series. Haseloff's characters embody the fundamental values—honor, duty, courage, and family—that prevailed on the American frontier and were instilled in the young Haseloff by her own "heroes," her mother and her grandmother. Haseloff's stories, in a sense, dramatize how these values endure when challenged by the adversities and cruelties of frontier existence. Her latest novels include THE CHAINS OF SARAI STONE (Five Star Westerns, 1995), MAN WITHOUT MEDICINE (Five Star Westerns, 1996), THE KIOWA VERDICT (Five Star Westerns, 1997), and SATANTA'S WOMAN (Five Star Westerns, 1998). THE KIOWA VERDICT won the Spur Award from the Western Writers of America in 1998 in the category of Best Western Novel.

June 8, 1871

Akia-ti-sumtau, Admired One, was coming his way. His father, Satank, was coming his way. Eagle Down Feather sat on his pony, waiting. He had brought his brother with him—the yellow-painted bones that were his brother's body with him. He had brought the favorite son for his father.

Eagle Down Feather waited in the morning sun, knowing that his father was coming soon. The young warrior had fled with the other Kiowas, getting their families to safety on the plains, when the chiefs were arrested. He had gone only a short way and had turned back, knowing there was something for him on this hill beyond Fort Sill, knowing exactly where to place his horse on the rise above the pecan tree so that he could see the Texas road. His power had told him these things.

Eagle Down Feather's power was young to him, but exceedingly strong. For a long time his father, Satank, worried about power, the transfer of his great power. He had two grown sons, and neither had sought or received power. Favorite Son and Eagle Down Feather had sat together listening to their father. "No one has offered to give you power," he said. "My powers have not spoken to me to give you power. Have you not been prompted to go and seek power?"

"Power is a heavy burden, Father," said Favorite Son. "You are always doing things for your power because among the Kiowas you have the most powers for peace and war."

Favorite Son spoke only the truth. Satank was surrounded by the signs of his power. He had the war bonnet for war and the sash and spear of the ten greatest warriors, the *Koitsenko*, who staked themselves to the ground and fought until they were killed or released by their brethren. These things and the Yellow Shield of the sorcerers, who could change a feather to a knife or a knife to a feather, fought for Satank as a warrior. In his lodge hung one of the ten sacred Medicine Bundles of the People. He was the keeper, protector. In this bundle, lay the power to care for the People, to make peace among the People. Satank quickly settled many disputes with his natural good sense and respect from the People. But when his human power was not enough, he would go to the Medicine Bundle and take the black pipe. If the disputants merely touched the pipe together, peace was made.

Each of these great powers had taboos or rules that had to be kept. For example, Satank could not eat food from a fire in which a knife had been dropped with the blade down. If he did not mix his tobacco with sumac bark, he would offend his power. He could eat whatever he liked, but he could not eat fish. He and his household were always conscious of disrespecting the powers. Power was a heavy burden that only a strong man could carry.

Everyone knew that Satank was afraid of nothing. They saw him stand in the midst of his enemies protected by his Yellow Shield, his war bonnet, his spear and sash. But very few people saw the small black stone arrow braided into his scalp lock. Sometimes, when he danced with the *Koitsenko*, he let it be seen. This was the symbol of his personal power that had gained him all the other powers and made him able to carry them all. No man knew what that power was. He never talked of it.

The sons born the same year had grown up knowing their father's respect for power. Before either could walk, he had talked to them as if they were already men and explained the loss of a war party. "These men went against the bear power. We heard the Comanches had killed a bear when we were going out with them. We went to them and asked them not to eat this bear. The bear is too much like a man. But they cooked it, and the smoke from their fires drifted over the Kiowas. Some of us struck our camp and moved away from the smoke. The next morning, we returned home, but some other Kiowas went on with the Comanches, saying they had not killed or eaten the bear. All but four of them were killed. A Kiowa does not offend the bear spirit. You better remember this," Satank had said to his infant sons. "Power is with you all your life. It can work good for you. But, if it is offended, everything you do will go wrong. You must respect power for it is much greater than yourself."

But neither of Satank's sons had power. Neither had received a gift from someone with great power to give away. Neither had received a prompting to go and seek power. Satank worried. Someone must take up the sacred Medicine Bundle when he was gone, or it would pass from the family. Yet Satank knew that power could not be taken dishonestly or insincerely without incurring the wrath of the power, so he kept quiet and waited.

All Favorite Son's life, Satank, or Sitting Bear, had doted on this son whose real name was Young Sitting Bear. This son was so worthy of power. He was beautiful and skillful in war. Even as a child, when he was in the Rabbit Society, this beautiful boy was given extraordinary feasts by his father, feasts worthy of a warrior. Perhaps, Satank thought, he was the one to have power. Eagle Down Feather also had feasts, but they were feasts for a boy.

Eagle Down Feather felt no jealousy over his father's

relationship with his brother, the favorite son. The whole family showed off Young Sitting Bear and took great pride in his achievements and in his beauty. He was the emblem of the family, the best hope personified. They gave him the choicest meat, the best leather and skins for his clothing, the finest horses. He carried weapons made by the tribe's craftsmen. He had a yellow and red lodge of his own while Eagle Down Feather lived in his mother's teepee. It never occurred to any of them that it was unfair to favor one son over the other with material things and their hopes. They simply celebrated the young man, knowing the fragility of life, knowing that he might die soon. His evanescence was theirs, and they could not think of fairness or mourning or bitterness while he was with them. Favorite Son was their feast. There was simply no time to waste on any other thoughts.

Eagle Down Feather, too, thought Young Sitting Bear was beautiful and worthy. He was himself much like his father—small and ugly. He had been born only a few months before Young Sitting Bear to Satank's second wife. Like all Kiowa children, he had been carried and held by the entire household. His individuality had been respected. He had come and gone as he pleased, had eaten whenever he was hungry, had ridden his pony, had listened to the tales of the old men, and had gone hunting or made arrows as he was asked by fellow Kiowas. He had not lacked love within his family. His brother loved him, also, and he loved his brother. He had not lacked his father's guidance and instruction. He did not feel deprived. He felt he was somehow exempt from the adulation heaped upon his younger brother. Eagle Down Feather enjoyed a freedom, a privacy to grow that his brother did not have. Eagle Down Feather could go about unnoticed and think his own thoughts. He had solitude and time.

"Father," Eagle Down Feather interrupted as Satank and Favorite Son contemplated the lack of power of his sons, "Father, I have been thinking. A man needs power even though it is a heavy burden. I am going to hunt for power."

That very day he had gathered the four things he would need—a buffalo robe with the hair still on it, a pipe, tobacco, and flint and steel. He washed himself and went to bed. The next morning, he got up very early and began to walk to a power-seeking place. He stopped four times and smoked and prayed. He had to go far enough from the village so that he would not be interrupted, but not so far that he could not get home again when he was weakened by four days of thirst and fasting. When he had gone far enough, he began to look for a sacred place. At last, he climbed high up into the Wichita Mountains where the world stretched out before him in every direction. He filled his pipe and smoked it to the east and to the west, to the north and to the south, to the sky and to the earth, and he prayed. He asked that he would receive power and that he would use it right. He rolled himself in the robe and watched the star bedecked canopy of the sky until he fell asleep. Whenever the cold awakened him, he would smoke again and pray again. This happened four times before morning. The next day he continued to wait, to smoke, and to pray. He did not eat or drink anything. No power came. He lay down for the second night and rose for the second day without receiving anything. He finally had to throw thirst away because it was trying to take his mind away from his seeking. "I have no interest in my thirst," he said. "I am here now seeking power. One day I will consider thirst again and drink, but not here, not now." And he waited.

He lost track of the number of times he filled and

smoked the pipe and prayed. This worried him because he was afraid he might come down too soon, before the four days required. And if he came down too soon, he worried that he might not be able ever to seek power again. And that was a great fear for him because he wanted power as he wanted to be a complete man, to do a man's part. He would wait some more and smoke and pray some more. He would stay as long as he could and a little more. He would go as long as he could and a little more. He was listening now with his whole body for any little whisper of power. There was no voice here but the wind, no sight but the earth, no time but the sunrise and sunset, the endless day and the endless night between them.

At last at the breaking of one day, a voice ran over and through him. He felt this voice going through the tissues of his body from cell to cell, layer by layer, deeper and deeper into him until it stopped in his center. "Look down," it said. And the boy looked down at the valleys and plains below his mountain. "No, look down at your feet . . . look to the humblest thing, the earth beneath your feet that bears you and every living thing. It is a mighty thing for it bears all and is always there."

The young man pulled his eyes away from the sprawling vista to consider the ground beneath his own feet. He struggled to focus his eyes, to see what was always there, but seldom seen. There were grass and rocks and the sandy red prairie dirt.

"What do you see?"

"I see the grass and rocks and the sandy red prairie dirt," Eagle Down Feather answered.

"Look closer."

The young Kiowa wove slightly as he bent closer to the earth. He put out his hand to hold himself, and there was a skitter in the grass. "I see a mountain boomer," he told the voice.

"Good," it answered. "You are like this little lizard."

The small yellow and green mountain boomer fixed a black eye on Eagle Down Feather. As the Kiowa watched, the little creature rose on its back feet and waved its forearms in the air, talking to him. "My power is your power," it said. "It is to be unseen everywhere and to hear and see everything. When you wish, you will be unseen in the camp or on the plains. Plants and animals will pay no attention to you. People will pay no attention to you. They will go on talking because you are unnoticed. They will teach you everything. You will become wise from so much seeing and hearing."

"This is a strong power," Eagle Down Feather said.

"It is the strongest power and gathers all other powers to itself." The little mountain boomer was not so little any more. It was standing on its hind feet, looking into the Kiowa's eyes.

"Are there restrictions with this power?"

"None that you do not already do," said the green mountain boomer. "Do not eat fish. Mix sumac bark with your tobacco. Everyone already does these, and they will not draw attention to you. When other powers come, they will bring their own rules. There is one other thing you must do. You must wear something tied to your scalp lock. I will show it to you as we go back to camp. I will always be with you now, even when you do not see me. Do you understand?"

Eagle Down Feather nodded, for he truly understood that what he did not see was stronger than what he did see. It was just as when he was ignored: he had great power for he entered into the thoughts of man and beast and earth without their knowing. He began to gather his things, and his strength returned. It was as if he were stronger than he had ever been. His footsteps were firm. There was power in his young arms again to lift the robe and all he had brought with him.

"Climb on my back. I will take you down the mountain." The mountain boomer in his green and yellow with his collar of black and white stretched out. Eagle Down Feather stepped onto his smoothly scaled back, and they ran down the mountain. As the lizard ran from rock to rock, he grew smaller and smaller until he was again the little ubiquitous lizard of the plains. "Look at the ground," he said to Eagle Down Feather. Eagle Down Feather bent over the red earth. Sticking up out of the sand was a small black point. His fingers brushed aside the particles. He sat and looked at the arrowhead that was exactly like the one his father, old Satank, wore. "Tie it to your scalp lock, Eagle Down Feather." The Kiowa grasped the obsidian, wrapped it with a piece of sinew, and tied it to the thin-braided shock near his forehead. A gust of wind blew his long loose hair over the scalp lock, covering it. "There," scrutinized the lizard. "You can go home now. From now on you won't see me, but I will be there. I will talk to you sometimes, and then you will know what to do."

So Eagle Down Feather went home the way he had come. He was tired now and moved slowly, but something was carrying him along, something that had never been there before—his power. He slept that night and started again in the morning. Without his knowing, his village appeared out of the ground, and he walked through the street toward his father's lodge. Favorite Son came running toward him. His brother grasped him and held him tightly. Eagle Down Feather felt the tear on his brother's cheek as he whispered: "My brother, my brother. You have been gone so long, six days and six nights."

Favorite Son took him to their father's lodge. "My brother is home, my father."

Old Satank looked at his first son closely. He found a drinking gourd and covered only the bottom with cool water and lifted it to the young man's lips. The old man was looking into his eyes. Eagle Down Feather knew that his father wanted to know if he had found power but could not ask. And unless the power told him, Eagle Down Feather could not tell what had happened. Then, he knew what to do just as the little mountain boomer had told him he would. Turning his side with the scalp lock to his father, Eagle Down Feather drank. As he drank, he pushed the long, loose hair away, revealing the obsidian point tied to the braided scalp lock. For just a moment Satank saw the shining arrowhead identical to his own, then Eagle Down Feather took his hand away, and the hair fell again over the symbol of his power.

"Your brother is tired," Satank said to Favorite Son. "Take my brave son to his mother's lodge where he may rest unnoticed."

"Thank you, my father," said Eagle Down Feather.

The procession of soldiers and wagons appeared in the dirt road, coming around the stone corral of the fort. There were mounted black troops to the front and rear of the two wagons. In the first wagon the old Kiowa chief, Satank, sat facing one guard and beside another. In the following wagon Satanta and Adoltay sat, bound as Satank, beside their guards. The three chiefs were going away—away to Texas to stand trial in a civilian court for the murder during robbery of seven teamsters on Salt Creek Prairie. One, ancient Satank, was not going to Texas. The sol-

diers did not yet know. Seeing him embrace Caddo George, they did not see him, the Yellow Shield warrior with magic power to turn a feather into a knife and a knife into a feather, take the knife. Hearing his song even as Eagle Down Feather heard it faintly on the wind, they did not understand his words. Seeing, they saw nothing. Hearing, they heard nothing. But the Kiowas and Caddoes knew. Eagle Down Feather knew. He and his brother had come to bear witness.

Finally seeking power of his own because his father still hoped it for him, Favorite Son had danced at the summer *Kado* the same year Eagle Down Feather had received his power. Favorite Son had seen Taime Man. He had seen the Kiowa man turn into Taime, the spirit man. The old man Taime had been all around the young warrior. Walking and dancing with the stick of old age, Taime had talked to Favorite Son.

"Because Taime showed himself as an old man," said Eagle Down Feather, "you will live to be old. I will care for you so that you will always be the favorite son."

"He told me wonderful things and terrible things," said Favorite Son.

"What are these terrible things he told you?" asked Eagle Down Feather.

"He told me that power comes to the man who can use it. If it is meant for him to have power, it will come to him whether he seeks it or not. It is his as much as his own heart or the sound of his blood in his ears," answered Favorite Son.

"Yes," agreed Eagle Down Feather, "but this is not terrible."

"Taime said the power was being given to me to pass on because I would not use it. Something is going to happen to

225

me soon so that I will not need this power of growing old."

Eagle Down Feather's heart shivered within his chest. He shook his head. "This is not good."

"But it is, Brother," continued Favorite Son. "You are not afraid of getting old. A man with power can stand to live to be old because even the worst things cannot come near enough to touch him. But a man without power should die young, because, if he lives a long time, something bad will touch him, and he cannot bear it because he does not have power. It may touch his body or his mind. It is better if it only touches his body. That is the way it is with me. I do not want power. It is hard to get and hard to keep. I have seen our father carrying his power. It is a great burden. It has not made him happy. It has just kept him alive to grow old. I want to be happy, my brother. I want life while I can enjoy it. I do not want to be old. I do not wish to carry a burden for myself or for the People. You are like our father. You are not afraid of burdens. So I am going to give my power to you to grow old and also to heal our People. You must now wear the small pink shell of the healer in your scalp lock, beside the arrow. You can use these powers. I do not want them. So we are both well served. That is sharing. That is the way between real brothers." Favorite Son stood up. "I'm going to tell our father that he now has only one son with power."

So Satank and Eagle Down Feather knew of the death of Favorite Son before he was gone. And the old man looked at Eagle Down Feather with new eyes, knowing that he would step forward and carry the burden of power. Just as he had called Young Satank, my Favorite Son, he called Eagle Down Feather by another name now . . . my Brave Son. For only a truly brave man could carry power.

Satank and Eagle Down Feather went to Mexico to get

the bones of Favorite Son when he was killed on a raid. All the young men of his Herder Society went with the men of the family. They were afraid when Eagle Down Feather cleared away the rocks that they had placed over the body of Favorite Son. They were afraid when Eagle Down Feather painted the bones yellow, the color of the society. They were afraid when Satank prayed over each bone and wrapped them together in a new blanket and placed them in the saddle of Favorite Son's pony. From then on, they were afraid, because Satank treated the bones just as he had treated Favorite Son. He talked to the bones as they rode home. He gave a lavish feast for the bones when they returned just as if the son had had a great victory. He had the women move the lodge of Favorite Son whenever the People moved, and he put the bones in the place of honor to rest. He led the robe-wrapped bones about with him for company and talked to them as he had talked to Favorite Son. The People were afraid of this behavior and the bones. But they knew that Satank feared nothing, and they respected him even more.

Since Satank had been in prison, Eagle Down Feather had had the care of his brother's bones. He, too, had been afraid of the bones when he touched them and painted them and gave them to his father. Then he was still a young man in power and did not want to attract death. But he loved his brother and his father, and his power said he was strong and should not fear death for it was always walking about, looking, seeking those without power that feared it. Now the People understood that Eagle Down Feather was his father's son—present, powerful, no longer an unfavored son.

From where he sat Eagle Down Feather saw a wagon

filled with children pull alongside the wagon carrying Satank. Caddo George Washington guided the mismatched team.

"I am sorry, Akia-ti-sumtau, there are no Kiowa children left. They have fled away with their parents, ahead of the evil wind of the soldiers. There are only Caddo children and some others from the school."

The old chief looked at the dirty children. "They will do. Take this message to my people on the plains. Tell them I died beside the road. My bones will be there. My people will gather them up and carry them away." He rode in silence for a moment, watching the road ahead. "Do you see that tree, old friend?" The Caddo nodded, following the direction of Satank's look. "When I reach that tree, I shall be dead."

One of the Tonkawah scouts, Captain Charley, rode between the two wagons, purposefully breaking the connection between the two old friends. He grinned, enjoying the sorry situation that the Kiowa chief was in. Satank knew his old enemy. All his long life he had despised the cannibalistic tribesmen. "You foul vermin, crawling over the white man's testicles, you may have my scalp. I, Satank, who killed every Tonkawah I could, give it to you, because you could not take it honorably. The hair is poor, thin, and gray now. It is not worth much, or I would not give it to such a nothing as you are. Still it is the best scalp you will ever get."

Satank turned away from the rider and began to sing again:

Iha hyo oy iya oiha yaya yoyo.
[Going away to die.]
Aheyo aheyo uaheyo ya eya heyo e heyo,
Ko-eet-senko ana oba hema haa ipai degi oba ika,
Ko-eet-senko ana oba hema hadamagagi oba ika.

[Oh, sun, you will live forever.
But we, *Koitsenko*, must die.
Oh, moon, you will live forever.
But we, *Koitsenko*, must die.
Oh, earth, you will live forever.
But we, *Koitsenko*, must die.]

Caddo George slowed his team, letting the wagon carrying Satank pull ahead. As Satank moved away, he turned the children's wagon and drove toward a rise that looked down on the road leading to East Cache Creek and the big pecan tree beyond. The children stood solemnly, holding the rough board sides of the complaining wagon as it rocked and swayed across the land. They were silent. Their large black eyes were innocent, accepting, and wise. They were witnesses. Eagle Down Feather saw them from the hill where he sat.

"Damn that noise is irritating," said the private in front of Satank. "Shut up!" He spat a stream of tobacco juice at the old man.

Sergeant Varily rode hootily forward. "That's enough of that! You will treat this man as a prisoner of the United States government. Is that clear, soldier?"

"Yes, sir," the black man said quickly. To his companion, he muttered: "I didn't hit him or nothing."

Satank pulled his head beneath his blanket, and the singing stopped. The soldiers laid their loaded guns in the bed of the wagon within easy reach. "Well, that's a relief," the private said.

Satank's head popped out of the blanket again. "Going away to die. Going away to die. Oh, sun, you will live forever. But we, *Koitsenko*, must die. Oh, earth, you will live forever. But we, *Koitsenko*, must die. My son, I will see you soon. I am coming to you. Make a little feast for me." He withdrew again to silence beneath the blanket.

The soldiers rocked in the heat of the June sun. Their eyes searched the land toward the horizon. They had been told to expect an attack, a rescue attempt. The June sun was hot on their blue wool tunics. The sweat that poured from them drained away their energy as they rocked back and forth, giving themselves to the rhythm of the wagon, to the rhythm of the alien land.

"Bet it's hot under that there blanket," the talkative private said. "But he's quiet under there."

Satank pulled the blanket from his head.

Corporal Robinson, sitting next to the old warrior, glanced at his companion opposite and grimaced. The private stared at the old man with small mustaches at the corners of his mouth. "Looks like there's blood on his mouth and teeth," he said.

Robinson leaned forward to see. Suddenly, the old Kiowa plunged a knife to the hilt in the man's thigh. The soldier grabbed the wound and howled. Standing up, staggering away from his attacker, he somersaulted backward out of the Indian's reach. The private rolled out the opposite side as Satank rose to his feet. He drove the bloody knife he still clutched into the end of the sash tied across his chest fastening it to the wood floor. He snatched one of the carbines from beside it. The warrior chief tried to lever a round into the chamber of the gun, but it jammed as an already loaded shell was poorly ejected. Satank fought the gun, trying to jerk it into action.

Lieutenant Thurston stood in his stirrups. "Shoot him! Shoot him!" Soldiers in the escort grabbed for their carbines searching the far horizon for attack. "Fire!" the lieutenant yelled.

Corporal John Charlton, who saw the action in front of him, raised his carbine, aimed. Tony Bordello, the driver of the front team, swung into his sights. He waited, found the Kiowa chief again. His index finger circled over the trigger.

Satank suddenly stood erect, throwing the betraying weapon from him, opening himself widely, embracing Charlton's first bullet as it struck him in the chest. Charlton fired again. The impact of the shots knocked the old man backward against the driver's seat. He reached for the second weapon, lying on the floor, and raised it over the side of the wagon.

"Fire!" yelled the lieutenant. More shots, now from other soldiers, pounded into the ancient warrior until he fell from the wagon to the road a few yards from the pecan tree.

Charlton felt a weight on his arm as he cocked the carbine again and stepped to stand above the fallen warrior. He looked down. Adoltay, the young chief, had placed his hand on his arm. "*Por favor. Por favor.* Please. You have killed him enough."

The thought fleeted across Charlton's mind: *Why had the young Indian not done that before? Why had he not tried to take the gun even as he fired it?* He glanced at the private facing him to see if he had the young Indian covered. The private had slipped onto the wagon floor with his gun raised toward the front over the wagon's side. Satanta sat quietly as before, looking back toward the corporal. Their eyes met for a moment, and Charlton knew that he had done exactly what the three chiefs had intended, had planned.

Colonel Ranald Mackenzie skidded into the confused escort under his command, shouting: "Deploy for the main attack! Where is the main force? Get ready, men." He drew to a halt above the lieutenant and sergeant who kneeled over Satank and hid his body. "What the hell's going on here?"

Lieutenant Thurston stood, revealing the warrior, propped against the wagon's front wheel. "He tried to escape, sir. He had a knife, seized a gun. I ordered the men to fire."

"Escape, hell! He was shackled hand and foot," said Mackenzie, dismounting. "Get some flankers out, Lieutenant. This is no place to stop. You're wide open. Surgeon! Patzki, where are you?" Mackenzie was kneeling over Satank as he shouted.

Patzki walked over and squatted beside the chief.

"I want a full report on this man's condition."

"Well"—Patzki wiped his hands on his handkerchief—"he's shot to hell."

"Could you be more specific, please, Doctor? Shot to hell is not an appropriate summary of the situation." Mackenzie kept looking about, expecting an attack to come from somewhere, feeling vulnerable and insecure in the open position. "Do this right, Patzki. Examine the man."

The surgeon felt the carotid artery in Satank's neck. "His pulse is very weak." He checked the dying man's eyes. "Pupils dilated." He moved down Satank's body, pulling the blanket and clothing away from the wounds. "He has at least five fatal wounds, Colonel, and a number of others that could, together, prove fatal."

Mackenzie glared at the arrogant surgeon. "Can this man live?"

"No," Patzki said.

Satank blinked and opened his eyelids slowly, lifting the gnawed hand that had let him slip the shackle. The men followed his gesture toward the rise beyond the pecan tree. A mounted warrior, naked of all clothing but breechcloth and moccasins, sat his mount beside another horse carrying a small, carefully wrapped bundle on its back. "My son, my Favorite Son, I am coming to you. Make a little feast for me." Satank sank back.

"Dead?" asked Mackenzie.

"Dead," affirmed the physician.

"All right, let's get this outfit firmed up!" shouted Mackenzie, turning to the next task. "We'll need an ambulance from the fort down here to take back the wounded and dead." He glanced down at his feet. "What the hell are you doing?" he asked the Tonkawah, Captain Charley, who had drawn his knife and knelt beside Satank's body. The scout looked startled, but grinned and gestured toward the scalp. Mackenzie kicked Satank's bloody, bullet-riddled blanket toward the scout. "Take that and get the hell out of here." Mackenzie shoved his foot into the iron stirrup and remounted his horse. "Post a guard over the wounded men and Satank's body. Move this party out of here, Lieutenant. We're sitting ducks." The colonel's eyes narrowed as they scanned the horizon. "Where'd that Indian go that was sitting on the hill?"

Eagle Down Feather had seen what he had come to see. He had brought his brother to witness, also. Now Eagle Down Feather rode slowly around the escort party back toward the plains. There was no great grief in Eagle Down Feather. Everything was as his father had wished. The old one had died honorably on the warrior's road he had ridden all his life. Eagle Down Feather directed no anger at the soldiers. They had done, without knowing, exactly what his father had wanted. The old one in his power had tricked them yet again.

He would soon gather his father as he and the old man had gathered his brother's bones in Mexico after he had been killed. He would bury them together. Eagle Down Feather was not afraid of the dead or death itself. *I know you, Death,* he thought. *You are nothing to me. I pass through you.* Nothing could come near him, even as he grew very old. The words of Favorite Son echoed in his ears: *Power comes to the man who can use it. If it is meant for him to have power, it will come to him whether he seeks it or not. It is his as much as his own heart or the sound of his blood in his ears.*

He knew now that just as Favorite Son shone in his father's eyes as that part of him that wanted to be beautiful, young, free, and unburdened, he was that part of his father who was brave enough to carry the burdens of his life and his people. Now the old one and his favorite son could rest together in the Land of Many Lodges. They would feast together as they had in life. Eagle Down Feather smiled at the thought of the two rejoicing together unburdened.

Eagle Down Feather saw himself, also. He, too, was feasting. He saw that he was not distraught or overcome. His power was true and strong. Although the world he knew was falling around him, the power let nothing touch him, even as he heard and saw everything. The burden was there just as Favorite Son had seen, but he, Brave Son, in accepting the burden had been given the power to carry it. And that was all that had ever been and would ever be, the living stream that ran through all time and made what was seen and endured small beside it.

About the Editors

Jon Tuska and **Vicki Piekarski** are authors or editors of numerous works about the American West, including Piekarski's WESTWARD THE WOMEN (Doubleday, 1983) and Tuska's BILLY THE KID: HIS LIFE AND LEGEND (Greenwood, 1994). They are co-editors-in-chief of the ENCYCLOPEDIA OF FRONTIER AND WESTERN FICTION (McGraw-Hill, 1983) which is now being prepared in its second edition. Together they were the co-founders of Golden West Literary Agency and the first Westerners in the history of the Western story to select and co-edit thirty-four new hardcover Western fiction books a year in two prestigious series, the Five Star Westerns and the Circle V Westerns. They are married and live in Portland, Oregon.